Bess froze in the doorway stood the boy had once been

He hadn't changed at all.

But the moment that thought surfaced, she knew it wasn't true. He was different. Seventeen years had lent him a hard maturity. On Zach Crandall, it was an exciting change.

Gone was the lanky whipcord strength of youth. In its place stood a form of purposefully hewn muscle and latent power packed inside faded denims and a snug black T-shirt. Hung over impressive shoulders was the expected black leather jacket. In younger years, it had made him look like a throwback to the rebellious fifties. Now it gave him a sleek, dangerous air. *Dangerous* was a word that had always described the Crandall boy.

But Zach Crandall was a boy no longer—and just the sight of him set off an earthquake of emotions within her.

Dear Reader,

Everyone loves Linda Turner, and it's easy to see why, when she writes books like this month's lead title. *The Proposal* is the latest in her fabulous miniseries, THE LONE STAR SOCIAL CLUB. Things take a turn for the sexy when a straitlaced lady judge finds herself on the receiving end of an irresistible lawyer's charms as he tries to argue her into his bed. The verdict? Guilty—of love in the first degree.

We've got another miniseries, too: Carla Cassidy's duet called SISTERS. You'll enjoy *Reluctant Wife,* and you'll be eagerly awaiting its sequel, *Reluctant Dad,* coming next month. Reader favorite Marilyn Pappano is back with *The Overnight Alibi,* a suspenseful tale of a man framed for murder. Only one person can save him: the flame-haired beauty who spent the night in question in his bed. But where is she? And once he finds her, what is she hiding? Brittany Young joins us after writing twenty-six books for Silhouette Romance and Special Edition. *The Ice Man,* her debut for the line, will leave you eager for her next appearance. Nancy Gideon is back with *Let Me Call You Sweetheart,* a tale of small-town scandals and hot-running passion. And finally, welcome first-time author Monica McLean. *Cinderella Bride* is a fabulous marriage-of-convenience story, a wonderful showcase for this fine new author's talents.

And after you read all six books, be sure to come back next month, because it's celebration time! Intimate Moments will bring you three months' worth of extra-special books with an extra-special look in honor of our fifteenth anniversary. Don't miss the excitement.

Leslie J. Wainger
Senior Editor and Editorial Coordinator

Please address questions and book requests to:
Silhouette Reader Service
U.S.: 3010 Walden Ave., P.O. Box 1325, Buffalo, NY 14269
Canadian: P.O. Box 609, Fort Erie, Ont. L2A 5X3

LET ME CALL YOU SWEETHEART

NANCY GIDEON

Published by Silhouette Books
America's Publisher of Contemporary Romance

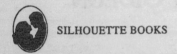

SILHOUETTE BOOKS

ISBN 0-373-07851-X

LET ME CALL YOU SWEETHEART

Books by Nancy Gideon

Silhouette Intimate Moments

For Mercy's Sake #648
Let Me Call You Sweetheart #851

NANCY GIDEON

attributes her output of over twenty-six novels to a background in journalism and to the discipline of writing with two grade-school-aged boys in the house. She begins her day at 5:00 a.m. when the rest of the family is still sleeping. While the writing pace is often hectic, this southwestern Michigan author enjoys working on diverse projects. She's vice president of her local RWA chapter and a member of a number of other groups. And somehow she always finds the time to stay active in her son's Cub Scout pack. Fans may know her under the pseudonyms Dana Ransom and Lauren Giddings.

Dedicated to the Iowa branch of the family for always
making me feel so welcome.

Chapter 1

Nothing energized a small town like whispers of scandal.

Before noon, no fewer than two dozen of Sweetheart's finest found their way into Rare Finds, Bess Carrey's used and rare bookstore, hoping to rehash old rumors. In Bess, they encountered a stone wall. Always admired for her closed-lipped approach to gossip, she could be darned frustrating when the talk turned as juicy as this new topic. Of course, Bess was friends with Melody Crandall and even with her brother Zach, himself, before he'd fled town in disgrace, but that didn't give her leave to be so sour on the source of the locals' excitement. Not in a town where last night's rainfall usually dominated conversation.

The news had traveled like wildfire on the lips of Alice Barbor, the town's acclaimed gossip. Even the cable news networks couldn't break a story faster. Bony features flushed, she had burst in on Bess the moment she'd unlocked the door to open her shop. Behind Alice's magnifying glasses, bright eyes glowed, homing beacons focused upon the tidbit of the day.

"Guess you've already heard."

Tempted not to pick up that dangled bait, Bess resigned herself to the inevitable. "What's that, Alice?"

"That no-account Crandall boy is back."

If it hadn't been nine in the morning and a comfortable seventy-five degrees, Bess would have blamed sunstroke for the sudden faltering of her system. Her knees refused to lock, going all rolling and wobbly beneath her knife-pleated skirt. Heat and emotion of Vesuvian proportion swelled up inside, threatening to blow as contrasting ice settled in the shaking fingers knotted about her bag.

"Fletch, Ross or Jordie?" Had that weak thread of sound come from her? Bess held her breath, waiting to hear Alice pick one of the younger Crandall brothers, even as her heart hammered out another name.

"I'm talking about Zach. You graduated with him, remember? Or would have if he'd stayed in school."

Did she remember? A chill of gooseflesh swept along her arms. Zach Crandall with his icy blue eyes shooting lightning bolts of intensity. Zach with his John Travoltaesque strut, cigarette dangling from the corner of a cynically curled smile, attitude sneering, "I'm good for nothing but bad." He'd roared out of Sweetheart on a cloud of motorcycle fumes and mystery over a decade and a half ago.

He was the last person on earth its citizens would welcome back. And he was the only person who could stir sparks in Bess's long-barren heart.

"Zach? I can't believe it."

She needed to sit down before she fell down.

Bess wove a kamikaze path down the center aisle and collapsed on a corrugated carton of Shakespeare's sonnets delivered too near closing time to be shelved. Alice followed, gabbing excitedly while her audience grew pale as the parchment in her old books.

"I couldn't believe it, either. He's got some nerve, that's for sure."

Dizzying impressions shivered to Bess's soul. Faint from the overload of sensations, she whispered, "Why?"

"Why?" Alice blinked owlishly behind her thick trifocals, not understanding the question that broke the smooth flow of her story.

"Why has he come back?" But she wasn't really talking to Alice. She'd almost forgotten the other woman's presence as she seized upon the earth-shattering fact.

Did it matter why? He was home.

"They're letting his mama out, from what I hear," Alice rattled on, never missing a beat. "Seventeen years. A whole lifetime lost for something she should have gotten a medal for…if she did it at all."

That mutter of speculation shook Bess back to the present with a jerk. A familiar defensiveness pressed for release, but, as always, she swallowed it back behind a mild smile.

"I've got to open my register, Alice."

So caught up in the drama she almost missed the brusque dismissal, Alice nodded absently, already planning her next stop. "I'll drop in later if I hear any more."

For Bess it was anything but business as usual.

The next hours went by in a haze, broken only briefly by visits from her neighborhood grapevine. *Zach.* Her pulse wouldn't stop pounding, as if she were again that seventeen-year-old girl infatuated with the first boy to look her way; the only one.

Smart and serious back then, as now, she hadn't been the type to inspire thoughts of romance. Homemade clothes of plain, unflattering cut, hair pulled back in a severe ponytail, no makeup, no trace of teenage vivaciousness, she had more in common with her peers' parents than the schoolmates who'd overlooked her.

Zach had been her one bright light, and oh, how hot he'd burned against the somber tones surrounding her. A fiery comet shooting across her horizon, leaving a glittering trail of memories even after the glow faded.

Memories still as bittersweet as the day they were made.

Now that he was back, would he light up her heavens again? Would he even remember her?

She bent to her work. Books to unload, count and shelve. Pain lanced her heart, slicing through it the way her utility knife slit packing tape on the shipping carton. Just because he was the most monumental force to affect her life, what were the chances that she'd made a dent upon his? In seventeen years, he'd never made a single attempt to contact her. No note to say where he'd gone. No card on holidays or her birthday. Not even a whisper of gossip to say he hadn't fallen off the face of the earth when he'd crossed the town limits. She jerked the box flaps apart with unnecessary force, spilling several of the weighty volumes out onto the floor. She stared at them blankly, her mind a world away from the musty odors of old paper and cracked leather.

Where had he gone? What had he done? Many times she'd started to ask Melody about him. She knew the other boys kept in touch with their sister. But Zach, the oldest, Melody's childhood champion, rarely did. Silence said it all. There was nothing in Sweetheart he wanted to remember.

Chiding herself for being a fool, Bess tried to shift her attention to the packing order. Zach Crandall hadn't come back to rekindle their ill-fated teenage romance. If she figured in his plans at all, wouldn't he have called her upon his return to town? It wasn't as if she'd be hard to find in a place the size of Sweetheart. She still worked in her mother's store. She still lived in her mother's house. Nothing had changed except that instead of rubber bands, she used tortoiseshell combs to hold back her baby-fine hair.

Had he changed?

Clutching one of the leather-bound volumes to her breast, she tried picturing how an extra seventeen years would wear on Zach. Certainly not like they had on most of the boys in their graduating class, who held up protruding bellies with their plate-sized belt buckles and hid thinning hair under John Deere green ball caps. They'd all rooted deep in the rich Iowa soil and grown with a solid predictability. But not Zach. He'd been transplanted to parts unknown. Had he found someplace to root? Had he...married? Did he have children who called him Daddy?

The achy heaviness in her chest kept growing. It wasn't fair for her to dislike the idea of his happiness. She'd given up her right to be a part of his life. Had she expected him to go on in some selfless vacuum, as lonely and isolated as she'd let herself become? Zach with a wife and children...settled down to domestic bliss. Someone else living the only dream she'd ever had. Hurt and confused, she blinked fiercely, denying the feelings that claimed she'd been mourning him since the night he'd gone away.

Why couldn't she just put him aside and move on?

But nothing about Zach had ever been easy. He was a tornado over their placid plains. And she was being sucked up and swirled around all over again. Used to stability, the feeling of not having her feet on the ground was as scary to Bess as it was exhilarating. She didn't know whether to cling or let go and enjoy the wild ride.

Maybe clinging all those years ago had been her biggest mistake.

With a sigh of regret, she stood and brushed at the dust circling her knees. Maybe what she needed was someone to come along and brush the dust off her before she became as dull and dried out as the books she secretly abhorred. Those staid, moralistic classics mocked her lonely existence. No one read them anymore because the plots were well-known and held no mystery. Flashy, action-packed pulp fiction was what sold, not the plodding prose lining her shelves.

She heard the door to her shop open and mentally girded herself for the ordeal of listening to yet another rush of gossip. The need to snap, "Can't you mind your own business?" tugged at her firmly set lips as she turned.

And she froze.

For there in her doorway stood a man where the boy had once been.

He hadn't changed at all.

But the moment that giddy thought surfaced, she knew it wasn't true. He was different. Seventeen years had lent a hard maturity. On Zach Crandall, it was an exciting change.

Gone was the lanky whipcord strength of youth. In its place stood a sturdier form, one of purposefully hewn muscle and latent power packed inside faded denims and snug black T-shirt. Hung on a rack of impressive shoulders was the expected black leather jacket with sunglasses dangling from the pocket where he'd used to carry a pack of smokes. In younger years it made him look like a throwback to the rebellious fifties. Now it gave a sleek, dangerous air. *Dangerous* was a word that always described the eldest Crandall boy. A boy no longer.

His features held a magnificent patina of years. Smooth, unshaven contours became compelling angles and stubble-shadowed hollows. Black hair once worn indifferently shaggy now sported a crisply cut aggressive bristle. Slashing black brows offset the familiar laser blue of a stare made more intriguing by the network of lines fanning from the outer corners. Dramatically shaped lips remained unsmiling, hoarding the wide, dimpled smile that was capable of charming any member of the female gender out of her virtue, when he chose to exert its hundred-watt dazzle. Age had brought a tough edge of character to his always startling good looks. And just the sight of him tripped an earthquake of emotions.

"Hello, Bess."

Her breath expelled in a noisy shiver. "Zach."

Silence stretched taut, as his icy gaze roamed over her. She tingled beneath that assessing sweep, every fiber coming alive, shaking off seventeen years of dormancy.

"You look great," he said. A blunt, factual delivery.

She'd never been able to modestly deny his compliments because they weren't meant as flattery. He stated observations with a flustering directness. Words she would have scoffed at from others were always believed when Zach spoke them. He didn't play manipulative word games. He said what he thought. That was the one thing that always got him in the most trouble. Except with her.

"I—I heard you'd come...back." She'd meant to say *home,* but how could he consider this town home after the way it had turned its back on him—the way she'd turned her back on him? Guilt twisted in her belly, adding to her agitation. "It's been a long time."

"Well, nothing in this place ever changes."

Truer words couldn't be spoken. Time stood still at the boundaries of Sweetheart. Days, months, years passed with monotonous predictability. She could have told him the bank now had drive-through windows and that the library had a link to the Internet, but those weren't the changes he referred to. He meant the heart and soul of Sweetheart; the attitudes of its people. And, no, they hadn't changed. Small towns had a way of fostering past prejudices and excluding anything outside the norm. Zach had been more than outside. He'd been on another planet. And that's where the town preferred he stay.

He left the doorway, coming farther into her store. Bess watched him move, fascinated as always by his potent animal-on-the-prowl swagger. Other men strolled, sauntered, stomped. Zach strutted, shoulders shifting with aggressive sensuality, hips rolling with an arrogant, "I'm the cock of this walk. Get out of my way or prepare to be moved." Back then most of the citizens of Sweetheart had scrambled to give him room. The few who hadn't usually had regretted it. Timid little Elizabeth Carrey was the only one who hadn't given way. She'd held her ground because she recognized that attitude for what it was: posturing, all for effect. The really dark and dangerous aspects of Zach Crandall weren't on the outside for everyone to see. They were deep and personal. And to Bess, very frightening.

He frightened her now. With his blatant sexuality. With his takeover intensity. With the way she quivered on command right down to her sensible loafers. No one but Zach had ever had that kind of control over her; the kind that was threatening yet voluntarily given. She'd given him everything once before. This time she vowed to be more cautious. There was much more at stake than a naive teenage heart.

She relaxed a little when he came to a stop just out of arm's reach. His penetrating stare left her and roved the crowded bookcases. Cold contempt settled in his gaze. "Still shut away in this tomb." Then he surprised her with his directness. "Where's your mom?"

Taken off guard, she faltered. "She—she's dead. Almost three years ago."

His stare snapped back to fix on hers. "Oh." No "I'm sorry," because she knew he wasn't. He wasn't a hypocrite. He could have easily said "Good." Instead, he studied her for her reaction, assessing what difference that fact had made in her life. Summing it up flatly. "And you're still here."

His comment said volumes. It said she was still the dependent daughter, afraid to take a risk, afraid to defy opinion, afraid to live. Knowing he was right in all those assumptions made her prickle up defensively. How dare he come back after seventeen years and make any judgments about her life.

"It provides a comfortable living for me."

"Comfortable," he echoed with a soft disdain. "Good. Good for you." But not for him. He would never settle for comfortable. Or safe. Or respectable. And that had always scared her, too.

It felt so strange, his presence crowding this room, her mother's bastion. Was she rolling over in her no-nonsense casket at the knowledge of him invading her sacred space? Part of her twitched with distress while another welcomed his bold intrusion. He was shaking off the dust.

"So, how long are you staying?" Did that sound too hopeful, too desperate?

"I don't know. I've got some unfinished business. Depends on how things work out." He said it casually, but his stare practically scorched her. Was she one of those loose ends? Was that something she should fear or anticipate? She was never quite sure with Zach. His motives were a mystery. And because she resented the anxious way his vagueness affected her, she struck back with her own touch of ice.

"Then what? You take off, like before, and no one hears from you for another seventeen years?" Hurt and anger trembled in her tone.

"Why not?" he answered coolly. His stare dared her to name a reason.

Bess blinked against the sudden burn in her eyes. She held her head up high to deny that he could still make her cry with the indifferent cut of his words. She didn't want him to see her as the same vulnerable teen, but rather as a woman with some degree of pride.

"Well, maybe we should just say our goodbyes now and be done with it." She turned away before tears fell in earnest, but he wouldn't allow a dignified retreat. His hand closed about her upper arm. Such strength in those long fingers, power he carefully channeled so as not to bruise her.

"I'm sorry," he said, this time meaning it. "I'm not leaving anytime soon."

When she turned, ready to forgive him, he stepped forward, bringing her right into his arms. Arms that curled easily to enfold her close in an unplanned yet instinctive embrace. Arms she'd longed for on many a wakeful evening. Arms that felt better than anything had a right to.

"I didn't come here to hurt you, Bess." He said that softly, as if he feared she might not believe it. His hands opened wide, between her shoulder blades, at the small of her back, pressing her into him, her soft swells flattening against his hard lines. Woman into man. The difference those seventeen years made quaked through her. His voice lowered a gravelly notch. "There are a lot of things I'd thought about saying to you, but goodbye wasn't one of them."

Bess knew she should pull away. It was the smart and proper thing to do. But he felt so good. She breathed in the scent of him. Worn leather, warm man, some woodsy cologne that sparked images of snuggling close in front of a fire. She had loved him for so long, not saying the words was agony. But she didn't say them, not now. She didn't dare.

Instead, she allowed herself the luxury of enjoying his embrace, losing herself in the storm of sensations as her sensual self was lured out of hibernation. She stroked the soft, cracked leather of his jacket. Zach and leather went hand in glove; both tough and resistant to the harsh things the world threw at them, yet soft and supple when well cared for. She remembered riding on the back of his motorcycle, squeezing her legs to the strength of his thighs, hugging him about the middle, cheek pressed to his shoulder while the wind tore through her hair. The closest she'd ever come to tasting freedom.

She hugged to him now, smelling the leather, taunted by whispers of freedom, tasting the bitterness of regret and sorrow. Too late to call back those memories. She stepped away from him.

"It's good to see you, Zach. I missed you." That was the closest she could come to telling him the truth.

He stared at her, an unsettling stillness surrounding him. "Did you?"

Before she could answer, the door opened behind them. She gave a guilty start, almost as if she shouldn't be caught talking with Zach Crandall. He noticed the reaction, and the glaze of remoteness she remembered so well sealed his emotions from view.

"Dare I hope I'm interrupting something?"

Zach turned from Bess's stricken expression to see a lovely teenage girl assessing him through bold eyes. Fifteen or sixteen, he guessed, pretty and confident of her appeal. A born flirt. She smiled, displaying sassy dimples and a twinkle of blue eyes.

"Who's this?" Speculation was ripe in her voice as her gaze cut between them.

"Faith, this is Zach Crandall. Faith is Julie's daughter."

Speculation deepened into a matured awareness as the girl met his stare. Then Faith smiled again. "So, you're the one."

"That depends," he said, extending his hand and one of

his devastating grins. Faith buckled beneath its charm, just as
Bess had at her age. And still did. "The one, what?"

Pressing his hand tightly between both of hers, Faith
teased, "Sweetheart's bad boy."

"Faith!"

But Zach's grin widened. "Guilty."

"I never thought I'd have the chance to meet you." Then,
realizing she still held his hand, the teenager blushed and
released it.

"Well, I'll be around for a while, so we can get to know
each other better. I always liked your mother. She was Sweetheart's bad girl."

"Zach!"

Faith giggled, looking proud as if being bad was the ulti-
mate compliment.

"How is your mom?"

"She's in Mexico on her honeymoon." She sobered. "My
dad died a couple of years ago. Diabetes."

"I'm sorry."

Faith warmed to the sincerity of his tone. "Thanks. Dave's
an all right guy, though. He can keep up with Mom, so that's
something."

"So I get to spend the summer trying to keep up with my
favorite niece." Bess stepped over to slip her arms about the
girl's shoulders. A protective move, revealing the depth of
love between the two. And that Zach was perceived as a
threat.

"I'm your only niece," Faith chided, but she returned the
hug.

The sight did funny things to Zach's insides.

"So," he said to Faith, "are you going to let me take your
aunt to the parade and picnic tomorrow?"

Wide eyes flashed up to meet Bess's equally wide eyes.
Then the girl grinned. "Sure!"

Zach's smile thinned as he looked to Bess. "Unless she'd
prefer not to be seen with the town bad boy."

Bess received the challenge like a slap, a punishment for

all the times it had been true. This wasn't going to be one of them.

"What time?"

He blinked. "What?"

"What time will you pick me up?"

His arrogant manner shifted, softening with a host of conflicting emotions. "Folks still line the streets by nine?"

Bess nodded, her courage fading.

"Nine, then."

Again, she nodded, too shaken to speak.

"It was nice meeting you, Faith."

"You, too," the teen murmured.

Then with a flick of his wrist, he snapped open his dark glasses, slipping them on to shield any expression from his eyes. Only then did he nod to Bess. She didn't exhale until the door closed behind him.

"Wow!" Faith sighed for her. "What a babe!"

"Faith Marie, he's old enough to be— He's an old friend, that's all."

"A totally *babe-alicious* old friend. And he's taking you out."

That gleeful teenage squeal brought home the consequences of what she'd done. She and Zach, on display before the entire town. The rumors. The whispering. A chill rattled through her with the force of her mother's reproach. A sacrilege in her mother's church.

"So what's the story?"

"Story?" Bess echoed with feigned innocence. She bent down to tear into the Shakespeare, hoping to avoid the issue. But Faith was like a terrier with a pull toy in her teeth. She wasn't about to let go. She stooped to help gather the books.

"Between you and Zach."

"There's nothing between us. Old friends from high school, that's all."

"Yeah, and I didn't step in on a scene hot enough to melt sand into glass!"

Books stacked all the way to her nose, Bess stood and

balanced the precarious pile as she walked to the section she'd cleared for the new arrivals. "Old friends," she insisted. "We haven't seen each other for—since graduation. You know, back when the dinosaurs roamed the earth."

"You're not *that* old, Aunt B."

"Well, thank you very much." But most of the time, she did feel ancient, positively Jurassic. Until today. Today she felt like a nervous kid again.

The girl came up to deposit her armful. Her gaze was patient. And persistent. "You were saying? About you and Zach?"

"I tutored him in geometry and English composition."

"A private tutor, huh? Cool!"

No, it had been hot. Very hot. Those private sessions that had evolved into a whole other kind of learning. She began shelving the books with brisk efficiency. "Anyway, he left town right before graduation, and I never heard from him again."

Faith plopped down on the coastered stool and leaned elbows on her knees. Empathetic confidentiality shaped her expression as she said, girlfriend to girlfriend, "And he broke your heart."

Bess gave her a quick glance, willing for the sake of harmony to admit, "Something like that. He was the only boy— Let's just say he was a babe back then, too."

Faith nodded, happy to share this common ground with her favorite aunt, who seemed suddenly all the more appealing because of her secret past. "Bad boy with reputation and squeaky-clean girl from the right side of the tracks."

Bess shook her head. "You make it sound like a James Dean movie."

"Who?"

"Never mind." Positively Jurassic.

"Were you in love with him?"

"I was seventeen."

"Were you?"

"Bring the rest of those books over, would you?"

"Not until you tell me."

"Yes," she snapped, then apologized with a glance. "But that was a long time ago. We were just children."

"And now you're going out with him. That is so cool."

"We're not—"

But Faith just grinned at her.

She gave up. What did it hurt if the girl saw her as less than a fossil because a handsome man paid her a little attention? It would seem incredibly romantic, seen through the eyes of a dreamy teenager. Love lost then returned. The stuff of dreams. Her dreams.

Foolish dreams, she reminded herself as she straightened and dusted off her hands. Zach hadn't come back to make her fairy-tale ending come true. The longer he stayed in Sweetheart, the greater the chance that he would find out exactly what part she played in all his family's pain. So much for the hope of a happily-ever-after.

It was crazy to encourage Zach Crandall.

More than that, it was dangerous.

Chapter 2

No, nothing ever changed in Sweetheart.

Sitting at the counter in Sophie's Diner, Zach felt the barbed stares of its disapproving citizens piercing his back. Not so easy to ignore were the haunted shadows lingering in his sister's eyes. That was something he'd hoped had changed.

Melody delivered his hot roast beef sandwich with a piece of advice. "You don't have to come in here and pay for supper. I get off in an hour. I could make you something at home." Her gaze scanned the booths and their scowling patrons nervously.

"Afraid I'll be bad for business?"

At his arid drawl, Melody melted into anxious apology. "I didn't mean that. Of course you're welcome to eat here. I just thought maybe you'd feel more comfortable—"

He smirked at her meaning. "They won't give me indigestion, but it looks like I've soured their meals."

"I'm sorry, Zach."

"What are you sorry for? Don't keep apologizing for them, Mel. It's not your fault."

His harsh correction only made matters worse. "I'm s—" She bit back her words, tears brightening her pale eyes. As she turned away from the counter, Zach reached across it to cuff her arm. He felt apprehension stiffen her body. Very gently he guided her back toward him. The blank daze of panic in her eyes made him think of their mother, the way she'd cringe away from the flat of his father's hand. He let Melody go, and she shrank back, rubbing at her arm even though he knew he hadn't hurt her. Not physically.

"Mel, I'll eat at home if it would make you more comfortable."

Because she'd rather drag herself over broken glass than let her brother believe she thought more of the town's opinions than his feelings, she gathered the necessary starch to claim, "Don't be silly, Zach. I like having you here. And they're just going to have to get used to it." She cupped the side of his face with her palm. He pressed into it like the affection-hungry boy he'd once been, the tense line of his jaw relaxing slightly. His stare was direct and somber.

"I love you, Mel. You know that, don't you? I would never do anything to hurt you."

Her fingertips traced down to his square chin as she smiled. "I know. Now eat your supper while I go see if anyone needs coffee."

For a minute he concentrated on his plate of food, but after a half dozen forkfuls under the watchful eyes of Sophie's customers, he lost his appetite. Their hatred and suspicion battered him. Nothing new. Wary glances always followed him, seeking to fix blame for any wrong done in Sweetheart. Like father, like son. He swallowed his last mouthful. It went down like sawdust. He rinsed it with coffee but the bitterness remained.

It was hell coming back. He'd worked hard to make a life for himself away from the soul-scarring memories of his youth. He'd crafted a career to be proud of, commanding respect, even awe. But one day back in Sweetheart stripped him bare, back to a sullen, angry boy crumpling under the reputation his father had carved out before him. He hadn't fought against it back then. His rebellious spirit sneered in the face of the town's censure. If he'd stayed even another year, all their predictions would have come true. He'd tried to tell Bess that. She hadn't understood. If she did, she was too scared to do anything about it. She'd let him go.

Even after seventeen years, the pain of that never dulled.

She was the one person in his bleak past worth remembering, outside his mother, sister and brothers. And in the end, she'd let him down, too. In the end, her faith hadn't been strong enough to break from the small-town prejudices that marked him as no good.

He'd proved them wrong. To spite them, at first. Then because of them. He'd worked long and hard to shatter the stereotype of bad seed. He didn't mind the ''bad'' part. Being a badass had its benefits in his chosen line of work. But he was as far from his father's footsteps as he could get. Yet here, in Sweetheart, that dark shadow surrounded him.

He smiled tightly to himself when he thought of the surprise to come, when the good folks of Sweetheart would discover what had brought him back. It was more than the desire to spend some time with Melody and to be on hand when his mother came home. It was to shove his success in their faces and rub it around. A petty revenge, he knew, when he wasn't even sure it was worth the trouble to change their narrow minds. He'd moved beyond them. What did their opinions matter?

But the instant his sister stepped before him with her tired smile and her spiritless manner, he knew he couldn't walk away, dismissing the past as unimportant. Not until he'd freed those he loved from its stigma.

Then there was the other, more private matter.

"Tell me about Bess."

Melody gave a nervous start at his turn of topic. "What about her?"

"I hear her mother died."

"Yes. Several years ago."

"How'd she handle it?"

"Like she handles everything. Competently. With no complaints. She and I have gotten to be pretty good friends lately."

Zach liked that. Melody had few friends. Though meek and self-effacing, she was still a Crandall, and the weight of that bore down heavier on her than upon her brothers, because she'd decided to stay behind when they'd all scattered and never looked back. He'd never given much thought to how hard it must have been on her, staying here to face the censure, the rumors, the hatred.

She and Bess were friends. Bess would be accepting when none of the others would, seeing the goodness, the sweetness in his sister, and Bess would nurture it. The way she had tried to in him.

"Is she seeing anyone?" He posed that as casually as he could, but Melody saw right through his indifferent act.

"No. No one since you."

A heavy sense of obligation came with that knowledge. But a part of him whooped in delight. Then cynicism set in. No one since him. Out of choice or because her association with him left her unacceptable? His hand clenched to a fist around his fork. Bess Carrey was old business and none of his, not anymore. Still, he couldn't keep himself from asking, "Was it bad for her, after I left?"

"If you cared so much, you should have written to her." But when his stare never flickered, she sighed in resignation. "She went away for a while. Her mother sent her to stay with her sister until after the trial. When she came back, it was like the life had been sucked out of her. She went to work in her mother's bookstore and was like a ghost up until the time her mother died."

"And now?"

"She smiles. She volunteers for town committees. But she

still sticks to that store and that house. Having her niece visit seems to have perked her up.''

"I met her. Spunky kid.''

Melody was silent for a moment. Then she spoke her mind in a burst of bravery. "What are you going to do about Bess, Zach?''

"Do?'' Her question took him by surprise, and he scrambled to cover his vulnerability. "I'm not going to do anything. She made her feelings pretty clear when I left.''

His sister's hands covered his as she leaned toward him in earnest. "She loved you, Zach. You can't blame her for not having the courage to go against everything she'd ever been taught.''

Yes, he could. And he still did.

He drew his hands away.

"Hi, Mr. Crandall.''

The cheery feminine voice caught him off guard. A friendly greeting within these city limits was something unexpected. He swiveled on his stool to see Faith and several of her teenage cohorts heading for a corner booth. She straggled behind and came over, unaware of how the others gawked in shock.

"How's the hot roast beef?'' She glanced at his half-eaten portion.

"Not bad. You and your friends here for supper?''

"Naw, just for some sodas and gossip.''

Guessing what their main topic would be, he smiled grimly. "You'd better go join them.''

"I'll see you tomorrow?'' Her hopeful gaze stirred that unsettling flip-flop again.

"Sure.''

She touched his sleeve shyly and bolted to the rear of the diner where her friends waited to surround her with hurried whispers of warning. Her gaze flashed over to him in alarm, then doubt, as she let herself be pulled down into one of the molded bench seats. He tugged out his wallet, mood souring. She wouldn't be so quick to greet him next time they met.

Not after her friends regaled her with stories of his sordid past.

He was surprised that that could still hurt him.

"I gotta go, Mel. I'll see you at home."

"Zach?"

He glanced up to catch her poignant expression.

"It's good to have you home."

He had nothing to say to that.

"I'm out here, honey," Bess called when she heard the back door slam shut. She waited, rocking the ancient metal glider in a steady rhythm, as the girl wound her way through the house to join her on the enclosed front porch. "Have fun?"

Faith frowned as she plopped down on the cushioned seat beside her. "I heard some things about Zach Crandall."

Bess's breath seized up in a painful spasm. So it started already. "Folks have always had plenty to say about Zach and the rest of his family."

"Is it true? I mean, he seemed so nice to me." Anxious eyes pleaded for reassurance.

"What did you hear?"

"That his mother is in prison for killing Zach's father to cover up the fact that Zach actually did it himself."

Whew! They hadn't held anything back. Bess arranged her hands atop the crocheted pillow resting in her lap. Her fingers worked the fringed edges restlessly. How much should she tell this impressionable child? The whole truth? The truth she'd never spoken aloud to anyone? Coward that she was, she started with the obvious.

The Crandalls were a small town's source of steady gossip. Sam Crandall drank, cheated, beat on his wife and terrorized his children. All four boys grew to be dangerous toughs, and the one girl, a shrinking shadow. No one was surprised when Sam Crandall was killed; the shocker was that his gentle wife Mary, one of the town's finest, whom they'd always felt married far beneath her, confessed to it. Rumors circled that the eldest Crandall boy, Zach, had done the deed. He and his father had come to blows earlier that same evening and Zach left town without a word to anyone that same night. The townspeople believed that Mary confessed to cover for his crime, knowing the law would go easier on a woman who'd suffered long physical and emotional abuse than they would on a hot-tempered boy already sporting a criminal record. But no one, not lawyers, not friends, could shake Mary Crandall from her story, and she went quietly, almost contentedly, to jail.

That was the official version spread by the town's gossips.

"Did he kill his father?" Faith's voice trembled slightly.

Bess squeezed her hand but didn't look at her. "No." Firmly spoken without a trace of doubt. "He had plenty of reason to, but he didn't."

"How can you be so sure?"

"I—I just am." It was a cop-out, and Bess felt terrible hiding behind it. But she'd been hiding the truth for so long, she didn't know when or how to tell it.

Zach Crandall had been with her at the time of his father's killing. He'd caught up to her on her walk home from the bookstore. He'd frightened her. It was more than the sight of his blackened eye, skinned knuckles and swollen jaw. It was the fierce gleam of determination in his stare. He had all his worldly possessions lashed down on his bike. He was on his way out of Sweetheart. And he wanted her to go with him.

She'd said no. He asked why, and she couldn't give a good explanation. He didn't try to talk her into it. He just left. If she'd known she wouldn't see him for another seventeen years, maybe she wouldn't have let him go.

She didn't speak the truth because she was afraid to lose the trust and affection of this lovely girl who meant everything to her.

"After all these years, why do they still hate him so?" Faith asked.

"Old habits die hard, Faith. Sam Crandall cast a dark shadow over all his boys." How well she knew it. It was easier to go along than to make the effort to change. She felt no pride in bowing to that weakness, herself. She patted the girl's knee. "You'd better get up to bed. It's going to be a long day tomorrow."

But instead of getting up to obey, Faith turned on the seat and surprised Bess with a warm embrace.

"Thanks for inviting me to stay with you this summer."

Bess hugged her tight, fighting down the swells of emotion crowding up to clog her throat. "Anytime, baby. You're welcome here anytime." Then she pushed away with a husky "Get up to bed."

"Wear that red outfit tomorrow, the one Mom got for you. It's hot" was her sage advice as she rose, then with a quick buss of Bess's cheek, bounded back into the house.

Bess sat out in the gathering night shadows, her hand to that cheek, her heart full of bittersweet tears. Happiness warred with long-standing regrets.

She'd spent half her life wishing for that night back, for Zach to ask again for her answer.

She rocked on the glider where she and a surly Zach Crandall had once sat while she'd tried to explain Euclidean geometry. At eighteen, he had almost a man's height and looks that could stop a heart. Hers had been beating like crazy: with curiosity, with agitation. He'd made no secret of his reluctance to be tutored. It was that or expulsion.

The education system, like all of Sweetheart, had written the eldest Crandall off as a lost cause. He was perpetually truant, had been caught underage with alcohol, he smoked on school grounds, showed no respect for authority and didn't care what anyone thought of him. Many of his teachers were afraid to confront him, even in the classroom. Not that he ever did anything to support their fears; he just had a latent air of violence about him. A violence he'd inherited. Discipline did no good. If calls were made home to his parents, he'd miss several days of school, then return with suspicious bruises but with no less arrogance. Everyone knew what was going on. His father was beating the hell out of him, the same

way he did his mother and brothers, and the town was afraid
to do anything about it.

Tutoring was the last straw, and Bess was the only student
who agreed to work with him. He was so menacing she almost withdrew her services. Until he'd growled that he had
no use for education. He was a Crandall, going nowhere.
Something sparked in her at that belligerently given
claim...because she'd heard a faint tone of remorseful anger,
of frustrated hurt. She couldn't stand the thought of anyone
or anything in pain. She'd turned on him with a snap of un-
common vinegar.

"You can be anything you want, Zach Crandall," she'd
told him. "You're certainly not stupid. It's ignorance holding
you back, the ignorance of a whole town, and if you were
any kind of a man, you wouldn't let them dictate your future."

He'd just stared at her. After weeks of studying together,
it was the first time she'd ever looked him straight in the eye.
She didn't back down, though she'd wanted to, in fear of his
reaction.

He'd kissed her.

It happened so fast. He leaned in while she sat fuming,
taking her by surprise. She'd never been kissed, but she'd
imagined what it would be like. The reality amazed her.

His mouth moved softly and so sweetly upon hers, steam-
ing the stiffness from her pursed lips, causing them to yield
to a sensuous shaping, giving her an exquisite taste of what
she'd only dreamed pleasure could be. Gentleness was the
last thing she'd expected from someone of Zach Crandall's
reputation. So was honor, yet he moved back, leaving her
shaking virtue untested.

And for the briefest instant, while they were breath-sharing
close, she saw a kindred longing in his long-lashed eyes, a
vulnerability he would deny to the last dying moment and
beyond.

Zach Crandall was a fake. He wasn't heartless or deviant

or anything like that. He was alone and afraid and hiding both behind a wall of blustering hostility.

It was then she realized she'd been as guilty as all the rest in prejudging him.

She vowed never to do it again. She would not listen to ugly whispers about his after-hour doings with an older, faster, more experienced crowd. She wouldn't let him get by with that chip of attitude keeping everyone else at bay. She would be his mentor, his confidante, his friend. And in the end she had been much more.

But she hadn't been able to keep her vow, and time hadn't eased the guilt for failing him. He'd needed her to be strong and she hadn't been. He'd wanted to trust her and she'd abandoned him.

She'd been seventeen, young and afraid. She'd never been beyond the limits of Sweetheart. She'd never broken her mother's edicts…except with Zach. He'd asked for more than she could give, and she'd never forgiven herself for buckling under pressure.

Just as he would never forgive her.

So why had he asked her to the parade and picnic? And why had she been crazy enough to say yes? Was the risk worth the danger? Was spending a few hours flirting with an old dream worth placing all her carefully constructed lies in jeopardy?

Then she remembered the feel of his arms curled about her, the scent of leather swirling around her senses.

And the answer was yes.

In the darkness, the simple two-story frame house seemed sinister. When he'd arrived during daylight hours, the homey touches his sister had added made it more appealing: colorful lemon yellow curtains, a flower garden bursting in riotous shades of purple, white and red, fresh white paint on the front gate and porch posts, hanging begonias. Like any other house on the block.

Crouching in the shadows, with no light of welcome glowing inside, it made a stark angular silhouette with steeply pitched roof and blank windows scraped by the fingernails of two ancient walnut trees. A haunted house. He opened the gate on soundless hinges, but in his mind he heard its rusty creak and could envision the hulking mass of his father rising up from the front porch steps, weaving in perpetual drunkenness.

"Where you been, boy?"

A cold sweat broke out as he made his way slowly up the walk. He could hear the echo of belt leather clearing the loops of his father's worn chino work pants.

"Answer me, boy. Sheriff Baines was by today asking after you. Seems someone broke out some windows down at the high school with empty beer cans."

Even before he could claim innocence, the crack of the belt brought sizzling fire. Prepared for it, he made no sound, not even when a huge cruel hand clenched in his hair, dragging him up the steps, flinging him through the storm door. Later, he'd sat stoically while Doc Meirs put the first of twenty-seven stitches in his face and hands, as his mother's thready voice claimed, "You know how careless kids are. He and his brothers got to roughhousing..."

The doctor couldn't look at her, because he knew. They all knew what went on at the Crandall house. Zach had been thirteen. His carelessness brought him to the doctor's office for broken ribs and arm, for fractured fingers and dislocated shoulder. No child was that clumsy. The doctor knew, just as the teachers who saw him slip into class late with his eye swollen shut or the imprint of a hand outlined in bruises against his cheek or neck. They didn't ask, and he didn't tell, and everyone wanted the unpleasant situation to go away.

So, instead of helping or stopping the abuse, they turned their backs, pretending not to hear the screams even closed windows couldn't shut out, looking away from the bruised features and battered hearts. Trapping a woman and her five children with a monster because of their own guilt and fear. How he hated them all for that.

Zach climbed the steps, soul steeped in resentment and helplessness as memories crowded close. His body tensed, hands fisted at his side, ready to protect against the horrors of the past as if they were something tangible he could strike. He wanted to strike and strike hard, but the target was long buried.

He stared at the front door, shaken by the ghosts hidden behind it. He never crossed its threshold without a chill of terror. Even though the years had brought a bubbling rage to ferment inside him, the fear remained. Ceaseless, shivering, desperate fear, for himself, his siblings, his mother, locked up like a wild thing within those rooms. He'd never spoken of it to anyone except Bess Carrey, who'd understood what it meant to be victimized and so alone that the spirit ached.

In that one fragile girl, he'd found the strength to break away from the cycle of fear. He'd done it because he wanted something better for the two of them, because she'd taught him that they deserved it. Only, she hadn't believed her own words as much as he had.

He'd left her behind and tried to forget everything the town of Sweetheart had done to him through its neglect. But no matter how far he traveled, how many years slipped by, he knew, he knew he would come back. For Bess Carrey. Because nothing in his life had ever felt so good as her respect.

Unable to enter that empty house with its whispering remembrances, Zach sat upon the front steps, leaning back against the porch post with eyes closed, listening to the sounds of the night, to the lazy rhythms of the small Iowa town. The prowling restlessness stilled as he pictured Bess with her prim spinsterish clothes and fresh-scrubbed face. No one since him. Her sweet lips had gone untasted, her generous heart untested. Were the men in Sweetheart all eunuchs? Couldn't they see beyond her shyness, beyond her effort to go unnoticed, to recognize the passionate fire simmering inside? He'd thought her hesitant glances sexier than the most sultry come-on. He still did.

The anger, the betrayal, the hurt still lingered in the heart that evolved from boy to man. Through matured eyes, he could understand her choice, yet could not condone it. She'd tried to explain it to him seventeen years ago, and he hadn't had the patience to listen.

Now, before he left Sweetheart for the last time, he would listen and he would know why his love had not been enough.

Chapter 3

"**W**ow!"

Bess stared hard at the reflection in her bathroom mirror, trying to justify Faith's earnest decree. She'd never been a "Wow!" before, not sensible Elizabeth Carrey who never showed bare ankles in public beneath her ever-present skirts. In the red-hot shorts set her sister had sent her, all she could see were immodest miles of leg, from strappy sandals to the barely there cuffs.

"I don't know..."

"I do, Aunt B. You're a knockout. Don't you dare change a thing. You'll have to set up metered parking for John Deere tractors out on your lawn."

"Great," she muttered. That's all she needed on top of the Sweetheart lonely hearts brigade trying unsuccessfully to match her up with every unmarried man between high school graduation and the seniors' center. Think of the speculation should Zach Crandall be the one to get her decked out like a show pony after she'd turned all the "respectable" men down. She sighed, wondering what insanity possessed her.

"Let me do your hair and face. Pleeeeease!"

Why not go the whole nine yards?

Bess surrendered, nudging her fanny back onto the bathroom counter with a sudden "Ooh!" as bare thigh connected with cold tile. She gave herself up to the artful handling of the teenage Jose Eber, enjoying herself despite her misgivings. She had no experience with this type of girlfriend-to-girlfriend behavior. Her mother refused to allow cosmetics in the house, saying a decent woman didn't need to paint herself up like a harlot to attract a man. The bathroom was for hairbrush and toothbrush, not the tools of vanity. Even now, Bess felt positively sinful applying a whisper of mascara and lip gloss. Her smile froze as Faith reached into her pastel box of facial magic.

"Go easy now," she warned, as Faith twirled up a tube of fire-engine red lipstick. "I don't want any of the children to mistake me for one of the clowns."

"Don't worry. You don't have the feet for it. You've got great lips. Are you sure I can't paint your toenails?"

"No!" Images of a flashy circus wagon came to mind. All she needed was gold fringe.

Faith examined her work critically, then nodded, picking up a hairbrush. Pale baby-fine hair crackled with new life under the girl's enthusiastic tutelage. Finally she smiled in satisfaction.

"All done."

When Bess tried to turn toward the glass, Faith caught her shoulders.

"Promise you won't scream. Give yourself time to get used to it. Promise?"

How bad could it be? Bess took a breath. "Promise." Then she looked.

And she stared at a total stranger with voluptuous red lips, beckoning blue eyes and delicate bone structure framed by loose waves of spun gold.

"Wow."

"Told you!"

Bess fingered the locks of hair curling against the collar of her sleeveless red vest. She never wore her hair down. It felt odd brushing her neck in a teasing caress. Faith plucked one fair strand up in a carefree loop, securing it above her left ear with a small red barrette, then hung tiny crystal hearts suspended on gold French earring wires to dance at her jawline whenever her head moved.

Who was this gorgeous free spirit, and what had she done with the mousy bookstore owner?

A soft knock at the front door startled Bess from her daze. The illusion of playing dress up vanished. Zach! Panic jolted through her as Faith squeezed her arms and warned, "Don't touch a thing! He's gonna love it!"

Then the teen dashed down the steps, leaving Bess confronting the somewhat threatening glamour queen in her bathroom mirror, one who exuded a confidence she could never claim. Nervousness fluttered in her belly. Anticipation tingled along all those inches of bare skin. The unnatural weight of cosmetics settled more comfortably as she tried a smile to ward off her fright. Stiffness eased in her expression, replaced by a warm glow that was neither artificial nor glaringly apparent. She exhaled shakily, amazed by the first recognition of her own loveliness.

"Aunt Bess, Mr. Crandall's here."

Her hands flew up to tremble against suddenly overwarm cheeks. She couldn't go downstairs, all lips and legs, in a Look-at-me! blaze of red. How could she parade around before the whole town of Sweetheart like a brazen advertisement for sin, on Zach Crandall's arm? She was on the library board, she sang a clear, rich contralto in the church choir. The thought of their horror shivered through her.

It would only take a minute. She could slip on a casual broomstick skirt and knee-highs. She'd twist her hair up into a no-nonsense knot. With a quick scrub of her face, no one would ever know this bold butterfly had ever emerged from its staid cocoon. No one but Faith.

She stopped her frantic thoughts, clamping down on her

panic. Faith would be so disappointed in her. Abruptly, the crushing of one girl's joy outweighed the whole town's censure. She couldn't be the one to purposefully snuff out the delight in a young girl's eyes. Even if she created a spectacle so shockingly out of character it got her regular customers checking their bifocal prescriptions. Faith was worth it. She'd prove to the girl that she wasn't hopelessly craven in the face of change.

Even if it was true.

So with consummate dignity and quivering heart, she left the bathroom to start down the stairs. The moment she took the turn on the landing, she saw him standing just inside the front door next to a proudly beaming Faith. For a timeless minute she couldn't move.

He looked so formidable, so out of place amongst her mother's antiques and bric-a-brac. The contrast accentuated his in-your-face virility to an alarming degree. Against the prim formality of Joan Carrey's front room, he was a slap of masculine nonchalance in a soft chambray shirt with sleeves pushed up over dark-furred forearms, in faded jeans worn white at the stitchings and creased with suggestive snugness at the inseam. A shock of bare ankles showed above low-cut running shoes.

His face tipped up toward her, and the effect of his intensely blue eyes was the same as plunging into the deep end of a pool: a shock of icy contact followed by the delicious chill of complete immersion. She might have drowned there if not distracted by the slow spread of his smile.

Never had a man looked at her quite that way, with such naked appreciation. And she smiled back, hesitantly at first, then with giddy thanksgiving that she'd managed to find the courage to change nothing about her lips or legs or free-floating locks.

"I was afraid you'd changed your mind," he said at last. The slight rasp of chiding nudged her back into full functioning. She continued down the stairs, very aware of the way his gaze followed.

"I told you I'd be ready." She reached the bottom of the stairs, pausing there as if stepping off that last riser meant free-falling into a dangerous unknown.

His gaze stroked over her again, this time, slowly, beginning at thankfully unpainted toes up the clean line of her legs, over the formfitting pleats in her short shorts and weskit top to the gradual flush coloring her cheeks. "You look ready for anything."

The rumble of innuendo held her mesmerized. What kind of signal was this "new you" look sending? Her breathing stopped as he reached out to pull a length of pale gold between the gentle pinch of his fingers.

"I like your hair this way."

She stood paralyzed until catching sight of Faith mouthing two words. Numbly, Bess verbalized them.

"Thank you."

"You look—" He couldn't find the right words.

"Great," Faith interjected, losing patience with their awkward ritual. "She looks great. Now, let's get going so we can grab a spot where we can see everything."

And everyone could see them…together.

As Faith rushed outside to snatch up the lawn chairs, Bess's resolve buckled.

And Zach said very softly, very firmly, "Don't be afraid."

His quiet command shook off her brief trepidation. What did she have to be afraid of? They were two old friends catching up on the past, not unlike three-quarters of the populace. But it was those who returned who were supposed to surprise with the change in their looks, not the ones who stayed behind. Bess had gone to bed Little Bo Peep and had woken up as Rapunzel.

Angling her chin a notch higher, she came down off that bottom step and boldly took his arm, pretending she hadn't heard his words, to say with feigned cheeriness, "After you."

And as she turned to close the door behind them, knowledge of her mother's disapproval speared her to the soul. Bess

swallowed hard, then looked up at her escort, smiling tightly.
"Let's go."

Town gossip hummed around Bess and Zach with the vo-
racity of hungry locusts sucking the life from a fresh crop.
Feeling like the last stalk of newly tasseled corn—in dangling
earrings—in the middle of that feeding frenzy, Bess stood at
the main street curb trying to be unobtrusive. Not likely when
her fire-engine red outfit made a bright bull's-eye, targeting
attention to the fact that she was with Zach Crandall. Not that
they stood out as a couple. There was no linking contact between them. But the way Zach framed her with his looming
presence left no question that they were together. Joan Carrey's daughter and Sam Crandall's son. A mind-boggling,
tongue-wagging combination.

Founder's Day in Sweetheart, as it was in many small Mid-
western towns, was the social event of the year. Its century-
and-a-half existence was recognized with a flag-waving
parade and class reunions, drawing those who'd ventured
away back home to be with family and friends for a weekend
of endless celebration. Inhabitants surrounded the town square
to watch and cheer as bands, baton twirlers, farm implements,
wagons and classic cars crept by on blacktop seared by Iowa's
August sun. More than one of the Harvest Queen's court or
Veterans of Foreign Wars marchers could be expected to
swoon by mid-morning as heat rose up in stifling waves.

Bess found the proceedings every bit as exciting as the big
spectacles televised from Macy's in New York, scaled down
to fit within Sweetheart's town center. She and her mother
had always commanded chairs outside the bookstore where
they'd sat demurely beneath its unfurled awning, following
the hour-long procession in silence, nodding to acquaintances
with an aloof dignity. This year, she felt like she was attend-
ing for the first time ever.

Anticipating the starting whistle with a childlike enthusiasm, Bess leaned out from her place on the curb to catch a
glimpse of the flag bearer and the high school band's twirlers.
Nothing could dampen her mood, not the murmurs of spec-

ulation, not the ever-growing temperature, not the restless
conscience that whispered she should contain her excitement
and act like a lady. This year she would behave as all the
others did, laughing, shouting, clapping. There was no harm
in it, no great sin in the boisterous revelry. If she wanted to
get loud, she could. If she wanted to bask in the pleasure of
Zach's presence, she would. A tremor of freedom sounded in
her heart, its tone as clear and vibrant as the sharp blast from
the drum major's whistle.

As all heads craned toward the approaching troop of Boy
Scouts bearing the emblems of country, state and council,
Zach only had eyes for the woman before him. He'd seen
enough Founder's Day parades to know the routine. He'd
been a closet watcher, never a participant. What he hadn't
seen before, what blossomed right in front of him, was a sight
more spectacular, more breathtaking: Elizabeth Carrey's delicate petals unfurling from the tightly closed bud.

She'd always been beautiful to him. He alone had seen
what wonders happiness and passion had worked upon the
solemn scholar. He held the knowledge close, a special secret
none of the other fools in Sweetheart had ever guessed. Until
now. When she'd come down the stairs to greet him, her
radiance blinding; a cool star gone suddenly nova bright. He'd
been dazzled beyond words, beyond conscious thought. She'd
become what he'd always dreamed he could make her—gorgeous, self-confident, free. Part of him rejoiced in her courage. Another simmered sullenly because she'd bloomed for
eyes other than his own.

Suddenly Bess turned to him, her features lit with sponta-
neity. They were close enough for her shoulder to graze his
chest, for her light floral perfume to tease up his nose and
steal his senses. In that instant the universe skidded to a halt
around him, slowly spinning up again only when she began
to speak.

"Look who's grand marshall. It's Mr. Ellis. He moved up
to Ames after he retired. He was our principal, remember?"

Zach looked beyond her to where a spindly old man sat up

on the back seat of Fred Meirs's gleaming Cadillac convertible, grinning at decades of past graduates. Zach's expression closed down tight.

At the same moment Arthur Ellis caught sight of the eldest Crandall, who'd spent three years in what could have been an assigned seat outside his office door. His gnarled hand froze in mid-wave. His smile died an awful death upon a shock of memory.

"Just sit there and keep your smart mouth shut. The law says we have to put up with you for three years or until you do us a favor and drop out. Let's not kid ourselves into thinking you'll leave here with any kind of education, but you make trouble and I'll see you're kicked out with a good start on your criminal record."

"I remember. Fondly."

The soft touch of Bess's fingers against the back of his clenched hand startled him out of his fierce recall. He glanced down into a gentle sea of empathy and remorse. Only Bess would recognize the scarring beneath his wry drawl. She'd always seen right through his cynicism. Once he'd basked in that sympathy. Now he pulled from it with a guarded smile.

"My memories aren't as good as yours, Bess. I try to keep them in the past where they belong."

Liar, his conscience shouted as he shifted his stare back to the parade. That miracle he'd never managed, no matter how many years, how many miles he'd put between him and the shadow of Sweetheart.

Idiot! Bess chided herself as he withdrew behind his practiced indifference. Of course he remembered. He remembered every slight, every sneer, every sorrow dealt him by the town he'd left behind. And standing here brought them all parading back before him: the principal who swore to have him expelled, the police chief who promised him a prison cell, the class of 1980 who went on to graduate without him, none of them at all surprised not to see him in their ranks. When she looked at the throng of people lining the parade route, she saw friends. What could he see except endless hostility from

the old ladies who swore he was the one who took a baseball
bat to their mailboxes; the peers who closed him determinedly
out of their ranks from kindergarten right through the final
months of high school; and the store owners who refused to
give him work, fearing a reputation that said he'd steal them
blind? A reputation complements of a father who'd lived
down to every expectation.

Why would he want to come back to a place so steeped in
old demons? To old memories that could only bring him
pain?

She touched his arm and felt the impact of his intense stare
as she gained his attention.

"We don't have to stay," she shouted over the brassy notes
blared out by the neighboring Corydon high school band.

His eyes narrowed, searching hers for a reason. "I thought
you liked this stuff?"

She shrugged as if it didn't matter. "It's nothing new."

"Let's walk awhile."

Bess cast about for Faith, finding her with her gaggle of
summer friends. They were throwing paper streamers at the
best-looking boys in the percussion section. The result was
several missed beats. Faith wouldn't notice her absence anytime soon.

"All right."

They backed out of the crowd, dodging chairs and coolers
and strollers filled with babies squalling their displeasure over
the loud rendition of "Summertime." But they couldn't avoid
the glares of those they passed, glares fixed upon the dark
figure from Sweetheart's past.

Escaping to the shaded seclusion of a side street brought
immediate relief from both heat and censure, and a buffer to
the noise. They walked side by side, not touching, not speaking, possessed by the awkwardness of two teens alone for the
first time together and the nervousness of two adults searching
for a common ground for safe conversation.

Zach's sudden laugh made Bess jump. He gestured ahead.
"The Dairy Dream. I can't believe it's still open. I used to

sneak cigarettes from Robby Benthem while he cleaned up after closing."

Faded and peeling, the ice cream stand weathered the passing decades tenaciously, fighting off the trend toward frozen yogurt and health food bagels to stick with good old hand-packed calories in twelve traditional flavors. Kids still hung out in the parking lot after sports events, and families swarmed the picnic tables throughout the long summer months gobbling steamed dogs and chili fries. The faulty neon sign flickered Open for Business in anticipation of thirsty parade-goers who would flood the front order windows in about forty-five minutes.

"Still like lime fizzes?"

Bess grinned, surprised he'd remembered. "I haven't had one in ages." Not since they'd shared their last one.

"My treat."

While Bess sat atop one of the scarred tabletops, Zach ordered from an oily-faced teen who had no idea about the notoriety of his first customer. Because watching Zach created a strange restlessness inside her, Bess concentrated on the graying planks supporting her, upon twenty years of devotion carved in initials and scratched out cuss words. Her stare fixed upon one lopsided heart proclaiming Z.C. and B.C. scored so deeply even seventeen winters couldn't wear it away. Her thumb rubbed over the bold groves as she remembered the blushing embarrassment of the young girl she'd been. And that same girl's secret thrill at having an eternal memento of her first...and only passion.

As Zach approached with waxy cups in hand, she scooted over, covering the bittersweet proclamation of a love that hadn't lasted.

"Here you go." She took the cold cup from him. "I had to tell the kid how to make it. I feel old." With that grumble, he settled on the tabletop beside her.

"Positively Jurassic," she murmured in agreement, then took a sip of the syrupy sweet drink. The cold shot up to numb her mind with a momentary headache. "Ooh, brain freeze." At Zach's perplexed glance, she smiled shyly. "That's what Faith and her friends call it. They're dragging me kicking and screaming into the nineties. A hopeless task. I never caught on to the slang of my generation."

"That's because you're a classic."

She wrinkled her nose, thinking of her mother's store. "Great. Now I really know I've been on the shelf too long."

Zach studied his straw as he stirred it through the icy confection. "That's not what I meant." His voice held the low raspiness of velvet nap. "You don't need to keep up with the trends. You're cashmere and pearls, a '62 Corvette. You'll never go out of style." He made a soft, deprecating sound, as if he'd spoken too much nonsense aloud.

Bess didn't know how to respond. His honesty unbalanced her arguments. Yet she couldn't quite believe all he said to be true. So she smiled slightly and took another sip of her drink, waiting for the beat of her heart to slow down from its frenzied gallop. Time to direct their conversation away from personal revelations. To the neutral things old acquaintances might speak of, instead of the uncomfortable familiarity between long-ago lovers.

"When does your mom get home?"

That brought back his moody quiet. "Sometime next week. Mel is taking vacation time to see she gets settled in."

"It'll be good having her back."

Zach didn't answer. She could guess how he must be feeling, returning to the home of his youth for a reunion with the ailing mother who killed his father. She could guess, but she didn't know. Sam Crandall reaped what he'd sown all his angry life. But the seeds he managed to plant before his violent exit from the earth still grew in Melody's haunted eyes, in Zach's brooding frown, in their mother's grim circumstance. Evil left a long-lasting residue that was hard to wash completely away. No, she couldn't imagine what he felt about it.

"I haven't seen her for seventeen years." That was said flat and factual.

"You never visited her?" That shocked Bess. She could understand him wanting to put Sweetheart behind him, but why would he sever ties to the one woman who'd loved him so unconditionally?

He shook his head, still staring at the sweating paper cup. "For a lot of years, it was impossible. By the time I was free to, I didn't think she'd want to see me."

Bess digested his words carefully and came up with a taste so bitter, she couldn't spit it out or swallow it down. *By the time I was free.*

He'd been in prison.

Awareness stunned her, but explained everything. Why he hadn't come back. Why she hadn't heard from him. A man with Zach Crandall's pride would never write to confess that he'd been thrown in jail: an admission that everything the town prophesied had come true.

Beyond the shock, questions surged up: what had he done? And why? How long was the term of his incarceration? Who knew about it besides her? Would this be another secret for her to keep from the rest of Sweetheart?

Anguished pity wrapped around a pang of disappointment as she studied his strong profile. She'd wanted to believe he'd made a good life for himself, but in the end he hadn't. He'd lived out the worst possible scenario. He was a felon, convicted of who knows what. And she was sitting alone beside him.

Then a flood of townsfolk converged upon the ice cream stand in the aftermath of the parade. Their privacy was invaded by families and uniformed band members, by 4-H members and veterans of the foreign wars. Noisy talk and an undercurrent of agitated whispers aimed in their direction destroyed their isolation, but not the anxious turn of Bess Carrey's thoughts.

Zach, a criminal.

Her mother's worst nightmare come true.

Chapter 4

"You're awfully quiet."

The sound of Zach's voice startled Bess from her moody reflections. She glanced up guiltily. "I'm sorry. What did you say?"

He wasn't fooled by her weak smile of attentiveness. "What's wrong?"

"Wrong? Nothing."

They walked leisurely back toward the town's center, where craft booths would dominate the grassy square for the rest of the afternoon. Mouth-watering smells of fair food beckoned as rides along the small temporary midway started up to the delight of squealing children and adults alike. But Bess had never felt farther removed from the embrace of community and fun.

What crime had he committed?

She couldn't think of anything else.

Robbery out of necessity for an eighteen-year-old on the run? Assault spurred by a too-quick temper? Nothing worse. *Don't let it be anything worse,* she pleaded within her panicked mind. Something involving a gun? Her palms slid damply against the sides of her shorts. Violence happened on the six o'clock news in places like New York and L.A., not in sleepy little burgs like Sweetheart; except in the case of the Crandalls.

Maybe Sweetheart was isolated and archaic, but it was safe—a safe place to live and work and walk the sidewalks after dark. Where doors weren't dead bolted and windows barred. Where the local paper's reports of crime involved juvenile vandalism or an occasional drink too many leading to a brawl or a fender bender. Nothing involving guns or hold-ups. The last holdup in Sweetheart was done by Jesse James, who'd politely asked permission from one of the local farmers to camp out on their property overnight, while unbeknownst to his host, he was casing the bank. Its brick still held the bullet scars from the gang's warning shots. Citizens spoke of the event fondly; their small piece of history over one hundred years ago.

But Zach brought the latent air of danger back to Sweetheart. It cloaked him like the familiar black leather. Standing so close to him, Bess felt its chill embrace.

What had he done?

Seventeen years was a long time. Like his father before him, had he surrendered to Darkness to walk an easier, angrier path? Prison wasn't known for releasing model citizens.

How safe were she and Faith in his company until she discovered all the details?

She almost jumped out of her sandals at the halting press of his fingers upon her forearm.

"Do you want me to take you home or would you just like me to leave?"

She looked up, eyes wide and a bit wild.

Yes. She should have said yes to either or both. *Just go and take your sordid deeds and upsetting presence and let me get back to my stable routine. I don't need the upheaval of you in my life again.*

That wretched cry shaped her lips but she never spoke it.

Looking up at him and getting lost in the looking, Bess was buffeted by past feelings in a dervish of desire and never-abandoned dreams. Her senses filled with every aspect of him, a blur of remembered textures and sounds: the scrape of his rough chin along her soft cheek, the moist heat of his mouth hovering above hers in forbidden temptation—irresistible temptation. The erotic music made by their mingling breaths and discovering sighs. The crunch and pungent odor of dried leaves beneath them on a chill spring night fraught with urgency and exploration.

All those things came back to her, prompting a feverish need to touch his face, to see if his squared jaw felt the same in the cup of her palm, to see if his kiss could wake the same wild magic within her slumberous spirit. She couldn't let the opportunity slip away without knowing, without experiencing, at least once more.

Without knowing, one way or the other, if she'd been wrong all those years ago.

So she pushed down the panic and the agitation and made herself relax enough to say, "I'm fine. Really. It's just the heat and the noise and...you." She let herself admit that much of the truth, knowing he'd understand without asking for further explanation. He knew what havoc he stirred in her staid, sensible soul, and would know it wasn't meant as a complaint.

Smart enough to know she wasn't being totally open with him, Zach held silent. For now. After seventeen years, she was entitled to her misgivings. He had them, too. There was a lot of ground to cover before they'd feel comfortable with one another. They couldn't do it in a single day.

If ever.

She hadn't been afraid of him since the first week they spent together. But she was now. He wondered why. And he wondered what he could do to change her mind. Years ago, he'd won her over with a kiss. It wouldn't be that easy this time. Bess wasn't the same naive girl willing to believe the best in everyone. He'd caught an edge of wariness when they met in her mother's store. Put there by him. She wasn't the only one with reason for wariness. He'd believed in her once and she'd failed him. He'd survived then, but a man could take only so much disappointment in one lifetime.

They continued walking.

Century-old oaks sheltered the town square, cooling its uneven brick walkways as the heat index soared toward one hundred. Iowa winters were long and cruel, shutting many of its occupants inside for the duration. Restless hands put the time to use producing unique goods to sell in area consignment shops or at community events such as this one. Woven area rugs, meticulously stitched quilts in Wedding Ring and Log Cabin patterns, crocheted pillow covers and yarn dolls in gaudy colors fashioned to catch young eyes, adorned tables and clotheslines interspersed with canned goods and jellies in this, their last round of taste testing before the county fair competitions.

Ordinarily, Bess would stop at each booth to admire the craftsmanship and share a few minutes of conversation with a lonely farm wife. Often she'd buy things she didn't need to help out those she knew were having a hard time making payments at home. Some were ritual purchases: Betty Schoop's quince jelly to last through the winter months; painstakingly crocheted wash rags from the arthritic Mrs. Mendleson; and flavored taffy, pulled by the girls' soft ball team.

This year she stayed on the walk, discouraged by the startled looks she received. Then the unwelcoming glares as attention fixed upon Zach. Each stare levied that same harsh blame, that same unforgiving judgment. Bad seed. Bad news. Bad to the bone.

Asking what was she doing with the likes of him?

Beside her, Zach walked tall, pretending he didn't notice that he was as welcome as a hailstorm before harvest. Despite the casual ease in his stance, his expression remained all sharp, angular lines, evidence of the strain he must feel pretending this was just another place, that he was just a regular guy out to enjoy the company of an old friend.

The people of Sweetheart weren't about to let him forget who he was. Nor could she ignore their shock and displeasure in seeing her as his escort, their sweetly sensible Bess Carrey, almost unrecognizable in her blindingly bright almost-not-there shorts. Traitor, those narrowed gazes accused her, churning up an acidy taste of guilt, anxiousness and anger.

Zach paused at one of the booths, picking up one of the handmade items. He didn't notice the way Helen Jeffers stiffened up behind the table, but Bess did.

"Think Mel would like this?"

Bess looked at the cinnamon-filled fabric tube coiled into a hot pad so that the heat of a serving dish would release its pleasant scent. She could imagine Melody's surprise at receiving the thoughtful token. "I'm sure she would."

Even as Zach reached back for his wallet, Helen Jeffers snatched the hot pad from his hand.

"That's not for sale. It's my last one. I'm using it as a sample so I can take orders."

He couldn't mistake the snap of her tone. Still he made himself smile and speak politely. "I'd like to order one then."

The woman's gaze narrowed. "I can't say when I'd have time to get to it. I've already got a whole season's worth of work ahead of me." And her thin smile implied that she'd make sure something else always took precedent.

Zach put his wallet away. "I appreciate your honesty." He stared at her just long enough to say he'd gotten the message then turned away from the table.

Bess lingered a moment, lifting the hot pad for a closer examination. "Mrs. Jeffers, this would be so pretty in my kitchen," she confided in a low aside. "If you're not taking any more orders, do you think I could have this one?"

"Well…"

Bess smiled hopefully, winning the other woman over.

"I guess so. That'll be four dollars and fifty cents." As she reached out for the money, she felt free to add, "That's a different look for you, Bess.'' Different, implying unappealing.

Bess felt color creep up into her face, nearly as hot and vivid as the ensemble. "Faith picked it out."

The woman nodded with a resigned lift of her brows, a "what can you do with kids these days?" attitude.

Feeling provoked and more than a twinge ashamed of herself, Bess paid, then rejoined Zach with the small parcel in hand. He glanced at it, his emotions veiled.

"Give it to Melody from both of us." She extended the sack covertly, but he didn't take it. She frowned, wondering if she'd made a mistake.

"Don't, Bess," he told her with a penetrating quiet. "I don't need your under-the-table charity anymore."

Her frown became a scowl. "That's not what it is."

"Oh? My mistake."

But he wasn't wrong. She'd purposefully angled so Helen Jeffers couldn't see the exchange. To protect the feelings of two people she cared about? Or her own image in the eyes of the town?

Flustered by the ridiculous conflict unfairly involving both heart and mind, she urged, "Take it, Zach. Please. For Melody. She'd enjoy it." She pushed the bag at him again, feeling his tense displeasure, refusing to back down before it. Finally he snatched the sack then leaned around her to meet Helen Jeffers's hostile glare. He lifted the bag, smiling smugly before mouthing a mocking, "Thank you." The woman blinked, betrayal bright in the aggrieved stare she turned on Bess. Bess looked away quickly and hustled after Zach's stalking figure. His mood telegraphed itself in each stiff-legged stride, so she stayed silent.

"You don't have to keep me company," he said with a growly snap. "It's not like I'm a stranger here. I'm sure you'd rather spend your time with your neighbors."

But Bess was beginning to wonder if he was a stranger to her. She was remembering the boy he'd been. What if there was no goodness left in the man he'd become?

"I see them all the time." She put a hand on his arm, apologetically, staying him, trying to sidetrack his anger. "I wanted to spend some with you."

He paused, casting a brief glance her way before glaring ahead at the scurry of faintly recognized townsfolk who were so busy eyeing him anxiously that they were bumping into one another.

"And I'm not making it very easy, am I?"

She didn't answer. What about Zach Crandall had ever been easy?

But she'd known that and still came with him.

"So what's on the Sweetheart agenda for this evening?" He didn't look at her. Paper cracked as his hand clenched and loosened rhythmically on the offending sack.

Wishing she'd never made the backfiring gesture, Bess replied, "Oh, the usual. Class reunions and a buffet in the high school cafeteria and a dance in the gym later. I'm working the refreshment tables. I've got to change first." Into something less glaring than the red shorts. Something sedate and more Bess Carrey.

Zach made an acknowledging noise.

"Thinking of going?" She didn't want to sound too obvious—like she was asking him out or anything. Wistfully she recalled all the dances in her senior year that had passed by uneventfully while she'd gone to bed early and fantasized about being in Zach Crandall's arms.

"I don't exactly have a graduating class. Think I'll pass."

"Oh." How stupid of her not to remember. He was the only official dropout from the Class of 1980. Not something he'd want pinned on the front of his shirt for all to see.

"It should be fun for you. You've got a lot of friends to catch up with."

This time she said nothing. Though she knew everyone in Sweetheart, how many friends did she really have? The kind who were confidants, the ones who shared secrets and gossip and comfortable silences? None that she could name. None except Zach. And they'd shared everything except a future.

They came to the edge of the square, having seen all there was to see. Zach turned to her, his expression stoic. He took a step back, widening the space between them. She stood against a backdrop of noisy fellowship, as one of the included, while he stood at the fringe, on the outside, ever looking in.

"Aunt B, come look what I found!"

Faith's energetic approach created an easy way to break from each other. Bess looked around, and Zach retreated to the street, meeting her return glance with a thin smile.

"I gotta go. I've got something to do before Mel gets off work." He hesitated, looking as if there was more on his mind, but deciding to say nothing more.

Bess hesitated, drawn toward him and at the same time, pulled back into the neighborly hubbub behind her. Again, she let him go with a wan smile.

"Thanks for this morning. It was like old times."

His smile never reached his eyes. "Old times." He made it sound very final, like there was no connection between then and now.

Torn by this, Bess nodded wistfully. Maybe it was better to leave the past in the past where Zach was concerned.

Seeing her answer in her eyes, Zach spun away, walking determinedly out of her life again.

How could she let him go?

She was just about to call out his name, when Faith tugged on her arm impatiently.

"Hurry, Aunt B. There's only one left and I've got to have it!"

Sighing, Bess turned from the sight of Zach Crandall's retreat and let herself be yanked back into the fold of Sweetheart tradition.

Tired and headachy after working a double shift, so the others could sneak out to enjoy the festivities, Melody Crandall let herself in the gate leading up to her quiet house. She started down the walk, sorting through the day's collection of bills and junk mail, and was halfway up the porch steps when a familiar odor reached her. Shock jerked her up taut as her wide gaze flew about, fixing in mind-numbing terror upon the figure of a man. Seated in the vine-covered darkness upon one of the side rails, he was faceless, just a large, intimidating silhouette with a beer bottle dangling from one hand.

An inarticulate cry tore from her as mail fluttered from nerveless fingers. She staggered back, knowing herself trapped, knowing she couldn't run as he rose up and started toward her.

"Mel?"

Confusion made her light-headed. She tried to breathe. It came out a funny little squeak. Afraid of passing out, she fumbled for the rail behind her with both hands just as late-afternoon light slanted across his face revealing the glitter of pale eyes and the strong, squared angles. Her knees gave out and the edge of the step cracked against her tail bone.

"Mel?" He dropped down in front of her, big hands bracing under her elbows to keep her from going over backward.

His voice...the concern crowding his dark brows.

"Zach?" She touched his features, her fingertips trembling. Then her arms lassoed his neck, tight, as she sobbed, "Oh, Zach, I thought—I thought it was—"

"Hush, baby. I know what you thought." He hugged her close, his own eyes squeezed shut as her fear and pain shattered through him. "It's all right. I'm sorry I scared you. I'm sorry, Mel."

"I—I smelled the beer and saw someone out here waiting—"

His embrace dragged her even closer. "It was just me. I'm sorry." He'd get rid of the rest of the six-pack without opening them. Remorse pounded in time with her frantic heartbeats. Gradually, her fright eased back into the past where it belonged and she pushed back from him with a nervous laugh.

"You must think I'm crazier than a rabid skunk."

He rubbed the tears from her cheeks with his thumbs. "No.

I don't think that at all. I do think you should have gotten the hell out of this house a long time ago.''

"I couldn't, Zach."

"Why?"

"I—I got married. We lived here for eleven years."

Where was the thud from his jaw hitting the steps?

"Married? When? To whom?"

"I don't want to talk about it now. Let me find the rest of my bills—" she was twisting away, fumbling for the letters "—and I'll make us some coffee."

"Mel—"

"Later, Zach. Please?"

He couldn't bring more anguish into her uplifted gaze. "Coffee sounds good. I've got some made inside."

The warm scent of cinnamon filled the kitchen, drawing Melody's attention to the hot pad beneath her coffee carafe.

"Like it?" He waited awkwardly for her response.

"You bought it for me?" She turned big eyes upon him, and as tears welled up along the lower lashes, he turned to complete mush.

"Bess and I did. I thought you might—" The rest was choked off by her sudden hug and the wad of emotion that remained stuck in his throat long after she spun away to wipe at her eyes and pour two cups for them. It punched home all over again just how difficult things had been if such a small gesture won a reaction of such magnitude. He'd make it up to her. He'd shower her with gifts until she could smile with delight upon receipt instead of bursting into grateful tears.

They sat in the bright kitchen, making small talk about the festival until Melody's hands grew steady and her breaths more regular. Zach wanted to ask about her marriage and why her finger was bare although, sensing her vulnerability, he stayed silent. But he couldn't leave it alone.

He knew how he could find out the details.

When the coffee was gone and Melody had cleaned up the kitchen, she bent over him, surprising him with a kiss upon the temple.

"What was that for?"

"For being here," she answered simply. She stroked his face, her own features growing wistful and sage beyond their years. "Don't let the ghosts drive you away, Zach. They will if you let them."

Bess spent the early part of the evening refilling the buffet table and ladling out punch. It gave her the opportunity to see and speak to everyone without the obligation to carry on conversations. She knew what everyone wanted to talk about.

They wanted to know about Zach.

Music started up in the gymnasium at nine, honoring decade after decade of nostalgic hit tunes. After she'd helped out in the kitchen, storing the leftovers and stripping the stained table covers, she thought about going in but quickly squelched the notion. She wasn't in the mood to twist to Chubby Checker with George Glover who'd come down from Ames wearing a horrible hairpiece, bragging about his successful car lot, or to fend off those determined to pry tomorrow's rumors from her. It had been a long day. The heels she'd wore with her wispy dress pinched her toes. The evening held no magic. Time to go home and soak up the solitude.

She didn't own a car. Everything in Sweetheart was within a five-block radius, and she liked to walk and savor the night air. There was no hurry. Faith and her friends would be at the carnival riding the Tilt-A-Whirl and gorging on elephant ears until eleven, so Bess set a leisurely pace, clearing her mind of the things that crowded her heart.

As she turned up her drive, she thought she heard music. She nixed the notion that it might be Faith. The teen wouldn't be caught dead listening to "How Deep is Your Love?" in Bee Gee falsetto. The sentimental old tune filtered out into the darkness from her front porch.

She paused, startled to see Zach Crandall sitting there on the stone steps with a miniature boom box between his feet.

"Zach?" Her voice quavered. "What are you doing here?"

He stood slowly, letting her take her fill of him with her bedazzled eyes. "There are a couple of things I wanted to ask you."

"Oh?" A croak of sound forced from a suddenly dry throat.

"About Mel."

"Oh." Fragile hopes scattered with the brief shake of her head. She started up the front walk steps toward him. "What about her?"

"I need you to fill in some of the blanks for me."

"Don't you mean a big blank? A seventeen-year blank?" She couldn't resist the needling jab. He didn't wince, so she sighed. "What can I tell you that you can't hear about from her?"

"Who did she marry?"

Taken aback, she blurted, "She didn't tell you?"

"If she did, I wouldn't have to ask you, would I?"

She could ignore his curt tone because of the apprehension behind it. He knew something was wrong, knew it was something he wouldn't like. And he was asking her to lay it on the line.

"Todd Nesman."

Zach mulled the name over, then shook his head. "I don't remember him."

"There's no reason you should. He was two years ahead of us in school. Red hair. A lot of big talk. Had a fast car and picked up some pretty good money on the pro stock circuit."

Zach's brow puckered then furrowed in deep horizontal lines. "I remember now. A real ass."

Bess nodded, dropping down onto the cement porch across from him.

"How did Mel get mixed up with him? I don't recall her seeing anyone in particular."

"I don't think they ever really dated." Bess paused, wondering how much she should reveal. She didn't want to cross the line between a friend's confidence and public knowledge. The private stuff should come from his sister, not from her.

Zach read her reluctance. "I came here to hear the truth. Don't sugarcoat it, Bess. I can take it."

Could he? She wondered. Could he hear the truth and not hate himself for leaving her alone to face such misery? She started talking, keeping her facts objective, betraying none of her own opinions in the candid picture she drew him.

"When your mom went to prison, your brothers took off in all directions, afraid they'd be placed in the foster care system. Melody was determined to stay, to try to hold on to the house so you'd all have something to come home to. You remember Mrs. Todd, don't you?"

"The social studies teacher?"

Bess nodded. "Melody stayed with them while the court was deciding about custody. She was underage, and there was no family."

Zach's features darkened, impatiently. He knew all that. "So?"

"So Todd promised to help her hang on to the house, if she'd marry him. She didn't have much choice. There was no one else for her to turn to."

Zach studied his fingernails with a fierce concentration. She didn't voice her comment as an accusation but he received it as one. He hadn't been there to help his little sister. She'd been forced to depend upon a stranger. "What happened?" he asked fatalistically.

"It wasn't a good marriage. She was looking for security and ended up...with someone like your father."

Zach didn't look up. The muscles in his jaw spasmed tightly. "Did he—did he mistreat her?" He was thinking of her glazed stare when he'd caught her wrist across the counter. Thinking it was his fault that she'd had to endure another monster.

."Not that she told anyone."

"So, where is he?"

Bess shivered at the deadly quiet in his words. The sound of a man sharpening his knives before beginning a hunt.

"I don't know, Zach. He left town. He took off with some bumper babe from the race circuit. Melody filed for divorce and got it." Bess added in a soft addendum, "He left with everything she had."

Zach surged to his feet with a violence that had Bess cowering back. What worked in his face was frightening to behold. Then it was gone, and somehow the lack of animation was scarier. "Guess I'll have to go find him."

"Zach, no." She grabbed his hand, hanging on when he would pull away. "Not without talking to your sister first. Promise me."

He stared down at her through eyes as opaque as pale blue ice. Bess knew a moment of pure fear, wondering if she had just unleashed a killer behind those impossibly cold eyes. Then Zach gave her a grim smile.

"Don't get shook. I'm not going out to stalk him on some lunatic vendetta. Life has a way of bringing back one's mistakes. I can wait."

Unconvinced, Bess continued to watch for signs of malice but Zach betrayed none. He seemed furious, justifiably so, and frustrated, also understandable. But no hint of maniacal rage steeped behind those emotions. He had his anger under control.

"Thanks for telling me, Bess. I appreciate the honesty." He rubbed her knuckles with his thumb, reminding her that she still possessed his hand. Blushing, she let go. But he made no move to leave.

"Was there anything else you needed to know?"

It was just the two of them, alone in the night. When he took his time in answering, Bess had a moment of distressing clarity.

What did she really know about this man? He could have been rubbing elbows with serious criminals for all she knew.

"There's one thing," he said at last.

She looked up, fixing her gaze within the power of his own. Making it impossible for her to break away as his voice lowered a suggestive notch.

"I was wondering if you saved a dance for me."

Chapter 5

He gave her no time to consider his seemingly odd statement. Not that she needed it. She'd dreamed of it too long.

He scooped her into a loose embrace, her fingers curled lightly in one big hand while his other rested low and easy at the small of her back. She'd never slow danced with anyone except the imaginary partner in her lonely teenager's room. Zach made it effortless.

His gaze held hers mesmerized, dissolving her tension so their movements sprang from an inherent inner rhythm instead of an awkward count of one-two-three. He moved her across the driveway gravel with the slight pressure of his hand, their unhurried steps slowing into a more-intimate shuffle as their bodies swayed ever nearer. The breezy print fabric of her summer dress caressed the backs of her legs as Zach eased her in closer until she could feel him imprinted through the thin material.

Dazed and compliant, she sought the comfortable lee of his shoulder as a pillow for her head. Her eyes closed and nothing existed beyond the haunting melody and her awareness of the man shifting against her with a seducing leisure. He rested his head atop hers, his cheek rubbing over the pale silk of her hair. Nothing could be so perfect this side of making love. Down from where her palms capped his shoulders, her slight form melted along his, riding the subtle bunch and relax of his muscular thighs as their dance slowed to a side to side rocking, then stilled altogether.

She lost track of how long they stood there in her driveway, leaning into each other, absorbing the sounds and sensations, fascinated by something as natural and ordinary as the harmony of each other's breathing. Finally, Zach's lips brushed, soft and warm, against the curve of her ear, sending a shudder through her every fiber. Then he stepped back. His hands lingered at her waist, a testament to his reluctance.

"I was just going to ask for the dance and talk for a while but I'm afraid I'm going to want a lot more than that unless I get the hell out of here right now." The low rasp of his voice rubbed her sensibilities raw.

"Okay."

He didn't know if she was okaying his urgent departure or his need for more. He didn't ask.

She didn't watch him walk away. Instead, she let her wobbly knees give way, flopping down on the stone steps leading up from the drive to the front walk so she could close her eyes and lose herself once more in the moment.

Things were getting complicated. It was only a matter of time before Zach would ask for more.

What was she going to tell him?

It was a Sunday tradition for Bess to stop in at Sophie's Diner for breakfast before closing out the week's receipts at the store and going to church. The booths were all filled by the time she arrived shortly after eight so she slipped onto one of the stools at the counter and ordered the eggs-over-easy special. She'd almost managed to consume her breakfast in peace when the spots on either side of her were filled by the Drabney sisters.

"Good morning, Elizabeth," one of the elderly sisters said, marking an end to her quietude. "I saw Herb Addison yesterday."

An innocent enough comment. Innocent, at least, on the surface. Bess reserved judgment as she stirred in the artificial sweetener needed to make Sophie's coffee taste less like forty-weight oil.

"He asked about you."

Bess took a swallow, grimacing at both the brew and the turn of conversation. She didn't favor the ladies flanking her with a glance that might indicate interest. "Did he?" Her tone remained carefully neutral. It wouldn't do to feed the flame. She watched Myrt Watson and Lorraine Freemiere exchange hopeful looks in the cloudy mirror behind the counter. Too late. The matchmaking sparks were at full blaze.

"He said he was looking forward to a taste of your rhubarb pie."

Bess stirred in another packet of sweetener, holding to her politeness with difficulty. "That's all he has a taste for, I hope."

Myrt made an aggravated sound but Lorraine, the older and more opinionated of the two sisters spoke right up. "And what's wrong with Herb Addison? He has his own acreage and no house mortgage. He'll own that fancy cultivator outright by next spring and I hear he's fixing to put in central air." Lorraine worked at the bank. She knew everyone's financial dealings. In her mind, a paid balance made for a good match.

"Well, that ought to cool down his taste for my rhubarb, then."

"Really, Bess," Myrt sighed. "You are the nitpickin'est woman. Herb Addison is a very nice man."

"Who forgets to put in his bridgework and still subscribes to those slinky ladies' underwear catalogs even though his Effie's been gone for over three years."

Lorraine chose to ignore her criticism. "He's just lonely and a tad forgetful. Nothing a good woman couldn't change."

"And what if I'm not such a good woman?" she asked archly.

Both matrons laughed at that a little too long and a little too heartily for Bess to feel flattered.

"Why Elizabeth Carrey," Myrt concluded, "you're as straitlaced as Wilbur Marlow's back brace."

She was thirty-four and already being compared to an old man's creaking back brace. Great. A real confidence builder.

"Well, if not Herb, how about Walt Sadler? There's nothing wrong with his teeth."

"If you like crocodiles," Bess murmured into her cup.

"Now, Bess, that's just plain unfair. Walt is a nice boy."

"I don't trust anyone who has that much to smile about and still lives at home with his mama and sister at forty-five years old."

Not to be discouraged, Lorraine said, "I happen to know his mother is quite fond of you."

Bess made an uncharitable noise somewhere between a snort and a groan.

Incensed by the younger woman's lack of appreciation for their relentless matchmaking efforts, Myrt said, "Unless you want to end up a wrinkled old spinster, you had better lower your standards. I doubt that Prince Charles is coming to Sweetheart, Iowa, anytime soon to ask you out to dinner."

"I'm leaving all my evenings open just in case. I hear he likes the more mature type."

The two busybodies shook their collective heads, wondering why they bothered with the stubborn creature. Except, like everyone in their small community, the two adored Bess Carrey and worried over her lonesome state. It just wasn't natural for a woman of her looks and sweet temperament to be alone. And so they told her every time they met, which was at least twice a day; once for breakfast at Sophie's and again when she brought her meager deposit to the bank. They'd named themselves the watchdogs of her fast-fading chances to snare a beau from the slim pickings in Sweetheart, and Bess couldn't help wishing their leashes were a bit shorter.

Seeing her with Zach made their efforts redouble.

"Have you made any plans for the fireworks tonight?"

Deliberately dodging their question, Bess said, "I'll have my usual tables out for the sidewalk sale this afternoon. Maybe someone will buy up my whole inventory and I can accept Ted Doolin's bid on the store. Then I can run off for some wild, wicked adventure. Maybe even to New York City."

Both woman scowled slightly at her levity. New York City equated to sin. But they both knew Joan Carrey's daughter wasn't going anywhere.

"That's not what I meant, Elizabeth," Myrt chastised in her former schoolteacher tone. "I meant social plans."

"I promised to take Faith to the rodeo."

Lorraine patted her hand sympathetically. "Chaperoning a sixteen-year-old girl is not exactly a social event."

Bess smiled. "I'm sure it will keep me busy. Half the boys in town are tying up my phone line."

"Do any of them have single fathers?"

"Really, Lorraine," Bess chuckled, sipping at the now unpalatably sweet coffee. "Romance is for the young, not for the soon-to-be-withered, like me." Before either woman could cut in with any comments, she added, "I have Faith for the summer and I mean to make the most of it until Julie gets back from her honeymoon."

"That gadabout sister of yours has always had the traveling bug."

Because it wasn't a harsh judgment, Bess didn't take offense. "Julie's always been the free-spirited one, that's for sure. I can't see myself prowling about Aztec ruins in Mexico. All I'd find is Montezuma's revenge. I get homesick watching too much of the Discovery Channel."

"Where is your niece? Isn't she helping out at the store?"

Bess smiled patiently at Myrt, who believed idleness meant an opportunity for mischief. "She's on vacation. She's sixteen. I didn't take her in to make a slave out of her."

"You spoil that girl, Elizabeth," Lorraine pronounced.

"You always have. I bet you went and got that satellite dish just so she wouldn't miss her MTV."

"Spoiling her is one of my greatest pleasures." She picked up her water-stained bill and her handbag. "If you would excuse me, I have a business to run."

"More like it runs you," Myrt mumbled. "If you weren't always buried in that musty old store, maybe you'd find more time for courting. Enjoy yourself once in a while."

"And what makes you think I'm not enjoying myself?"

Neither woman could answer, for Bess never complained about her lot. She always smiled as if everything was wonderful. Since her mother died, she'd come partially out of her shell, committees at the school and library, volunteering for fund drives, working tirelessly, efficiently at any task put to her. No one in Sweetheart could complain that Bess wasn't a paragon of all that was good and decent. Just like her mother raised her.

Except for that unfortunate incident with the red shorts that nearly sent poor Walt to the cardiac ward...and the business with that Crandall boy. Surely good-heartedness didn't need to extend quite that far. Zach Crandall was hardly a stray dog to be taken in and pitied.

And they worried for their guileless young friend.

"Shall I give Herb your best?" Lorraine called optimistically.

"You can tell him I baked lemon meringue this year."

"I'm sure he'll want you to save him a piece for the barbecue. All it would take is a little encouragement from you. And you wouldn't want folks to get the wrong idea after seeing you with that Crandall boy yesterday."

Bess took a breath and held it until her temper was under control. She knew it would come down to that. Plain, lonely Elizabeth Carrey so desperate for a man that she should settle for the likes of Herb or Walt without complaint.

What would the two busybodies say if she announced with shocking deliberation that she had been hipbone to hipbone with Zach Crandall under the moon last night, and that he was so damn hot and sexy, she'd considered dropping with him right there in the driveway for some madly passionate lovemaking?

Either they'd have a stroke just imagining that changing sheets for Herb Addison wasn't half as appealing to her as rolling around in them with Zach Crandall, or they'd have her locked away for her own good. Since she'd been locked away most of her life from anything that might be construed as mildly pleasurable, she said nothing beyond a soft, "Thank you for your concern, but I'm a big girl now."

She went to the cash register and counted out the approximate coins, thinking it would serve them right if she started disgracefully chasing after one of the high school boys. Maybe that would stop them from trying to shove moldy old widowers down her throat.

Or maybe she should develop a backbone and give Zach the encouragement he needed, proving once and for all that there was just a trace of bad girl in her after all.

She stepped out into the early-morning sunshine and glanced around the quiet streets before taking the shortcut across the town square where the only reminders of yesterday's craft fair were the holes from table legs in the grass. There was no hurry in her stride. It wasn't as though she had to balance the national budget. If she had a half dozen people wander in and out of the store all day, it was a good day. She didn't kid herself about making a million in the used and rare book business. A good month was making the bill payments. But the house was paid for, and her father's family had left her a tidy little trust from which to draw if she needed any extras. She was comfortable.

As she breathed in the sultry scent of late summer, her annoyance with the meddlers at the diner mellowed. It was hard to stay angry with those who genuinely cared for her well-being. Sweetheart residents considered themselves all one big close-knit family with the right to meddle wherever they chose. And like a big family, the town harbored few secrets and fewer surprises. She loved the intimacy of the town square, the fact that everyone knew everyone and that all looked out for each other. She'd never had that sense of closeness in the confines of her own family. That was why her sister had gotten out at an early age. Maybe Bess had been a little envious, but she'd never resented Julie for being brave enough to make the break. It was a courage she could never claim.

How different her life might have been if she only had.

She was content with her life, content with her freedom. No one to answer to. No one to obey but her own common sense.

And no one to share herself with.

Fishing in her shapeless woven bag for her keys, Bess walked along the pre-Civil-War and turn-of-the-century store-fronts to pause at time- and weather-worn steps. She unlocked the heavy door with its leaded glass and brass fittings and swung it inward. It struck her an almost physical blow, that smell, the moldy stench of things old and forgotten. She braced against the memories hanging upon that stale odor. Since the store had been shut up all the day before, it was worse, stronger, thicker, almost heavy with neglect. The stagnant scent of her youth, shut away and unused. Sometimes, even after she'd gone home at night and showered, she could still smell it, the musty reminder of dreams shelved, growing thin and fragile with age. On those nights she'd cry herself to sleep, hating the store, hating her life and the woman who dominated both.

She'd had the chance to escape once before and let it pass her by. Had that chance come again?

If so, could she gather the courage this time to take it?

The sense of having been caught in a confining time warp followed Zach all day as he made the rounds of Sweetheart's festivities. Businesses surrounding the square held their annual sidewalk sale after lunch in tandem with the Friends of the Library's bake sale. The setups, the faces; everything unchanged. Including the suspicious looks he drew wherever he went. None of them saw a grown man, matured by the passing years. They saw the rowdy, restless boy and the menacing father before him. They were waiting, to a one, for him to step out of line, as if it were only a matter of time before his true colors would unfurl.

When those colors showed themselves first thing Monday morning, he thought with wry amusement, would they ever be surprised.

And resentful. And probably scared.

More trouble to deal with, but he was trained to handle it; with tenacity not temper. Let them get used to seeing him walking their streets proudly, meeting their eyes without apology, because he wasn't going away anytime soon. Their hostile welcome was expected, but their respect would be demanded. He'd been looking forward to it for a long, long time.

Time to pull the name Crandall up out of the mud where his father had wallowed. Time to pull his family back together.

Every day, every hour, he saw as a step toward that goal. Regimented thoughts from a disciplined mind. He'd laid his plans out carefully, meticulously timed to rock the calm of Sweetheart like a nuclear assault. He wouldn't sneak back as if ashamed of who he was. He meant to march right down Main Street in full view of everyone. Let them stare. Let them grumble. Let them get used to the fact that Zach Crandall was—home, this time to stay.

He stopped his aggressive campaign trail, pausing at the edge of the square to take in the other reason for his return. Across the street, outside the antiquated front of the bookstore, Bess Carrey, with her practical upswept hairdo and modest blouse and skirt, stood straightening, talking classics with Miss Fitch, the reference librarian at the high school. His mood softened without his awareness of it as he watched the graceful gestures Bess used to punctuate her speech. Her sweet smile, the kindness in her eyes, acted upon the man the same way they had the boy, gentling the anger always simmering under the surface, quieting the darkness residing in his soul.

He hadn't told her the complete truth about his return to Sweetheart, a deliberate omission. Part of him; the anxious, wary part of him, wanted to see if she would accept him back into her life unconditionally, unquestioningly. A selfish, unworthy test, perhaps. Loving Bess Carrey would be too easy—if only he could overlook the baggage that came with her in the form of her mother's moralistic memory and the censure of a whole town. Bess hadn't chosen him over them in the past. This time, he wanted a no-holds-barred victory.

He wanted her to take a confident stand beside him against the tide of the town's disfavor.

Bess paused in mid-sentence when she saw him. Her expression lit up with a secret pleasure, then she glanced away to continue her conversation. She didn't wave, she didn't call him over. She didn't acknowledge him except with that brief, covert smile.

Not good enough.

Not damn near good enough!

He continued along the edge of the square, his stride picking up an exaggerated bounce as he shifted unconsciously into his too-cool-for-this-place strut. His hard, provoking arrogance drew in trouble like a magnet.

"Hey, Crandall. What're you doing back here? Thought we cleaned out the trash back in the eighties."

Zach kept walking, but his steps grew light and alert as he tried to get a fix on the coarse voice.

"Think you're too good to look me in the eye? Guess again."

The speaker closed in on him from behind, flanked by two others. Abruptly, Zach stopped and spun, setting the trio back in alarm. His mood was just dark enough to relish an in-your-face confrontation. He leaned forward, intimidating with his posture, with the menacing squint of his eyes.

"This is the nineties, that was the eighties." He spoke quietly, with the compact velocity of a .44 silencer. "Some things have changed, but not you, Web. You were an ignorant SOB then, and you're an ignorant SOB now. Still hiding behind your daddy's badge, or are you man enough to back that mouth of yours?''

Obviously Web Baines wasn't, not in the middle of town, especially when his two friends were busy backing away. Too sullen and just plain mean to let it go without a final jab, he sneered, "Oh, I'll back it. Just you wait and see."

Zach checked his watch. "My time's valuable, Baines. Maybe you should make an appointment."

Then he turned with a majestic indifference to the danger and strode away. Web Baines wasn't about to do anything out in the open. He was an ambush kind of guy. And despite Zach's show of calm, he knew from now on he'd have to be ready for the coward to strike.

He had few friends in Sweetheart. And more enemies than he could name.

A fact of life, inherited with the name he carried.

The afternoon hours crept by, slow and sweltering. Except for that brief glimpse, Bess didn't see Zach again. It did no good telling herself she wasn't disappointed.

A visit from Herb Addison hardly alleviated it.

"I was hoping that book on the Spanish-American War was going to be on your sale table, but I don't see it."

"I'm sorry, Herb. One of the Boxstander twins picked it up to do her history report. I would have saved it for you if I'd known you were really interested."

Herb came by her store several times a week to browse, though she was certain he didn't have any literature over magazine length in his home. He was an earthy man of simple tastes, and reading wasn't one of them. Finding a new wife seemed the greater priority. Bess hadn't given him any encouragement there, but she wondered if someone—or a pair of someones who happened to be sisters—was. She didn't dislike Herb. He was a fine citizen, a fairly good friend. But he wasn't husband material—at least not for her.

Now to convince him, gently, of that fact.

Today he didn't seem in the mood to listen.

"You would have known I wanted it if you'd been paying attention," the farmer grumbled. "You've been mighty distracted lately."

Bess's goodwill took a frosty turn. "I've been busy, Herb."

"Busy strutting around in those shameful shorts," he muttered under his breath. "Busy flaunting yourself with that Crandall guy. Old friends." He made an uncharitable noise and continued poking through the books. "I was looking forward to your rhubarb pie, like I do every year, but I would have settled for the lemon."

Bess locked her teeth against words she'd regret later. Instead she mentioned, "It's over at the library—"

"*Was* over at the library until *someone* bought the whole darned thing. Guess I don't need to tell you who that was."

"I'm afraid you'll have to because I don't have the slightest—"

"Zach Crandall, that's who. Who else has been hanging all over you, taking up all your time after appearing out of nowhere."

Conflicting emotions collided: the unexpected pleasure of Zach's purchase and the ugly undercurrent she was getting from Herb. He sounded all too possessive and she didn't care for it in the least.

"Zach and I *are* old friends, Herb." She made sure he caught the edge in her tone, telling him she resented having to explain something she didn't think was his business.

"Zach Crandall is trouble and not the kind of man you should be involved with."

Every human being had a limit, and Bess found hers.

"If I need someone to tell me how to run my personal life, Herb Addison, I will certainly come to you first, since you feel you have the right to comment on it so freely. And if you find yourself hungry for pie anytime soon, I suggest you try Sara Lee."

While Herb's jaw sagged, threatening to drop his wobbly bridgework, Bess snatched up her cash box and marched inside the store. After slamming the door, she flipped the sign over to Closed, then stood trembling, panting, in the aftermath of her first temper blowup.

She took a breath, then another, deeper one. What possessed her to explode like that? She should find Herb and apologize—

No. No, she would not! He was the one in the wrong, not her. She wouldn't say she was sorry...because she wasn't sorry. In fact, a liberating sense of satisfaction lightened the niggling sense of guilt. Why shouldn't she tell nosy old Herb Addison that her love life—which did not include him—was none of his affair.

And unfortunately still nonexistent. A few pulse-racing moments with Zach didn't equate to a love affair. The town was jumping to conclusions.

And unfortunately, again, so was her heart.

The bell on the door jangled. Bess turned, ready to fillet Herb Addison out like a trout. Her features froze in indignation.

"Aunt Bess?"

Her self-righteousness deflated like a pin-pricked balloon. "Faith..."

"Are you all right?"

"Of course I am. I just decided to close up a little early."

The teen frowned skeptically. "Oh. I thought maybe someone had said something to you."

"About what?" She bent to open her small floor safe where she'd store her earnings until the bank opened in the morning. Not that there was much to steal.

"About you and Zach."

Blood pounded to her head. Somehow, she managed a level voice. "What about us?"

"That the two of you are having a passionate affair. If you are, how come you didn't tell me?"

Chapter 6

"Who gave you—and the town—that crazy idea?"

"Zach."

"Zach?" His name quavered from her. "What— Why—"

"Probably when he bid thirty dollars for your lemon pie at the library auction."

"Thir—"

"I thought Mr. Sadler and his mom were going to have strokes. I didn't know you were that great at baking." The girl's eyes twinkled mischievously.

Bess rocked back on her heels, gripping her tented knees in an effort at control. "All this is over a pie?"

"That and something about the two of you lip-locked in the driveway last night." Faith grinned wide in her delight.

"Lip— We were no such thing! Zach Crandall is an old friend. I was just being nice to him. We were dancing." Heat sizzled in her cheeks. It had been more than dancing. She'd wanted it to become more scandalous than a kiss. Was it the rumor upsetting her...or the fact that it wasn't true?

"You don't have to convince me," Faith insisted. "I know

it was just you and your dotted swiss nightie in your bed last night.''

"They're saying Zach and I— That he and I were together in my house—in my *bed?*" That last came out a hoarse whisper.

"They're saying everything shy of the two of you running off to Las Vegas to get hitched in the Elvis Presley Honeymoon Chapel."

"Oh dear!" She sat back hard on the floorboards in a graceless slump, shocked, stunned, *horrified!* She couldn't think. She couldn't react. After all she'd gone through, all the hell and heartbreak, to protect the one precious private slice of her past. She'd been so careful, so fearful of anyone finding out the truth.

And now everyone thought they knew everything. She could picture the gossips huddled close, suppositions and innuendoes flying on the winds of salacious rumor. Her name, her feelings, her morals dragged through the mire of scandal her mother fought so hard to save her from. What an irony that a lie should have the effect the truth could not.

How could she ever repair her reputation?

"If it's not true," Faith said with the clear-cut naiveté of youth, "why don't you just tell them it isn't?"

Fat chance! Like anyone would choose to believe her! No one noticed a small retraction on page twelve refuting a front-page headline. How was she ever going to hold her head up again? Joan Carrey's demure daughter, shacking up with the town's ex-con under the same roof where her young niece was sleeping! Imagine!

Bess could imagine. And she went numb inside.

What would her mother say? The thought of her harsh censure knotted Bess's stomach into a painful half hitch of dread.

Worried by her aunt's pallor, Faith knelt down to slip a supportive arm about her rounded shoulders. "Why should you care what they say? Heck, I'd be in seventh heaven if they had me horizontal with someone like Mr. Crandall—I mean, if I were older."

Someone like Zach. Someone considered a town's worst nightmare. Someone who'd stirred her life into a frenzy, then disappeared from it for seventeen years without a word. Someone who went to prison for who-knows-what crime then casually returned without a word of apology to set her world on its ear again—without her permission.

It would be different if she were guilty of something sinful. Then she'd deserve the frowns, the whispers. But for Zach to purposefully create the idea of guilt by association in indifference to her reputation, well knowing—*knowing!*—how afraid she was of loose talk...

Her shock thawed to a roiling boil.

How dare he play loose with her standing in Sweetheart? She was a businesswoman, single, with temporary guardianship of an impressionable young girl. Didn't he realize what harm such talk could do?

Of course he did. He was one of the Crandalls. He, more than anyone, knew how vicious rumors could become.

With the clatter of the midway going full tilt and the enticing scent of barbecue heavy on the air, people gathered in the shady square. With lawn chairs and blankets spread, they anticipated an evening of speeches and music that would culminate in a dazzling display of fireworks.

Bess laid out their blanket toward the edge of the gathering where she could escape easily and without much notice. Founders' Day programs were notorious for their long-windedness and the questionable talent of their performers. The mayor's wife had center stage, belting out an off-key medley of show tunes with an enthusiasm that made her too-tight, beaded dress strobe and flash like a mirrored disco ball. No one had the heart to tell her what a spectacle she made in the garish dress, with her face made up like a big-city streetwalker. In her own eyes, she appeared elegant and sophisticated, so her friends smiled as she hit or missed notes, indulging her the fantasy.

Faith, not being small town like the majority of them, gawked in dismay and winced in pain. Bess poked her.

"Be kind."

"Shoot me, please," the girl muttered.

Bess hid her grin of agreement. Then her amusement drained away as she spotted a lone figure leaning back against one of the century oaks. Zach Crandall, all dressed in villainous black, stood staring not at the stage but unblinkingly at her, his expression grimly unsmiling, his eyes laser-beam direct. She gasped and looked quickly away. He couldn't have drawn more attention to them if he'd been sitting on the blanket beside her. A few good citizens already noted the focus of his attention, and she cringed beneath their questioning frowns. It couldn't continue. She had to do something before Faith noticed the commotion.

"I'm going to get a soda," she announced, reaching for her billfold. "Do you want something?"

Faith raised her can of pop. "I'm still fine. Some aspirin would be nice. Ear plugs would be better."

Bess tried to shame her with a scowl but the teen was incorrigible. Finally she had to chuckle. "I'll be right back."

Faith nodded absently, her interest already captured by a cadre of senior boys who just happened to swagger by in front of her.

Freed of her pretense, Bess hurled a meaningful glare at Zach, then wound her way to the back of the square where children were romping with gleeful indifference to their surroundings. She began walking, heading behind the skill booths set up to lure the hard-earned coins of the unlucky. It took Zach less than a minute to catch up to her. She rounded on him in an immediate attack.

"Just what exactly are you trying to do to me, Zach?"

A host of unspoken answers filtered behind his steady stare, some protestingly innocent, which she didn't believe in the least, and some provokingly intimate, sparking more anger to cover her vulnerability. Finally he turned the tables with a bland question of his own.

"Just what is it you think I'm trying to do, Bess?"

"Don't you think thirty dollars is a little excessive for a pie?"

"I like lemon pie. And it was for a good cause."

She huffed indignantly. "And you never once stopped to consider what people might say?"

"I've never been one to listen to what other people are saying, but apparently you still do. What are they saying, Bess?"

Her cheeks flamed with humiliation then awkwardly spelled it out for him. "They're saying... They're spreading rumors that—" Her voice lowered to a hoarse whisper. "They're saying that we're sleeping together."

"Because I bought your pie at a charity auction?" His brows lifted. "That's an excessive leap of logic, don't you think?"

His lazily unconcerned attitude threatened her control. Her voice grew shrill. "Not for this town, Zach, and you darned well know it!" She glanced around nervously to see if they could be overheard. "Someone saw us last night. In my driveway."

He shook his head, dismissing the significance. "So? We're two single adults. It's not like we were rolling around naked on the lawn."

Bess swallowed down her guilty thoughts to snap, "Why are you doing this? I thought we were friends."

His gaze chilled. "I thought we were more than friends."

His lethally quiet claim gave her a moment of frantic pause, then she scrambled to recover. "That was a long time ago."

He said nothing, challenging her statement with a penetrating stare. Goading her to speak more harshly than she normally would.

"You left. You never once tried to get ahold of me." Accusation strengthened her tone.

"You let me go," he added, mildly.

"I was seventeen years old!"

"So, what's your excuse now?"

What was her excuse? For an instant, as she followed the provoking purse of his lips with mesmerized attention, she forgot. Those lips. The thought of his kisses. The air seemed too thin, making normal breathing difficult. Then, the slow, decidedly arrogant spread of his grin proved a reminder. Her temper rallied.

"This is my home, Zach. I live here, work here. I face these people every day. Even if you don't give a damn what they think, I do. I have to." She was too incensed, too upset, to be shocked at her own uncharacteristic use of profanity. "You left. I had to stay here."

"No, you didn't," he corrected. A touch of her temper began creeping into his modulated voice as well.

Bess grabbed for breath and stability. She'd never been good at confrontation. Her stomach ached. Her heart pounded. But she had to make him understand. So maybe she could understand.

"I've been lonely all my life. I couldn't have friends, I couldn't join clubs or go to parties like the other kids. I didn't know how to make my own choices. Julie was the brave one, not me. I was the good kid, the dutiful child who stayed home and caused no problems. Do you know what it's like, day in, day out, suffocating on your own fears?"

"Yes."

She ignored his soft reply because she couldn't afford to soften her resolve.

"I spent years taking care of Mother and the store, shut up in that house or in that store. When I buried my mother, I was the one who escaped being buried alive. This town has become my family. They took me in. They've shown me more love and acceptance than I ever knew existed."

"How nice for you." His drawl held a cutting edge. "I'm sure the good folks of Sweetheart were just as generous to my sister when she was left dangling on her own. Come on, Bess, wake up to what they are. They're narrow-thinking, closed-minded hypocrites! And you want to be just like them."

"I do not!" Her objection validated all he said without her knowledge of it.

"You don't see a difference between the way they treat a Carrey and a Crandall? How many of your fancy functions does Mel belong to? How many of these good people have gone out of their way to make her their friend?"

"I have."

"Have you? Or is it just lip service, like you gave me? You don't want to be seen with us. What would they think?"

His words twisted everything around, making her motives seem self-serving and shallow. Forcing her to question what she'd so happily embraced. She wouldn't listen. She couldn't believe, not without accepting the brunt of the same searing hatred he held for the rest of the community.

She couldn't bear to be held with such contempt, not by him. So she couldn't let it matter.

"I will not pretend that I don't care what they think," she protested valiantly in her own defense. "I do, Zach. I do care. If I get all wrapped up in you again, I'll never earn back that sense of belonging. And someday you'll up and leave, and where will I be? I'll be here, alone. I can't spend the rest of my life that way, growing old and isolated and bitter like my mother was."

She didn't realize she was crying until Zach reached out to brush her tears away. "I don't want to hurt you, Bess."

She jerked back, away from his touch. "You are! Can't you see that? You come breezing back in here and expect me to pretend that seventeen years haven't gone by. You torment me with what I might have had, who I might have become. You ask me to risk everything I have on some wild dream we shared when we were kids. I can't, Zach. I can't walk away from my responsibilities. I can't thumb my nose at people who've been good to me. People who've stood by me for all those years you were gone. It's not fair, Zach. It's not fair for you to demand so much from me and offer so little in return. You don't even trust me enough to tell me where you've been."

He'd been watching her face as she spoke, his gaze intensely focused. His expression gave nothing away when he asked, "Should it matter?"

Bess sniffed back her runaway emotions, her reply as candid as she could make it. "I don't know if it should, but it does."

He blinked, and everything about him changed. A subtle, almost indiscernible difference, but to Bess it was a wall of ice crystallizing between them. Instinctively she wanted to throw herself against it, to begin chiseling it away. But a self-preserving logic held her still, allowing the distance to thicken into an impenetrable barrier.

"I'm sorry." He spoke the words flatly. They could have meant anything. But to Bess, they meant goodbye.

She hesitated, knowing she could yet tear down the wall by simply reaching out to him. Her touch had always crumbled his most determined barricades. She held back, clutching at the sides of her skirt to control her wayward hands. This time she was the one walking away.

Maybe that would make the loss of him easier.

Somehow she didn't think so.

Zach let her go. He could have stopped her, but it would just postpone the inevitable. He had his answer. Now he'd have to live with it. She'd found strength in the passage of years. Unfortunately for him, it was an inner courage, protecting herself and her hard-won independence. Or so she thought. But in Zach's mind he knew she was just replacing one domineering force for the suppression of an entire town. And apparently, preferred it that way.

He was sorry. Sorry it hadn't worked out. Sorry she hadn't given him more of a chance. But not sorry that he'd tried. Never that.

What now?

He didn't expect the answer he got.

He turned, planning to go home for some heavy-duty brooding, when he heard an odd whistle and felt air against his face.

Then the whole world exploded.

Chapter 7

Bess almost reached the square before she remembered the excuse she'd given Faith. Supposedly she'd gone to buy a cold drink. It would invite all sorts of questions she wasn't ready to answer if she returned empty-handed.

And it would give her a few extra minutes to compose herself. Faith had built-in radar and wouldn't be easily fooled by a placating "Everything's fine." At the moment, she feared she wouldn't fool a deaf, dumb and blind man. Her eyes felt raw and were most likely red. Her hands shook. Her breathing rattled. And within her chest a heavy weight sat still and cold where her heart once beat with renewed joy.

She stopped, stilling her thoughts, blanking her mind to things that would haunt her nights forever.

Right now she had to think, first and foremost, about Faith and the people of Sweetheart. No stranger to hiding away her own emotions for the benefit of others, she took a few deep breaths to still her trembling, then started back to get her soft drink.

That's when she heard the sounds of a scuffle.

Curiosity brought her cautiously around the corner to the back side of the midway. Alarm held her there, frozen with silent horror.

Whatever they used to hit him smacked the side of his head with sledgehammer force. He went down like a felled steer, saved from meeting pavement when his arms were grabbed from behind. His head whirled.

"Not such a tough guy now, are you?"

Web Baines.

Zach let his weight sag, giving him time to collect his senses, letting them believe he was worse off than he was.

Baines gave a rusty laugh. "We're gonna teach you what happens when trash like you gets the idea they're good enough for a fine woman like Bess Carrey. You're mama was a fine woman, too, until your daddy got hold of her. That ain't gonna happen again." A hard punch to the ribs was added to convince him.

There were two more added to the original three, each hard, mean and bovine. Two held his arms pinned behind him. The other pair flanked Baines like cowardly coyotes eagerly waiting for leftovers. The obvious place to start was with Baines. The odds didn't bother him. He'd been up against worse.

Gradually he shifted his center of gravity, balancing lightly on the balls of his feet, waiting for the opportunity to surprise the hell out of the brawling loudmouths.

Then they all got a surprise, as meek little Elizabeth Carrey launched herself onto the back of one of the burly men holding Zach. She clung like a cat, all spitting fury and sharp claws. Howling as her fingernails raked the side of his whiskered face, the startled fellow released Zach's arm. And that was all the opportunity Zach needed.

Zach brought his knees to his chest then kicked out. Both feet connected in the center of Web's chest. With a stunned "Ooof!" Baines pinwheeled backward, falling hard to the ground. Before the man holding his arm could react, Zach went down on one knee, dragging the heavier man over his shoulder and flipping him to the pavement.

Not expecting a swift, lethal attack, the other two stood there, jaws hanging until Zach closed them with a couple of precise uppercuts. One went down, out cold. The other staggered in a tight circle only to meet with another flying fist the minute he went the full three-sixty. He, too, collapsed with a groan.

Bess rode the last man standing with the tenacity of a bulldogger. One arm locked about the man's thick neck, the other covered his eyes. And Zach filled the space in between with a solid jab. The big oaf tipped over, landing on Bess before she could scramble out of the way.

She hit the ground hard, the bulk of the man on top of her squeezing the breath from her lungs. Her vision wavered as she wheezed and tried to wriggle out from under the dead-weight. Then Zach bent down, shoving the dazed beast off her. He clasped both of her hands, hauling her up with an "Are you all right?" filled with concern and a deeper admiration.

She forced the words, "Look out!" from her constricted chest.

Zach spun, pushing her to safety behind him. Web Baines tottered drunkenly, but the knife in his hand was dangerously steady.

"No scum like you makes me look like a fool," Baines snarled, waving the blade before him in tight figure eights.

Zach was all cool business. "You don't need me to make you look like a fool."

His disdainful remark had the desired effect. Baines lunged at him with a roar, his attack fueled by rage rather than skill. Zach greeted him with a disciplined response. He dodged to one side to let the knife jab past him, clamping down on Baines's wrist with a grip of iron and collecting a handful of unkempt hair in his other hand. He brought up his knee at the same time he smashed Web's head downward, both actions meeting like a traffic accident in the middle. Zach tossed the unresisting Baines aside then retrieved the knife; seven inches of retractable steel, each inch illegal. He pocketed it as he swept the area for further signs of aggression. The five men were efficiently docile.

Bess stared at him. She'd never seen anything like it this side of the matinee screen. More frightening than the exacting violence was the concise way it had been dispensed; quickly, dispassionately, without hesitation or remorse.

She shrank back slightly when Zach came toward her. He didn't miss her anxious move. He stopped and said, "We'd better get out of here before there's more trouble."

Not from the five sprawled on the ground. They wouldn't give anyone trouble for a long, long time. And they'd think twice before trying to assault Zach again with anything less than an armored urban attack vehicle.

Her knees started knocking in delayed shock.

Then she saw Zach sway, hugging his arm into one side. She forgot her reservations, focusing on his bloodied lip and bruised brow.

"You're hurt." She approached him, gentle fingertips touching his face. His nervous system jump-started with a jolt as he pulled her hands down.

"I'm all right. You'd better get back to your niece. You don't want to get involved in this." He pushed her away, insulating her from the situation. She should have grabbed at the chance to escape.

But she didn't.

"Wait right here," she told him with no-nonsense intensity. While he frowned in bewilderment, Bess jogged back to the midway, spotting the mother of one of Faith's new friends.

"Sarah, could you keep an eye on Faith for me. I ran into an old friend, and we're going to get some coffee."

The woman waved. "Sure. What time do you want her home?"

"By eleven."

"We'll drop her off."

Calling her thanks and surprised by her own lack of guilt at telling such an inventive tale, Bess hurried back to where Zach was checking the wallets of the fallen men. At first she stood horrified, thinking he was robbing them. But all he took were their driver's licenses, tossing the rest of the billfolds, untouched, down beside their motionless forms.

"Zach?"

He glanced around, and she couldn't help wincing at the sight of his battered face.

She urged, "We'd better go before someone gets curious."

He nodded and stepped over Baines to take her arm. "What about Faith?"

"She's with friends. I'll take you home."

"Not a good idea. I'll see you to your house. You don't want to be seen at mine."

How suddenly absurd that sounded. "Zach, I don't—"

But he started walking in the direction of her street so she trotted beside him, too shaken by what transpired to argue with him.

She'd helped him beat up five of Sweetheart's citizens. Well, she hadn't actually done much, but she was, in fact, an accomplice. Would Baines and the others implicate her? Great. She could just see Faith trying to raise bail money for her delinquent aunt. The idea didn't strike her as particularly funny.

Zach guessed at her worries.

"They won't say anything," he told her tersely. "They'd never admit that I took the lot of them on and beat them." He grinned at her, a sudden dazzle against brutalized features. "With some capable assistance."

Bess didn't return his smile. She was scared, alarmed by her own actions. She would swear she'd been temporarily out of body if she believed in such things.

When she'd seen Zach seemingly at the mercy of those thugs, a foreign fury had taken possession of her. She'd jumped in without thought, regardless of the fact that she was wearing a skirt and was at least one hundred pounds lighter than the brute she tackled. She could have been seriously hurt. Since she had no idea how or why the tussle started, she might even have been in the wrong. Her trembling returned. Unconsciously she clutched Zach's arm.

When they reached her house, they went up the drive and to the back steps. There, Zach began to pull free. His expression remained inscrutable.

"I'd better go."

Her gaze flew to his ravaged face in tender anxiousness. "You will not. Not until you let me look at those bruises."

He smiled, small and tight. "Just like old times."

"Then you know better than to argue with me." She dragged him up the steps and into her tiny kitchen, where she'd once nursed injuries far worse than these by the faint glow of the stove light so as not to wake her mother.

"Sit."

Unquestioningly, he drew a chair up by the sink, blinking against the abrupt glare of overhead fluorescents as Bess flipped the switch, then turned on the tap to wet a clean cloth.

"Look up," she commanded. When he did, she dabbed at the gash on his lower lip, pausing as he flinched, continuing when he steadied.

"Who started it?"

Strangely moved because she'd asked instead of assuming the answer, he murmured, "We had some words earlier. I should have been better prepared for the inevitable. They're not the kind to let things go."

"They're not the kind you go poking sticks at, either." She paused the cloth a second time. "Will they come after you again?" *Or me,* she wondered in a quiet panic. Somehow she didn't think her being a lady would keep Baines and his friends from roughing her up to prove a point. Nor did she think their sheriff was likely to do anything about it.

"I don't think they'll be that stupid again."

When she met his uplifted stare, she found a steadying assurance in his gaze. She chose to believe him. He had more experience, after all.

He waited patiently for her to fold another cloth into a small square. She wet it thoroughly then touched it to the swelling at his temple. She was, just as he remembered, unfailingly gentle.

"Hold this there."

He replaced her hand with his, the slight brush of passing contact nudging the mood toward subtle tension. Especially when she reached for the hem of his T-shirt.

"I want to take a look at your ribs."

"Nothing's broken." His protest rumbled in a lower warning register as he twitched away with what she might have thought modesty if she hadn't known him so well.

"Sit still," she ordered, amused and aggravated by his objections. "It's nothing I haven't see before. Don't make me call Doc Meirs."

He sat still, breathing shallow and fast while focusing fiercely on the collection of china teacups lining the opposite wall. Bess hesitated a moment, wondering if he were more badly hurt than she at first supposed. Carefully, she lifted his shirt, and her breath caught in her own chest.

She was wrong. There was plenty she hadn't seen before.

His body was hard and dangerously fit. Smooth sinewy youth had metamorphosed into the solid power of adulthood. A thick mat of black hair hugged a meanly sculpted torso, built, not by bale lifting but by deliberate design. Its cruel beauty mesmerized her for a long moment until she noticed another change.

A thin pale scar carved a harsh diagonal across his rib cage.

She traced it with quivering fingertips, causing a jerk and a taut flutter in his abdomen.

"Did you lose this one?" Her voice was oddly gruff.

"No. Just careless, and he knew what he was doing."

Her hand inched lower, to the puckered seam disappearing beneath the waist of his jeans.

"And this one? Another fight?"

"With a surgeon." She glanced up to find dimples capping his broad grin. "Appendix."

She looked down, embarrassed, intrigued, breathless. Her palm loitered against the heat of his skin until she realized her preoccupation with the indentation of his navel and the gradually shifting contours within his denims. Her gaze jerked up as she exhaled shakily. His grin faded to a slight, bemused curve. Then—

"Owww! Geez!"

"I'm sorry!"

He eased back onto the chair, protecting the tender spot on his side from any more unintentional prodding. Her lips pursed at the sight of ugly bruising mottling the area.

"I bet that hurts like a son of a gun."

"You'd win," he hissed from between clenched teeth. Gradually he expelled his breath and made himself relax. "But like I said, nothing broken. You don't forget what a broken rib feels like."

Bess kept her gaze fixed on the discolored flesh. "Did you learn that where you learned to fight?"

"Yes."

"Oh."

Her fragile response alerted him. She wouldn't look up until he filled in the blanks. "I was division boxing champ in the marines."

Surprise rounded her eyes. "The marines? I thought—" She bit back the rest.

"You thought what?"

"I— Nothing, Zach. A misunderstanding."

He caught her chin in his palm before she could evade him. "Where did you think I learned it, Bess?"

She couldn't meet his eyes. "In prison," she whispered weakly.

He was silent for so long, she finally risked a peek. She couldn't tell what moved behind the granite set of his expression.

"I've never been behind bars, Bess," he explained with a scary lack of inflection. "At least not for longer than overnight in the care of good Sheriff Baines. Why would you think I was?''

''I—I don't know.''

He pressed her chin between the vee between his thumb and forefinger. His low, flat tone distressed her. ''Did someone tell you that, or did you just suppose that's where I'd end up?''

Catching the accusation beneath that smooth question, she made herself reply unfalteringly.

''It was something you said, about being unable to contact your family. I thought you—I thought wrong,'' she finished miserably. ''I'm sorry, Zach. I should have known better.''

His grip loosened, evolving into a slow caress of her cheek and jawline. ''Why, Bess? Why shouldn't you have thought the worst? Everyone else did.'' His touch was soothing, his tone was not.

Her gaze grew direct. ''Because I knew you better than everyone else.''

He studied her, assessing her flustered shame, her remorseful eyes. She'd thought he'd been in jail and yet invited him into her kitchen while they were alone, not knowing what crime he might be guilty of. Whether it was trust or naiveté, it humbled him completely.

''I was in basic, Bess. Then I did a tour overseas. In Germany. I had a lot of things to sort out. A lot of things to put behind me.''

She nodded unhappily, knowing she was one of those things. Her sad eyes lowered, a glimmer of dampness rimming her lashes. ''I shouldn't have assumed the worst.'' But she had then, and just a while ago, when she thought he was stealing from the men he'd beaten senseless. She knew better. She knew the real Zach Crandall.

Before the first tear fell, he was kissing her.

The reacquainting sweetness of his mouth on hers twisted sundry emotions through her, weaving them into a delicate pattern of dreamy delight. It was very much like the first kiss they'd shared: light, soft, almost chaste, a tender tease of what might follow. She leaned into it, wondering at the wisdom of opening up, of inviting him in to make himself at home once more.

It was so easy to fall completely under his spell. She missed the exact second she caved in. Probably when she slit her eyes open to scan the floor, to see if the linoleum was clean enough for them to roll around on. When she forgot to care if Faith walked in on them. That she was no more protected than she had been the first time. Or the fact that this was her mother's house.

Nothing mattered but the exquisite taste of passion reborn.

A passion that wasn't raw edged with cigarettes, bottled beer and desperation, but a mellow lingering taste of clean, crisp promise. Of forever rather than goodbye.

And it made her hungry to savor the heat and urgency of a real kiss.

He pulled back, seeing capitulation in her softly flushed cheeks, in her slightly parted lips, in the smoky longing clouding her gaze. He could have taken her to the linoleum or to the moon. But before she could ask him to, he stood, her words from earlier that evening tempering passion with a cautiousness. If he cashed in on the invitation in her eyes, it would be a moment's weakness not a lifetime decision.

She gazed up at him, dewy-eyed and desire drugged, everything he wanted there for him to have…but not hold. What was one brief moment of heaven in her arms if it meant spending an eternity in hell without her? She wasn't ready for that all-or-nothing commitment. Without it, he'd still have nothing.

With a hoarse "I'll see you tomorrow," he was gone.

For a long restless night, Bess thought about the possibility of those linoleum tiles, cool and hard beneath her, while Zach Crandall moved hot and hard above. And not even the high setting on her window fan could ease the heated flush of her skin.

She knew the harsh words she'd said to him earlier were more truth than temper. And he'd meant every one of his, as well. The pull between them intensified with every meeting but answered none of the difficulties they couldn't overcome. The entire town of Sweetheart, for one. Like how they could ever breach the barrier the past placed between them, for another.

Then, there was the big one: how could she risk more involvement without telling him the entire truth?

One truth had hit her unfairly while she'd tended his hurts in the kitchen. She wanted Zach Crandall.

Seventeen years ago he'd taught her the basics of sex. This time she wanted him to elaborate on the intricacies of making love.

And all the pressure to deny it, from both conscience and community, didn't make a dent in discouraging that desire.

He heard the shushing strokes of a broom mingling with the soft hitch of his sister's sobs. There was no light on to illuminate the porch, but Zach could see Melody's slumped figure highlighted in shadow as he raced up the walk.

"Mel? Melody, what's wrong?"

By the time he bounded up onto the porch, his vision had adjusted to the lower level of light, and he could see what she was doing. She was cleaning up a mess. All the pretty blooming pots she'd hung from the ceiling beams lay in smashed piles of broken pottery, soil and scattered petals. Metal hooks dangled above, as empty as the look in his sister's eyes.

"Why would someone do such a thing?"

Zach lifted her up from where she'd been meticulously brushing the remnants into a dustpan. He removed the broom and the pan from her hands and put his arms around her, offering shelter a little too late. He wished he could say he didn't know the answer to her question, but he did know. He knew who and he knew why.

He brought heartbreak back into his sister's life with his return, making her the target of an indiscriminate hate.

And as Melody wept against his shirtfront, he felt a familiar darkness freeze through him, a mindlessly vicious anger he'd always equated with the sound of his father's belt clearing its loops.

That cold black fury lived in him, too; an inheritance from Sam Crandall. The temptation to let go, to let the anger out like something wild and deadly, had never been so close to overwhelming him. He'd learned a thousand ways to kill a man and a thousand more to make that same man beg for death. He'd ended a man's life more than once, and on one of those occasions had been perilously near forgetting all that was civilized and good. He'd vowed then and there he would never allow himself to approach that point again.

So he held Melody close and he used his love for her as a center, focusing, forcing the darkness down until it was manageable.

There were ways to deal with Web Baines and his friends. Ways in his command.

And first thing in the morning they'd realize their mistake in making his sister cry.

Bess sipped her morning coffee at Sophie's, forcing her mind to remain on the workday ahead when it preferred to stray to Zach's husky claim of, "I'll see you tomorrow."

Once, long ago, she'd lived and breathed for Zach's brief appearances, lighting up when he was there, feeling cold and bereft when he was gone. She had the excuse of youth then. As he so deftly pointed out before, what was her excuse now?

She had to tally her sidewalk sales amounts, to plan her front window display, to decide on whether or not to make a daring trip to a trade show in Chicago to bolster her tired inventory. But all she could concentrate upon was the remembered feel of hard muscle rippling beneath her palm.

She sighed, exasperated at her own sorry state. She had a worse case of hormonal hysteria than Faith and all her friends put together. But she was a grown woman who knew what to do about it.

Could an affair with Zach satisfy her cravings for intimacy,

or would it leave her desperate for more? A *more* she knew
he couldn't give her.

While she stared into her cup as if she could find the answers there floating in grounds that had somehow slipped
through the reused filter, the stir of excitement all around her
gradually broke her from her trance. She glanced up, then
frowned in puzzlement.

The counter girls gathered at the front window, whispering,
pointing outside. They were joined by the early bird customers who added to the agitated murmurings. On the walk Bess
could see passersby stopping to stare over at the town center.
Something was going on.

Not one to involve herself with gawking and gossip, Bess
tried to ignore the situation until Myrt Watson looked her
way. The woman's features were a caricature of amazement
as she called, "Honey, you'd better come see this."

Bess slid off the counter stool, taking the time to smooth
her skirt before going to the window. She didn't want to seem
too eager to elbow into the foray. She had to stand on tiptoes
to get a good look at the object of their attention. Then she
stood as stunned as the rest of them.

For strutting right through the center of the square, bold as
brass, heading toward the sheriff's office, was Zach Crandall
wearing the proudly creased uniform of the Iowa State Police.

Chapter 8

The look on Sheriff Lloyd Baines's face was worth it all.

Every minute of hell going through basic. Every lonely night watch in a foreign land. The disbelief of his friends and superiors when he announced he had no plans to reenlist to take the career opportunity of a lifetime.

Who would pass up a request to join military intelligence to ticket highway speeders in the cornfields of Iowa?

They didn't understand. They had no idea what this moment meant to him.

Watching Sheriff Baines's flabby jowls quiver, his hard, mean little eyes pop wide open in shock as moisture beaded up on his bald head like rain on a Simonize shine, paid a multitude of past debts in full. It made up for the cold terror that had gripped him every time a patrol car had pulled up in front of their house. It erased the brutality of the "questioning" he'd endured while refusing to admit to something he hadn't done. It eased the memory of sleepless nights in the back, curled up on an unyielding cot, terrorized by the knowledge of what was going to happen—not at the hands of the law but at those of his merciless father when he was finally sent home with a reprimand or a fine.

But nothing could wipe away the haunting image of his mother's tears the first time she'd watched handcuffs snap closed on her eldest son's wrists. So Zach took his time peeling down his dark glasses, reveling in the sheriff's astonishment.

Surprise, you son of a bitch.

"Good morning, Sheriff Baines. I'd like to say it's professional courtesy bringing me by to say hello on my first day on the job, but unfortunately," he let out a slow, searing smile made lopsided by the swelling of his lower lip and concluded, "it's business."

"Crandall." That's all he could manage.

"You remember me. I'm flattered. I remember you, too." The icy smile melted down to a cold, thin frost line. "Fondly."

Shock wore off, becoming instant hostility. "What the hell are you doing here like that?"

Zach deliberately misunderstood him. He reached into his uniform pocket and withdrew five driver's licenses. "I want you to pick up these men on assault charges, and that last one for assault with a deadly weapon, for starters."

Baines took the cards reluctantly without looking at them. "Who's filing charges?"

Zach tapped his forefinger against the spectacularly discolored bruise behind his left brow. "I am. I'll be back on my lunch hour to fill out an official report, but I suggest you catch up to these boys before they do something else stupid. Like get in my face without bars between us."

Scowling his displeasure, Baines thumbed through the licenses, pausing at the last one. "No way. I'm not doing this."

"Why, Sheriff, a fine upstanding lawman like yourself wouldn't want to be guilty of obstructing justice, now would he? You wouldn't want to force me into taking action against a fellow officer of the law." He withdrew Web's switchblade from his trouser pocket and clicked up its tongue of steel.

Baines stumbled back. With a blur of motion, Zach reversed the handle in his hand and drove downward, embedding the blade in Baines's desktop. "Log that as evidence."

Baines looked from the shivering blade to the bare steel of Zach's stare. His face grew florid, veins throbbing in his thick neck and temples. "My boy ain't gonna be found guilty of no crime in *my* town. Especially for beatin' up on the likes of you."

"Sheriff, we don't tolerate anybody beating up on anyone. Not in *my* state. Have a nice day." With another grim smile, Zach nodded and turned toward the door. Baines shouted after him, panic touching his voice.

"How did you get Pat McEnroy's job? Who's idea of a sick joke is this, anyway?"

Zach paused and glanced back at him with a gratified smirk. "It's mine."

And he pushed out into the warm morning, scattering the half dozen citizens who'd crowded up on the front step to peer through the frosted door. They froze up stiff when he issued them a genial good morning.

Time to go to work.

"He's coming over here."

The cry from Myrt sent the patrons of Sophie's scuttling back to their seats. All but Bess. She couldn't make her legs function even when the tinkling of the bell announced Zach's arrival. She took in the sight of him—admiration, pride flickering in her suddenly moist gaze.

He'd done it. He'd proven it to everyone.

Zach Crandall wasn't a loser with only jail time waiting in his future.

She'd known it all along. The only thing missing from her satisfaction was her mother here to see it for her own doubting eyes.

He glanced at her in passing, noting her shock and the deeper evidence of her pride, without betraying his own reaction. Greeting each of the customers by name, he made his way to the counter.

"Coffee, please, Gert. Very large, very black."

"Sure thing, er, Zach."

Silence sat heavily as he waited for the harsh dark brew, but he seemed immune to the flabbergasted stares. Either that, or he was enjoying them. Bess wasn't sure. But she did know his dramatic, jaw-dropping appearance in uniform was carefully calculated for effect.

"Thanks, Gert." He took the huge foam cup and laid down a dollar. Gert stood too stunned to notice the size of the tip. Coffee in Sweetheart was still fifty cents with refills.

This time Zach paused at the door, taking his time before directing his translucent stare toward Bess. He waited for her to say something.

"Why didn't you tell me?" she asked at last.

"You didn't ask where I was going, just where I'd been," he replied in a tone as meticulously camouflaged as his gaze. "I wanted to know if it would make a difference to you." Then, with the incremental lowering of his eyelids, she knew the depth of his disappointment. "Guess I got my answer."

Then he pushed out the door, wading through the gawkers to walk across the square once more toward the new state post on Palmer.

"The wolf guarding the lambs," someone muttered behind her.

Set on guarding those sheep or devouring them? Bess wondered. If Zach was the wolf, did that make her Red Riding Hood? What other disguises concealed the real purpose of Zach's return?

"This can't be allowed in our community, and we want to know what you plan to do about it!"

A sweating Mayor Howard Anderson looked at the agitated members of the town council assembled in his office for an emergency meeting. Ted Doolin, Sweetheart's council leader and banker, as usual, was leading the pack and stirring up the most trouble. Howard checked his watch. Twenty minutes until he had to pick up his grandson for a promised fishing excursion.

"I don't know that I can do anything about it, Ted."

"You're not going to weasel out that easily, Howard," Lloyd Baines growled with menace. The mayor swallowed hard. Baines wasn't a man you wanted to cross.

"I'm not trying to do anything of the kind, Sheriff. Listen to me, all of you. I've seen the transfer orders. Everything's in order. Pat McEnroy recommended him."

"What?" Doolin yowled. "That backstabbin'—"

"He was always sweet on Mary, you know, Ted," Fred Meirs added as if that would explain the unexpected treachery from one of their own.

"You don't look so surprised about all this, Doc," Baines said, suspicions alerted by the calm way the old man sat polishing his glasses. "Could be you knew about it and didn't say nothing."

"Could be right, Lloyd." The doctor restored his spectacles and stared at the seething sheriff with a mild amusement. "Pat and I discussed it at length, and I agreed with his choice."

"And you didn't say anything to us?" Doolin was the first to accuse.

"Why? It was a state matter not one for local concern."

"Not for local concern?" Baines stared at him. "Are you nuts? Crandall coming back to this town sporting a badge in front of that attitude of his? You're forgetting who he is and what he's done, aren't you?"

"I delivered the boy, Lloyd, and I know him and his family a sight better'n any of you. It's not what he's done that got you all haired up, it's what you all did to him. And you're shaking in your socks wondering if it's redemption or retribution that brought him back. I'd be worrying, too, if I were you."

"That was a long time ago," the mayor put in hopefully. "Surely you don't think—"

"You're damn right, that's what we think," Doolin clarified for the others. "That's why we've got to do something. Now. We can't let someone like that have power over us."

Doc Meirs chuckled. "Kinda uncomfortable having that shoe on the other foot, eh, Ted?"

"Shut up, you old fool. Maybe you should be worrying, too. After all, you never wrote up one complaint in those files of yours to report suspected abuse, did you?"

Meirs looked down at the blue-veined hands knotted in his lap. "No, I didn't. None of us did anything. Maybe now's the time to apologize for it."

"What?" Baines roared. "To Crandall? Him, most likely a murderer? Hell, let's just give him the keys to the city, why don't we?" He turned upon the mayor again, causing him to shrink back into his fake leather chair. "There's got to be some way to get rid of him. Isn't there something about him having to finish school? He dropped out in his final year, you know."

Howard glanced unhappily at the records on his desk. "And it says here that he took his GED before entering the military. Gentlemen, the man has a sterling record—military police, overseas tours, commendations—"

"Let's elect him mayor, why don't we?" Doolin sneered. "I don't care what those papers say. We know what Zach Crandall is. We had to suffer his daddy for years. Do you want to go through that again? This time it'll be worse. He'll have the law on his side. Look what he's done to my boy and Lloyd's. Picked a fight with 'em and now they're in jail. It could be your son, Fred, or your brother, Howard."

The other council members shifted uneasily, picturing the vengeful havoc Crandall could level upon their town with complete impunity.

Howard held up his hands to quiet their murmuring. "All I'm saying is there's nothing we can do about it, legally. Like Fred said, it's a state matter. He works for them, not us."

"So we're just gonna let him run loose, threatening our families and our businesses?" Elmer Grant muttered from the

back. He owned the local Super Value grocery store and held
the leases for several other small area shops along the square.
Fear hurt business, and when profits were threatened, Elmer
took it personally.

"Has he done anything to anyone?" Howard demanded.

"Not yet," Elmer grumbled. "Do we have to wait until he
does?"

"Yes, we do. The man's got a right to live and work here
as long as he doesn't step out of line. If he does—"

"You mean 'when' he does," Doolin interjected.

"—then we have support for a complaint."

"And until then, a murderer walks the streets with our
wives and children," Bernie Sacks, the high school counselor
asked, quickening the anxiety once again.

"No charges or suspicions were ever made against Zach,"
Doc reminded them.

"Not officially, but we all know what really happened between Crandall and his daddy." Doolin paused, gathering all
their attention with that dramatic hesitation. "He and his old
man had it out that night. Sam smacked the crap out of him,
and finally the kid got fed up and hit back. We could have
just shrugged it off, garbage taking care of garbage, if the
coward hadn't skipped and left Mary to take the blame."

Nods and murmurs of agreement brought Doc Meirs to his
feet. "That's nonsense and you know it. Mary confessed—"

"To protect that piece of crud boy of hers. If Mary Crandall killed her husband, why wasn't the murder weapon ever
found? Huh? You're so damned smart, Doc, answer that
one."

Meirs gripped his mouth shut at Baines's taunt. He had no
answer. He, like the rest of them, never believed for a minute
that Mary Crandall was guilty. But unlike the rest of them,
he didn't think Zach had done the crime, either.

And that meant someone else, maybe one of them in that
room, had done it.

But after seventeen years, it didn't seem worth picking at

old wounds. Mary had willingly taken the blame, and peace had returned to Sweetheart. Until now.

"Let the boy alone," he advised wearily. "Haven't we done enough to persecute the whole family?"

Baines jabbed a finger at him. "Just wait, Doc. He'll show his true colors, and you're going to be the one apologizing to us."

"Time comes, I will. Until then, we really don't have any cause to take action."

"Maybe if we called him over and asked what his intentions are?" Bernie suggested.

Elmer turned to glare at him. "You want to go get him, Bernie? Go ahead."

Bernie scowled and stayed silent.

"All right! All right!" Mayor Anderson checked his watch, then stood up, assuming the guise of authority, if not the real thing. "There's nothing we can do for now except keep an eye on him. Anything happens, you come to me first. Then we'll convene a special meeting and hold Crandall accountable. That agreeable to everyone?"

All muttered, but none challenged his decision. Doc Meirs shook his head, thinking them all frightened fools, but he knew they had their reasons.

Sam Crandall had been a plague upon their quiet community, drinking hard, tearing up anything that got in his way, acting mean and basically scaring the liver out of anyone who crossed his path. They avoided his wrathful outbursts and preferred to forget the unfortunate five who couldn't. No, Doc couldn't cast blame on the rest of the council.

Because he'd known and he'd done nothing. Zach had as much right to hate him as any of them.

If Zach Crandall was his father's son, there'd be hell to pay in the town of Sweetheart.

"Rare Finds."

"Dinner?"

Bess jumped, shocked by the electricity just the sound of

his voice sent jolting through the phone lines. Glancing at the two customers rummaging through her back shelves, Bess turned her back to them lest her expression betray her.

"When?"

"Tonight. If the two of you are free."

His inclusion of Faith relaxed her for a moment, but then the buffer was gone. "Faith was planning to go to the soft ball tournaments over in Chariton. I could ask if she—"

His voice dropped a persuasive decibel. "Why don't you ask if she minds her aunt going out to dinner alone with the town's bad boy?"

"Mind?" Bess pictured Faith's gleeful delight. "I don't think she would. Where did you have in mind?" She grimaced at the anxiety her question implied. Would he assume it stemmed from an unwillingness to be seen with him? His smooth reply gave nothing away.

"I thought we'd go to Haven's over at the interchange. Mel's working tonight, and Haven's sirloin tips win out hands-down over Sophie's mystery-meat burgers."

She laughed nervously. The receiver slid, damp in her palm. She changed hands. Was he remembering the first time they'd sneaked off to Haven's? Her stomach did funny little flip-flops as she struggled to sound calm. "That would be fine."

"Bess, do you have the first volume for this?"

Placing her hand over the mouthpiece, she called back, "I think so Mr. Thomas. Just a minute. I know right where it is." When she uncovered the receiver, she discovered she was trembling. "Wh-what time?"

"Six too early?"

"All right."

"At your house or...someplace else?"

She almost named a neutral spot where she could go off with him, unseen. But she'd already disappointed him enough for one day. "My house."

A pause. Then, "Wear a jacket."

The line went silent.

"Where did you say it was, Bess? I don't see it on this shelf."

It took her a full minute to set the receiver upon its cradle. "Wh-what? Oh, it's there in the back. I'll get it." She hustled to the rear of the store, her step light, her heart barely tethered.

A date. She mulled it over and over in her mind all afternoon. By the time she was actually getting ready, the prospect assumed gigantic proportions. She hadn't gone out with anyone since her senior year. Well, a couple of group gatherings to the multiplex theater over the Missouri line. But never alone, just her and a man with only steaks and the burden of conversation between them.

She didn't question her change of heart too deeply where Zach was concerned. She didn't want to think her willingness to go with him had anything to do with his sudden elevated status.

Because she was afraid it did.

And that would make her no better than anyone else in Sweetheart who judged him by name rather than by individual standards.

She wanted to go. To be with him. To talk. To ask where he'd been and how he'd come back to Sweetheart.

She wanted him to know how very proud she was of his accomplishments.

And maybe, just a little, she wanted to apologize for all her preconceptions.

She'd thought him a criminal. Ironic, considering.

She'd rummaged through her closet for just the right dress, something fancier than her normal conservative work attire and nothing as reserved as her Sunday best. She pulled the dry cleaner plastic off a dress way in the back, one that had hung there since Julie had come down for their mother's funeral. She'd brought the delicately feminine outfit as a gift, never explaining the occasion.

It fit beautifully, skimming her figure, lifting her mood. Hearing Faith galloping up the stairs, she held her breath, then turned to tell her the news.

One look at her flushed face gave everything away.

Faith grinned. "Where's he taking you? Someplace romantic? Please tell me it's not bowling!"

"Haven's."

The teen's gaze went dreamy. "Ooooh!"

"Would you do my face for me?"

Faith grabbed her hand and hurried her down the hall as if they were a pair of giggling contemporaries instead of a budding teen and her ancient spinster aunt.

Though questions were percolating, Faith asked none as she applied the makeup. Bess observed the result, prepared for the difference. Liking it.

Still, she asked, "Not too obvious, is it?"

Faith inspected the total package: the glowing features, the soft chiffon print over a solid sea-foam-colored slip dress, which just brushed the kneecaps. Its spaghetti straps bared smooth shoulders. She smiled.

"Yeah, obvious to anyone with eyes that you're gorgeous."

The low growl of a motorcycle brought Bess to the window to see Zach arrive on the side street of her corner lot. Instead of rounding the corner and coming up the drive, he nudged his big bike over the low curb, cut the engine and silently coasted down the slope of the backyard, braking at the back steps. He made a dark, mysterious figure, all in black from helmet and sunglasses to leather coat, slacks and boots. Straddling the powerful machine, his identity concealed, he was dark, sinister and sexy as hell. The stuff of any woman's fantasy.

When he slipped off the helmet and glasses as she came out the back door, he became hers.

His icy blue stare slid over her, trailing shivers along her skin. Bess clutched the matching jacket about her, not to shield herself from his appreciative look, but to hide the way she trembled.

"Ready?" His voice purred, a low vibration matching the

growl of his bike. It was all Bess could do to tear her gaze away from him to give instructions to Faith.

"I know," the girl interrupted, "lock the doors behind me, take a coat, don't eat too much junk, have fun, don't be late." The teen embraced her, brushing off her worries with a whispered, "The same goes for you." She leaned back from her flustered aunt and grinned at the black-clad knight errant. "Hi, Mr. Crandall. Take care of her."

He grinned back. "Yes, ma'am, I will." He patted the seat behind him. "Let's go."

Zach fixed his helmet over Bess's pale hair, adjusting the chin strap for a snug, safe fit, then waited for her to slide on behind him. Once she was settled, her hands resting lightly at his waist, her legs nudging up shyly alongside his, he switched on the bike and coaxed it down the drive with a quiet roar.

They rumbled through the streets of Sweetheart as inconspicuously as possible under the noses of its citizens. But there was nothing inconspicuous about the muscle cycle and its grim-faced rider, whose identity couldn't be hidden under a bushel basket. It was the woman wrapped around him, her features hidden against the back of his jacket, showing a sleek length of thigh and a whisper of blond hair that got them asking questions.

Who was slipping out of town with Zach Crandall and into sin?

The instant they hit the smoothly paved highway, Zach throttled back. The motorcycle rocketed ahead like Chuck Yeager's X1 test plane out to break the sound barrier. Bess hugged in closer to Zach, her arms banding tight about his middle as they pushed against the ripping wind. The formidable span of his shoulders created a sheltering break as she huddled behind them. It took a moment for her to get past the idea of their vulnerability as they hurtled down the road; for her to remember there was nothing reckless in the way Zach controlled the big bike. He was one for pushing the limits, not for foolishly shattering them. That sense of safety allowed her to relax, to lean into the wind, to feel freedom chilling her face and hurrying her heartbeats.

The sense of excitement was like sweet liquor, rolling through her veins, warm and seducing. As aware of the man as she was of her own emotions, she had to ask how she ever could have given it up without more of a fight?

Part bar, part intimate hideaway, Haven's sat at the interstate crossroads, flashing a neon invitation to weary travelers. Known for its pricey menu and low-lit atmosphere, it was a favorite spot for romantic interludes and celebrations. Surrounded by high-backed booths and beaded curtains, with sultry blues tunes murmuring from the public area, privacy made an irresistible lure for courting couples; the illusion of escaping small-town familiarity and stepping into a world of big-city sophistication.

The first time she'd visited, Bess had been too anxious to appreciate the ambience, afraid of being found out, afraid of the urgent feelings twisting inside when she thought of being in a place like this with Zach. A trickle of those same apprehensive worries crowded close when they were shown to their table, but Bess forced them back. She was an adult, responsible to no one for the decisions she made.

Besides, who in Sweetheart would see her here?

As their host held back the curtain to their booth, Zach stepped behind her to take her jacket. As he peeled it back, his thumbs stroked slowly along the ridge of her collarbone, scaring up a rash of gooseflesh along her arms as he bared them. She scooted into the booth and arranged her skirt primly while he slipped out of his well-worn leather.

Against the smoky backdrop and husky music, his manner easy, his physique fluidly detailed in a dark knit pullover and soft pleated trousers, Zach Crandall could have been a corporate executive or wealthy urbanite closing a business deal. No trace of the rough-edged rebel remained. The man who slid in opposite her appeared self-assured and comfortable in

the upscale setting, erasing the ghost of a defensive teen awkwardly wrestling with the menu selections, then anxiously
counting out his cash under the table to see if he could pay
the bill.

He ordered wine, pronouncing the French name without
difficulty, then asking if she was agreeable to his choice. She
nodded, unwilling to express her ignorance. Wine was something swallowed obediently during communion at Easter, not
sipped over dinner with a man who was suddenly a total
stranger.

They ordered, Bess a modestly priced chicken, Zach, the
thickest slab of beef on the menu, then he leaned back in a
pose of suave negligence. She might have bought the whole
picture, except for one thing. There was nothing restful in his
gaze. His stare cut through the layers of civility in which he
tried to cloak himself, laying bare his unchanging nature, that
of something half-wild and wary, and waiting to pounce.

As always, his first remark knocked reason askew.

"You are so beautiful." His lips twitched in a thin smile.
"But I guess you're used to hearing that."

"No."

The quiet honesty of her reply started a slow burn in the
back of his stare. Before he could follow up with more dis-
concerting praise, Bess flanked him.

"So," she began softly. "I know where you've been.
Where are you going? Is it too late to ask?"

"I'm not going anywhere, Bess. I spent a lot of years trying
to make someplace else work, but nothing fits like being
home."

Even when that home resented his presence and swore to
rid itself of the past he represented? Even when his first act
in a position of authority was to lock up the sons of the town's
two most prominent citizens? He read those questions in the
pucker of her brows and smiled with indulgent determination.
"Even when," that look told her.

"Zach, you could try something easy, like making a pair
of alligator skin boots while the alligator's still wearing it."

His smile hardened into a cynical curve. "It won't be the first time I've been bitten a time or two before I've gotten what I want."

"And what do you want, Zach?" It was the question all of Sweetheart was asking. And his answer would send them all, including Bess, into a panic.

"Justice."

Chapter 9

Bess sat quietly, eating but not tasting her chicken, drinking too much wine, listening to Zach talk about his time in the service. Behind her polite, attentive smile, her mind whirled frantically.

Justice. What exactly did that mean? Had he returned to Sweetheart in a lawman's guise to punish the town for its neglect? He'd had good cause for running in Web Baines and his bullying friends, but would it stop there or extend to petty grievances? Lloyd Baines abused his power that way, maintaining control through intimidation. So could Zach. She felt the difference in him as she watched him talk. A hard core of confidence underlay his words, a strength of will to match a strength of body. Whereas Zach the teen would have vented with volcanolike steam and heat and erupting violence, Zach the adult made her think more of an earthquake: a cool hidden force, striking without warning yet no less devastating in the end. Maybe the strict mores of Sweetheart needed the shake-up to stir them from their placid lives. But would Zach stop with minor tremors, or did he mean to cause the earth to open, swallowing them whole?

Her with them.

What kind of justice did he have in mind for her offences? She was more vulnerable than he might guess.

"Bess?"

She blinked like a deer caught in headlights. "What?"

"How's your meal?"

She glanced down at the neatly dissected dinner, scarcely touched, then at his empty plate and the waiter standing patiently for the order to clear the plates. "Fine. It's fine. I guess I just wasn't very hungry. You can go ahead and take it." She felt guilty sending so much costly food back to the kitchen, but Zach seemed unconcerned as he dealt out his credit card without even checking the bill.

"Coffee? Dessert?" the waiter suggested.

"Coffee would be nice," she managed with a smile.

With the table barren between them, Bess sat anxiously waiting for Zach to start up the conversation again. But he leaned back, studying her in his intense fashion until she began to fidget.

"I've heard nothing but my own voice for the past forty-five minutes," he said at last. "I think it's time I listened to yours for a while."

She toyed with her linen napkin. "What's to tell? You know everything about me already."

"I know where you've been. Tell me where you're going."

She shrugged. "After Faith leaves, I guess it's business as usual."

"Your mother's business." He said it casually, without censure or accusation, but she winced, anyway. Then grew defensive.

"Yes. What's wrong with that?"

His gaze never wavered, pinning her like a fluttering moth to a specimen board. "Nothing. If it's what you want. Is it, Bess?"

"Rare Finds is a part of Sweetheart history. My grandfather started it up from a library his grandfather ran."

"And you probably still have half of his original inventory sitting in the back."

Bess bristled at his wry observation, certain that he was ridiculing her ambitions—or what he saw as a lack of them. "What's your point, Zach? That it's not a big-city superstore? That it's not earning me a cool million? That I'm no competition for the malls or mail-order catalogs? I know that. Rare Finds is a family business, handed down from generation to generation. Ted Doolin's been after me to sell it so he can develop the whole block, but I won't. It's not the money or the lack of it. It's the sense of preserving the community, the history. Family tradition. I'm proud to be a link in that chain."

"What difference does it make, if you're going to be the last one?"

She gulped a quick breath, surprised by his too-accurate thrust. She'd forgotten how merciless his candor could be. It took her a moment to regroup her emotions. "I thought Faith—"

"Does Faith want to be tied down to that dusty old albatross? Have you asked her?"

She stared at him, injury giving way to a protective chill. "Thanks for letting me have it right between the eyes, Zach. I'd say you've a right to be bitter, but I don't remember you being mean. It's not an attractive quality."

She reached for her water glass, thinking to drown out the hurt, but he intercepted the move. His hand covered hers, shocking her with the sudden warmth of contact. His fingers closed before she could pull away. He was stronger, so Bess let her hand go limp, showing her rebellion in her passivity. He hesitated and she saw him questioning the wisdom of the move, cursing the bluntness of his claim. But he didn't let her go.

"I'm not subtle, Bess. I didn't mean to give you a right hook but I'm not going to apologize for speaking the truth.

And I'm not going to pretend that the thought of you locked away in that store doesn't make me crazy.''

A pause came with the coffee, then Bess took the offensive once more. "I don't want you to pity me because my dreams are tied up within the town limits. Just because you and Julie had to get away or suffocate, doesn't mean others can't be satisfied with a simple day-to-day existence."

"Are you?"

She responded to his soft challenge truthfully. "Yes. Yes, I am." Or at least that had been true before his return. Having Zach Crandall back in her life had a ripple effect, unsettling every aspect of who and what she was. The rest of her answer was even more defensive. Perhaps because she was working to convince more than just him. "I don't have elaborate needs. I don't wish for pots of gold. I like what I have. I like who I am."

"So do I."

His statement startled her, but not so much as the light figure eights his thumb sketched around the knuckles of her imprisoned hand. He studied the contrasts between them; hers pale, delicate, engulfed by his powerful, coarsely furred grip. He framed his next words carefully.

"I'm envious, Bess. You belong in a way I never could."

His poignant claim melted her guard.

"Don't envy me, Zach. You, you've seen the world, you know what it's like to be free."

His laugh held a metallic ring of irony. "Free? Is that what you think? I've been beating my wings against the bars all my life, but I've never flown." He released her hand, then looked up as their waiter presented his card and the receipt which he signed with an aggressive scrawl. Zach nodded to the "thanks and come again" speech and stood.

"Let's air out this conversation before it gets too claustrophobic," he suggested with a tight smile and the offer of his hand. Bess took it shyly, letting him guide her from the booth.

Unaware that in the bar area, one of the town council members chose that moment to glance up from the pretty young thing he was charming with drinks and flashes of his over-stuffed wallet. Unaware of his resentful glare as Zach slipped her jacket over her fair shoulders then shrugged into his own. Unaware of the dark schemes turning within an even darker soul as they stepped out into a surprisingly cool night.

They roared up the highway, along the thin white ribbon illuminated by the bike's single beam. Zach yelled something back at her but the wind snatched his words away. She leaned in closer.

"What?"

When he turned his head, she was right there, her chin on his shoulder, her mouth only inches away. Too much distraction for the speed they were going. He looked ahead quickly.

"Are you warm enough?" he shouted again.

"Fine."

But her arms tightened, maintaining that flush contact, her breasts flattened to his back, her face tilted up to taste the wind over his shoulder. He tried to keep his eyes on the road, away from the airy chiffon fluttering back to bare even more firm thigh. His body thrummed in time to the growling machine.

The feel of her against him quickened memories of another time, of a hormonally supercharged eighteen-year-old driven to urgent madness by the clutch of Bess Carrey's legs around him. He'd been a quaking libidinous mass all during that first awkward dinner, and it had taken all his willpower to keep the motorcycle on the road as they headed home. Finally, to save their lives, he'd pulled off into one of those roadside rest areas where a chained-down picnic table and waste can offered a respite to travelers, and to one sexually ravenous pair of teenagers. Shaking with uncontrolled eagerness he'd turned to the fresh-faced innocent behind him to say the first incredibly artless thing that entered his desire-drugged mind.

And as he cut the motor, seventeen years later and took off his sunglasses, the words felt just as clumsy.

"So, do you want to neck, or what?"

Bess remembered the place, the event and even the tactless question. A husky chuckle vibrated through her. "Such a smooth, worldly approach. No wonder I fell for it."

Zach laughed at his own gracelessness. There was a catch to the sound. "Have a heart, Bess. I was a kid. You had me backed up so bad, my eyeballs were swimming."

"Oh, that's a delicate turn of phrase. You are such a poet, Mr. Crandall." She eased off the seat, still feeling the bike's power quivering through her. Or was that her response to Zach and her own memories. She walked to the rickety table, needing to put a little room between her and the object of those long-ago fantasies. "I seem to recall being more than ready, myself."

When she closed her eyes briefly, she could feel, again, the hot desperate yearning to "go all the way" with Sweetheart's least-favorite son. The want, the fear, the guilt and defiance had pulled her in a million different directions at once as he'd retained the presence of mind to lay his jacket atop the carpet of leaves, providing a cushion as he'd laid her down for the first time on that frosty spring night to claim her virginity just as he'd claimed her heart and soul; with a rough uncertain sweetness.

They both sat in the darkness a lifetime later, remembering how it was, consumed by the curiosity to know how it could be.

"So?" Zach asked softly, still straddling the motorcycle. "Do you?"

She said nothing, her gaze wide, welcoming, in the moon-light, as she watched him approach. She didn't move as his large hand fit to her cheek, tilting her head back as his mouth came down. Hers was already open, ready to receive the reac-quainting thrust of his tongue. Her low moan spoke a lan-guage of pure sensation.

His free arm curved around her waist, lifting her, dragging her up against him so she could feel exactly how much he wanted her now, as he had then. The knowledge made her tremble all along his rugged planes as he tore his mouth off hers to plant scorching kisses to the arch of her throat, feasting on the chaotic rhythm he created as passion thundered in her blood. His hands clasped her small waist for a restless moment, then began to push upward over the filmy chiffon, to heft the weight of her small breasts, shaping them to fit his palms, spreading his fingers upward to hook the thin straps of her dress and brush them off her shoulders even as she shrugged to let her jacket fall. The night air brought a sudden shiver that matured into a shudder of exquisite passion. Her back arched in tangible evidence of need.

It never occurred to Bess to say slow down or stop. Her own desires had all but run away with her last scrap of coherent thought. Her physical being was alive, her sensory self crying out to experience everything he might give her. Then surprisingly, the braking power of restraint came from him.

It was hell to pull back while his head whirled and his blood ran thick and hot. But this wasn't how he wanted their reunion; not with the same hurried carelessness of two kids afraid of being caught in the forbidden. Bess deserved better. He wanted more. So he reined in hard, prying himself off her soft lips, defying the attraction of her nearly bared breasts and the intoxicating scent of her flushed skin. The years of military discipline served him, not well, but well enough. His thumbs restored the straps of her shift to their proper place, but as he lifted his head, his noble intention was almost thwarted. Bess caught his face between the press of her palms, holding him for the sudden ravishment of her kisses.

"Bess," he murmured against the eager mash of her lips over his, fighting for his sanity. "Not like this."

She paused, breathing hard and fast, not comprehending. Especially when she opened her eyes to see that the hungry flicker started over dinner now raged, a hot blue flame.

His hands moved upon her bare shoulders, not in caresses but with gentle distancing pressure. "This was a bad idea. I wasn't planning...I'm not prepared," he ended lamely.

"Zach—" His name rumbled from her, all throaty invitation as she pushed against his bracing palms.

He stepped back so quickly she almost lost her balance. She stumbled forward, catching herself, peering up at him in bewilderment.

What was meant to be a gentle discouragement came out all wrong.

"Bess, I can't afford to make another mistake with you."

Few things he might have said just then would have jolted her out of her dazed and desirous state. But those words had the shock value of ice-cold water. She blinked rapidly and swallowed. Her mouth moved as if to say something but then gripped tightly shut.

"I'm—"

She cut him off brusquely. "Don't say you're sorry. I understand and I agree. Take me home, Zach."

"You don't understand, Bess. I meant—"

"I know what you meant."

But as she strode back to the motorcycle to pull the helmet down over the tousle of pale hair, her agitated movements said she didn't. She had no idea what was behind his words, for she heard something entirely different.

She heard her dreams die on the one word: *mistake*.

Zach hesitated, sensing he'd fouled everything up somehow, but there was no time to fix it. He'd promised Melody he'd pick her up from work. She was afraid to go home, alone, to their empty house after discovering the vandalism the night before. Cursing under his breath, he swung astride the bike and waited for Bess to settle behind him, which she did at a frigid distance. Her fists touched his sides gingerly as if she were loath to get closer. He caught them and yanked her arms around his middle, hearing her gasp as she bumped against his back.

"Hang on," he ordered in a tone so taut she didn't dare disobey him as he angled the cycle back up onto the road and jammed through the gears to send them flying.

A mistake. Bess blinked hard, blending blurriness into tears that the wind wiped away. That was how he saw the treasured relationship they'd had and the blessings that sprang from it.

That was how he defined their getting back together. No way
she could misinterpret that message.

Her anguish numbed her to the approach of danger until it
was right on top of them.

The car came up behind them from out of nowhere, headlights glaring, blinding, not intent upon passing them but in
running right over the top of them. Bess screamed as the wide
chrome grill loomed up at her back like a shark on the attack.
She clung to Zach as metal rasped against rubber with a stunning jolt. She buried her face in his jacket to blot out the
reality of their impending deaths.

For just as the big automobile bore down on them from the
rear, the road swung into a tight curve. A camper lumbered
toward them from the opposite direction. Instead of slowing
down to combat the hairpin angle of the road, Zach opened
the throttle wide, jolting the bike forward, steering it purposefully into the oncoming lane. The camper's lights glared
briefly as the blare of its horn cut through the night. Zach
didn't return to his lane, aiming the cycle for the far shoulder,
where they slid precariously on gravel as the camper roared
by within a yard of mangling them.

As Bess squeezed her eyes shut and prayed aloud, Zach
fought the loose stones threatening to upend them. Finally he
muscled the cycle to a shuddering stop. The large dark car
that had come up from behind continued on as if the driver
had never seen them.

Zach twisted on the seat, adrenaline pumping.

"Are you all right? Bess?"

Her fingers were imbedded in the leather of his jacket. He
had to pry them loose to drag her up in front of him to take
her in his arms. She remained stiff and still against him until
shock rolled through her in a loosening spasm.

"Oh, my God! We could have been killed!"

Her arms banded his neck in a choking circle, and he simply held her as her teeth clattered too fiercely for her to speak.
He unfastened the helmet, letting it fall to the gravel as he
stroked her hair, trying not to think of how close he'd come

to losing her. His insides knotted with nausea, then were steadied by a calmer anger.

By then Bess had recovered enough to sit back and look up at him. Her features were stark and pale. Her brows knit with fear and agitation.

"What was wrong with that guy? He almost ran us down. How could he not see us?"

He couldn't. It was no accident. Zach kept that piece of grim news to himself as he rubbed her arms so the friction would restore her body heat.

"Sorry I scared you. I couldn't ditch on the other side. There was a drop-off."

She bought his explanation, saying gruffly, "Sorry? That was the best bit of driving I've ever seen. You saved our lives."

Yes, he probably had. If the incident was meant as a warning, it was an intense one.

Their lives weren't in jeopardy, his was. Who was bent on taking it wasn't quite as important as the fact that they'd been willing to sacrifice Bess to have it. That scared him so deeply, so profoundly, he fell into a pattern of instinctive preservation. He had to get both Bess and Melody out of the line of fire as quickly as possible. If someone was out to end his life, he wouldn't risk theirs by association.

Something was going on in Sweetheart. Something darker and more dangerous than just a rebellious teen's return.

And he had to find out before it killed him. Or anyone close to him.

"C'mon," he said to the still-trembling Bess. "Let's get you home."

"Shouldn't we report this to someone?" she argued with a bit more spunk.

"Yeah. To me. I could write up a report, but there's not much to go on. Did you get a make or model or license number?"

"I was too busy wondering what I'd wear to my funeral."

Under the fragile exterior, she was a gutsy piece of work.

He fought the need to kiss her wildly, desperately, until passion devoured his fears. Instead, he smiled thinly.

"A big dark car of uncertain make and model tried to run us off the road. Not much of a report."

She frowned. "Guess not. Probably some drunk or some salesman driving on too little sleep." She looked up at him for confirmation.

"Probably."

"I'll say this for you. Being with you is never dull, Zach." She touched the collar of his jacket, punctuating her bittersweet claim with a reluctance to let him go. He was *this* close to collapse when she let her hands drop and bent to retrieve the helmet. His gaze sketched over the tempting curve of her hips, increasing his self-imposed torment. Only Bess Carrey would cause him to require a cold shower atop a near hit-and-run, to cool down his libido.

Bess slid off the bike at her back door and handed Zach his helmet. He said nothing, not with words, not with his expressionless eyes. She couldn't quite make herself say thanks. Not after he made it clear there was no future for them—at least not the future she'd hoped for. She schooled her features into a matching impassivity while her heart broke quietly within.

Don't leave me, Zach. Not after I've waited all these years for you to come back for me.

But apparently she wasn't included in the reason for his return.

After fixing the helmet on his head, he geared up and rumbled off into the darkness.

Chapter 10

Mary Crandall came home to Sweetheart.

It wasn't the usual welcome a convicted felon received, for Mary was one of Sweetheart's own; well loved, well respected and much pitied for the lot she'd chosen as a foolish young girl. Her only crime in the eyes of the town was falling for the wrong man. In marrying Sam Crandall, she'd stepped outside Sweetheart's protective circle, and for the years that followed, though old friends might shake their heads in sorrow, none would lift a finger to help her escape the terror her life had become. Folk minded their own business. What lay between a man and his wife was no one else's concern.

At least, those were the platitudes the good citizens hid behind to excuse their cowardice and shame.

The fact that Mary blamed none of them, at least not directly, only made them feel more wretched and eager to make amends. They respected Melody, even after the scandal of her divorce. She never made trouble for anyone nor made her problems theirs. She worked hard to maintain a private life, a quiet life, and they pretty much left her to it. The only stumbling block between the town and the Crandall women was Zach. His presence kept them from crowding close to exorcize their guilt, as Mary, older, frailer, spindly as a delicate water bird, was carried up the front walk in her eldest son's arms.

Bess heard all the details as the rumor mill came and went through her store all that day. She didn't run to gawk, herself, feeling the family deserved their privacy. Feeling she wasn't exactly welcome to intrude. And deeper down, afraid to face Mary Crandall with so much weighing upon her heart.

Still, she couldn't escape hearing about it, over and over, just as she'd listened to step-by-step descriptions of Zach's every move all week long. It didn't help to pretend she wasn't interested. Since the pie incident, the entire populace considered it their duty to protect her from making Mary's mistake all over again. Zach Crandall was no good, just like his daddy. The uniform didn't change the man inside. He'd only hurt her. He was taking advantage of the friendship she'd given a troubled boy to weasel his way back into the town's good graces.

The longer he stayed away, the easier it grew to half believe them.

She might have been able to, except for one thing.

She knew Zach hadn't killed his father. And her silence fed the hostility of a whole town toward an innocent man.

Better she stay away from the Crandalls before her secrets were dragged to light. There was more than her own future at stake.

The homecoming exhausted Mary Crandall. Prison was a poor place to recover from heart surgery, especially with the added stress of awaiting her release. By the time she was able to breathe free air again, she was almost too weak to enjoy it. The ride home was strength sapping, but she hung on valiantly for the sake of her children, as always.

Though she'd said nothing of her fears, her return to the site of so many nightmares filled her with dread, but in the end the expected trauma was absent. Instead of taking her to the room she'd shared with her husband, Zach laid her down on the comfortable bed in Ross and Jordie's room. The interior was newly remodeled in soft pastels and fresh flowers, a balm to her weary senses. Though so many things remained for her to do and say, to her dismay, she fell instantly and deeply asleep, to wake hours later to a darkened room on the edge of hell.

His silhouette filled the door frame, brutally big and oozing inevitable violence. How had she truly believed she could escape him? Evil had a way of latching on and never letting go. This time, he was going to kill her, then the children, just like he'd always threatened. She tried to cry out in alarm, to pull herself up and out of harm's way but her worn-out body wouldn't respond. So she lay there, weeping silent tears, waiting for the worst to come, for the only release she could ever find from a beast like Sam Crandall.

"Mom, are you awake?"

Her breath expelled shakily. "Zach?" It took a moment for her thoughts to adjust. Her hands swiped the tears away. "Come in, honey. Turn on the light."

He crossed the room, his size, his features so chillingly familiar, but the moment the room flooded with mellow reality, Mary saw the differences. Her son was not the monster her husband had been. She'd saved him from that.

"How are you feeling, Mom? Did you get some rest?"

He hung back, expressing the words of concern with an odd aloofness. All she wanted to do was hold him tight, but Zach wasn't like her other children. He'd always been cautious when it came to his emotions, guarding them zealously as the only things of worth truly in his control. He'd let them slip once in a while with Melody and, she suspected, at one time with Elizabeth Carrey, but never with her, figuring she had enough worries on her mind already.

"I feel better now," was all she said.

"Can I get you anything?"

"You can talk with me for a while."

He hesitated. "I don't want to wear you out."

"You won't."

He began to pace the room, strong steps, caged energy, but unlike his father's it was under tight control, even when he was anxious about something, like now. She didn't ask. She knew she'd have to wait until he was ready to talk about it.

"State Police," she mused with a smile. That brought him to a halt at the foot of her bed. "I'm so proud of you, baby. I knew you'd make good if you had the chance."

For a moment he didn't move, then by tiny increments as she watched, the wall of his reserve begin to crumble. It began with his jerky swallowing, followed by a thinning about his mouth. Finally, the cutting blue of his eyes grew wavery. When he spoke, his voice was a low rasp.

"You gave me that chance, Mom. If I'd have guessed what it would cost you—" He broke off, turning away.

"Zach," she called softly. "I would have paid any price."

He shook his dark head as it hung low in inexpressible grief. "I'm sorry. I'm sorry."

"It was bound to happen, baby. We all knew that. The law wouldn't do anything. He would have killed one of you or me. No one could have stopped him."

"I should have. Long before then. I should have done something. I never should have let him hurt you the way he did. I was afraid of him." His shoulders slumped at that admission, shoulders that had never bent under years of punishment, broken only by his failing to protect those he loved.

"We were all afraid of him, Zach. He was a dangerous man. You did the right thing. I never blamed you. Not ever."

He shook his head again, still not looking at her. "It was my fault. My fault. I never should have hit him. But when he knocked you down and you didn't get back up, I just went crazy. Nothing ever felt so good as burying my fist in his face."

Mary winced at the harsh slash of his tone but she understood the hate, the anger. And she understood the fear, too, when he continued in a quieter voice.

"I should have stayed to make sure you were all right. I shouldn't have run and left it to you. But if I'd have stayed, I would have become him, right then, that night. I knew it and that scared me more than he did. I had to go. I know you can't forgive me for that, and I don't expect you to. I haven't thought of anything else all these years. I couldn't face you in that place. It should have been me. It should have been me."

"No, baby. Never. Zach. Zach, come here."

He turned slowly, head still down so she couldn't see his features. He came to take up the hand of absolution she offered, clutching it with a tender desperation as he went down on his knees at her bedside. She drew his bowed head up against her, stroking his hair the way she had when he was young, before he'd learned to handle his own hurts with such fierce independence.

"I love you, Zach. I love all you children. I would have made any sacrifice for you. Don't you dare think you owe me anything. All those years I watched him mistreat you and did nothing. I never filed a complaint. I never tried to leave him. It was my fault, baby. I would have done anything to make up for not keeping you safe. Anything. I know you had to get away. I'm glad you did. Look what you've made of yourself." She hugged him in tighter as her frail voice toughened with pride.

"You did what you had to do, Zach. It was bound to happen sooner or later. I'm just so thankful it was him and not you. That's what I thought of all these years. Thank God it was him, not you. He was a man who needed killing. If you hadn't done it, I'm afraid to think what might have happened to the rest of us."

Time stopped for Zach Crandall.

"What?"

"Don't ever say you're sorry, baby. I just did what I had to do, too."

He raised his head, his shiny eyes blank with shock. "What

do you mean if I hadn't done it? Mom—Mom, I didn't kill him."

She smiled faintly, brushing his wet cheek with unsteady fingertips. "I never let them say you did. I couldn't bear the thought of you going to jail for saving our lives. It was the only thing I could do to make up for not stopping him before. It was the only way I could let you know how sorry I was for failing you, the only way I could stop him from ruining the rest of your life. And I was right, Zach. A lawman." Her eyes grew teary. "Look what you've made from all my mistakes."

A cold, fearful realization began to spread through Zach's belly as he told her again, more forcefully, "Mom, I didn't kill him. I—I thought you did."

Bess was finishing up the supper dishes while Faith stacked them away when the girl went still, plate dangling from one hand as she stared out the window.

"Aunt B, there's someone in the backyard."

Bess leaned across the sink, squinting out into the deeper darkness, her first thoughts ones of mild alarm. "Probably kids cutting through," she murmured to reassure them both. But after a moment, when her eyes adjusted, she could make out a single figure far in the back, where an old swing set stood. She wrung out her dishcloth and laid it out to dry across the sink divider.

"I'll be back in a minute."

The quiet tone alerted Faith. "Who is it?" When she got no answer, she jumped to her own conclusions. "Will you be back in time for Mom's call?"

"If I'm not, tell her hello for me."

She walked up the slight slope of the yard as if in a remembered dream. Each step felt as familiar as the emotions crowding up inside. The swing set was a remnant left over from a time when she'd baby-sat for the neighbor's early-elementary-aged twins. Its legs were sunk in cement so it had remained long after the little girls grew up to have kids of their own. The silent figure rocking slowly to-and-fro on the low board seat, waking creaks and groans from old hooks and chains was a ghost from the past, as well.

She didn't ask him why he was there. It had been their rendezvous spot in the late evenings after her mother had retired for the night in her front bedroom. He would be there, rocking, waiting for her, when his mood was dark and troubled.

The way it was now.

"Zach, what's wrong? Is it your mother?"

He didn't look up right away, giving Bess time to crouch down beside him as his long out-flung legs flexed to move the ancient swing. She heard the hoarse draw of his breath and the hard swallow that came next.

"I shouldn't be here," he mumbled thickly. "I just didn't know where else to go."

"It's all right."

She followed that soothing sentiment with an easy embrace, one arm sliding across his broad back and the other about his middle. He doubled over, head hanging between his knees, fingers lacing at the back of his neck. And he leaned into her, not much, but enough so she knew the support was needed.

"It's all right, Zach," she told him, holding him the way she had when he was a frustrated, frightened teen. "It's all right." She began to rock with the gentle movement of the swing. "You can always talk to me. You know you can." Caught up in the moment, in the memories, she curved her body over his, forming a protective shelter he'd seek from no one else. With her cheek pressed to the top of his dark head, she asked, "What's wrong? Tell me."

A slight negating shake. "Not yet."

She understood, holding him, giving him the time he needed to force the right words to the surface, humbled by his trust, by his need for her just as she'd been all those years ago. A man like Zach Crandall didn't break easy, but when that hard exterior began to crack, it sheered apart like a rending fault line, with violence and force, in an awesome release. Bess waited, willing to absorb the tremendous snap and the shaky aftershocks that would follow.

"Let go," she coaxed, and the first fierce wave shook through him. He lifted his head so she could kiss his brow, his cheek, tasting the salty dampness as he angled for her lips. Mouths moved together, hurried, healing, quieting the pain with passion, as Bess heard the faint ringing of the phone within the house that meant Faith was out of sight...out of mind.

She wasn't sure who moved first or it if was a joint decision that took them from swing set to cool grass. She was too busy kissing him to care. She welcomed the weight of him leveling out over her, pressing her into the warm earth as he pressed into her warm peaks and valleys. An avalanche of sensation swept over them, pushing them along the path with an unstoppable urgency. Bess's fingers raked through the short bristle of black hair as Zach's palms rubbed over the jut of her hipbones in restless, seeking circles. His tongue plunged deep as he rocked into her, his jeans barely able to contain him. His mouth slid slightly, just enough for him to ask, "Are you sure it's me you want?" in a voice too rough to be recognizable.

Her hands went down to push into the back pockets of his jeans, kneading hard muscle, encouraging a more aggressive movement while she whispered, "I've been waiting seventeen years."

He went still over her, breathing hard, his cheek pressed tight to hers. Strung taut, muscles bunched, he didn't move as a fierce battle of will against want shook through him.

"I can't do this." His words dredged up raw and harsh.

Bess clutched at him, her senses spinning, her breathing thin, her chest aching, as expectation trembled, then slowly receded. She understood. He wasn't here for sex, though they could have easily tumbled into it. Her restlessness eased as she contented herself with the feel of him, heavy and hot above her. He'd come to her to find comfort, not release. It wasn't the time to confuse the two. She touched his hair, stroking, calming until his tension waned.

"I need a friend right now, Bess. Not a lover."

"I know. It's all right." She kissed his temple to prove that it was, while packing the rebellious passion he'd ignited back where it had lain dormant for so long.

He stirred at last, his cheek brushing against hers as he lifted up, gathering his elbows and knees beneath him. She mourned the loss of his covering, lying still with eyes closed. He was silent for so long, she feared he meant to stand and leave without regret or remorse, without saying anything of what had brought him to her. But then she heard his heavy exhalation as he stretched out on the lawn beside her and began to talk, telling her in toneless brevity of the exchange he'd had with his mother.

"She walked in that night on an argument between me and my father. I told him that I was going to enlist after graduation and get as far away from him as I could. He laughed at me, Bess. He was drunk, mean drunk, had been all day. He said if I wasn't planning to hang around to pay him back for the wonderful upbringing he'd given me, he wasn't going to support my dead ass another day. That's when Mom came in, saying I was going to finish school, that I was going to amount to something, that she wasn't going to let him throw me out. He hit her, hard."

His mother told him what little she could remember. That, from her dazed position on the floor, Mary had heard father and son exchange blows, their fight growing more violent, moving outside into the garage while she dragged herself upstairs, falling unconscious upon the bed. When she'd come to, hours later, the house was silent, the younger kids having gone to a double feature before the commotion and Zach, just plain gone. And on the floor in the kitchen, she found her husband, the back of his head caved in from the force of some tremendous blow.

"She called the police, and when Baines showed up, she told him that Dad started in beating her and she'd killed him for it. She confessed because she thought I'd done it and run away. That's what they all thought—my mom, my sister, brothers, the whole damn town. They all thought I ran and left her to take the blame.

"I didn't even know he was dead until months later. I read about it in the paper. By then she'd already been sentenced. I figured he came back after I'd gone and they'd gotten into it again, since I wasn't there for him to take it out on. It never once occurred to me to think she didn't do it. She had every right to. Every right."

His voice trailed off, and for a long time he just stared up at the stars.

Bess studied his strong profile, her own emotions tangled up in his anguish, in her own guilt. On that night, like this one, he'd come to her, bruised, overwrought, on the edge, unwilling to talk about what was eating him alive. Only, they'd made love on that night, fiercely, frantically, and he'd fallen asleep afterward. Sleeping for hours like the dead, until the time pinpointed as the approximate moment of Sam Crandall's demise was long past. She'd watched him then, too, loving him, afraid of him and for him, for the violence he couldn't escape, for the secret she couldn't share. Torn apart by the decision she had to make.

When he'd awakened, unaware of how much time had passed, that's when he'd told her he was leaving Sweetheart with just what he was carrying...and her, if she'd go with him.

She'd never told another soul that they'd spent the long hours of that evening together. No one except her mother.

Zach turned toward her, his eyes quicksilver in the moonlight. "Did you believe it, Bess? Did you think I killed him?"

"No," she told him honestly, then writhed inwardly at his relief.

He reached out, curling one arm about her shoulders to draw her up against him where she nestled in, as if she belonged. Where she'd always wanted to belong. "You always believed in me when nobody else would. I don't know why."

She could have said it was because she loved him, but that wouldn't have been answer enough. It was more than that. More than she realized until she saw him wearing the State Police uniform. His success had been hers, as personally as if she'd won it herself. By playing a small part in pushing him ahead, to achieve, excel, to move on, she'd allowed herself a taste of what it might be like to escape and fly.

She'd made her choice seventeen years ago, and the reasons still bound her to them.

"Why didn't you get hold of your family, Zach? You could have found all this out years ago."

He sighed, the strength drained from him, his mood quiet, self-contained. "I couldn't, Bess. I was afraid if I did, I'd get pulled back here out of guilt or responsibility. I wasn't ready to come home. I couldn't look back. There was too much here that still had a hold of me." He didn't say she was one of those things. He didn't have to as his lips moved lightly across the silken tousle of her hair. "I kept track of Mom through Pat. He was the one who told me about her first heart attack. I'd been thinking about leaving the service. I got what I'd wanted from it. Anyway, after talking to Pat McEnroy, I took a post with the state up in Des Moines, and we timed it so his retirement could coincide with my transfer and Mom's release."

"So you planned everything." Her tone was soft, admiring, yet still a trace anxious.

He had planned it all. Methodically. Painstakingly. How he would use his authority to impress and influence the opinions of Sweetheart, how he would use their approval as a stepping-stone to Bess's heart. By smoothing all the obstacles in advance, he'd leave her with no objection to his suit. He'd considered every angle, every detail. Almost everything, he admitted to himself as he cuddled Bess close. Everything except how she would still rock his senses like the kick of a mule and get him thinking with his heart instead of his head.

Everything except the misunderstanding that had sent his mother to jail and left him in exile from those he loved.

Everything except how to deal with both those things.

Then through the calm of his spirit slithered a thought as dark and unwelcome as a serpent in the proverbial garden. If neither he nor his mother was guilty of his father's murder, someone else in Sweetheart was.

As Bess nestled against him, trusting him with a humbling innocence not to hurt her, he gathered the detachment of mind and body it would take to deliberately push her away. Because he cared too much to put her at risk once he went after the real killer. The killer who had most likely tried to run them off the road once already.

Anyone near him was going to be in terrible danger.

"You've been a great friend, Bess. Thanks."

He shrugged her off his shoulder and sat up.

"I gotta go." He could feel her confusion, even though he lacked the courage to watch it cloud her expression.

"Are you all right?" Her tentative concern held the blunt impact of a fist to the solar plexus. Affixing a thin smile, he glanced down at her.

"Yeah. I knew I could count on you to listen. Thanks, Bess. I feel better now."

She blinked, stunned by his dismissal. He could see her uncertainty, the way she weighed their earlier desire against his casual classification of what they were to each other. She recognized the inconsistency, but thankfully hadn't the experience or confidence in matters of the heart to call him on his lie. Thankfully for him, devastating for her, who'd looked to him for so much more.

Dammit all, anyway! He took advantage of her bewilderment to stand and brush off her pain the way he did the grass clippings from his jeans.

"Zach—"

"I'll see ya. Okay?" And he began to walk away from where she huddled on the shadowed lawn, without waiting for her response. Because it would kill him to see it.

Chapter 11

"Asking questions, that's what he's doing. Can you imagine?"

"As if he didn't know the answers."

Bess rubbed her temples, trying to soothe the persistent ache behind her eyes. And having about as much success as she was with closing out the sound of the two sisters' hushed gossiping at her elbow. The last thing she wanted to hear about over breakfast was the early bird report on Zach Crandall. For the past few days, he was the town's only topic, making Bess wish for a crop-threatening storm or some other natural disaster to turn the talk to something less distressing.

"As if anyone remembers after all this time," Myrt grumbled, casting a covert look to see if Bess was still listening.

"As if anyone believes someone else actually killed the man," Lorraine agreed. "He can't think we're so stupid we can't figure it out. What do you think, Elizabeth?"

"What?" She glanced toward the two expectant hens with a disappointing blankness.

"Can you believe that Crandall boy thinks to fool anyone

by stirring up talk about his daddy's killing? It isn't like we don't already know who the murderer is.''

"I believe the court said it was Mary Crandall." Both ladies tsked at her naive response, but she didn't plan to give them time to educate her. "I've got a shipment of damaged books to return this morning, so if you'll excuse me—''

Myrt caught her wrist, halting her rise from the counter stool. Bess stared at her, surprised by the firmness of the old woman's grasp. And by the solemnity of her voice.

"He did it, Bess. You know that, don't you? Sheep's clothing doesn't change the wolf underneath.''

Frustration and lack of sleep left her vulnerable to a sudden sidestep of reason. She jerked her arm back, startling the ladies with her abruptness and the gruff tone of her voice.

"I know nothing of the kind and neither does anyone else in this town. Don't you have something better to do than spread malicious rumors that ruin other people's lives?''

The round-eyed shock, greeting her outburst, rattled Bess back to a tentative sanity. But she didn't apologize, *wouldn't* apologize, thus giving her permission for more of the same to continue. She'd heard enough speculation. Each question rounded back on her, chipping at her conscience, prodding her to do something, say something. Pushing her toward a risk she would not take. Toward a stand she could not make.

Instead, she snatched up her purse, leaving the nearly untouched breakfast she'd ordered without real appetite as she turned toward the door. And stopped, the breath slammed from her lungs as Zach and Melody Crandall entered the diner.

Their eyes met as Zach held the door open for his sister. The lack of any tangible emotion in his laser-blue stare had Bess scrambling to conceal any response within her own. She would not stand there with whipped-puppy-dog eyes welling up in a confusion of hurt, begging to know what she'd done to be treated so badly. She did have some pride left, even though he'd managed to mangle most of it with humiliating ease.

"Good morning, Melody. Zach." The syllable crystallized as Melody's curious gaze jumped between them.

"'Morning, Bess." Melody touched her brother's shirt-front, the gesture not as much to display affection as it was to gauge the runaway tempo of his heartbeats as Bess slipped past them. Melody stretched up to kiss the granite line of his cheek, startling him into a slight thaw. "Thanks for walking with me. Be here at seven?"

"Sharp."

"I'm probably just being silly...."

"No problem, Mel." His firm tone dismissed hers. She had more to worry about than she knew. He waited until she'd gone behind the counter to secure her apron strings before nodding to the gawking sisters and startling them with his warmest smile. "Good morning, ladies."

For a moment they blinked and moved their mouths like fish out of water, not sure how to react to his polite attention. Then came the expected snub as they turned back to their coffee and oatmeal. He let it roll off. He'd wear them down eventually. For the moment he had other, more pressing matters to attend to.

He started across the shady square, sticking to the diagonal paths instead of tromping through the grass and flowerbeds the way a defiant boy once had. He was only now beginning to realize what a pain in the butt that kid had been. They'd been grand gestures at the time. Looking back, they were signs of delinquency. No wonder he ran up against so many suspicious faces when he was decked out in his official khakis. It was quite the leap from surly rebellion to honorable intentions, and the people of Sweetheart couldn't be pushed into making it. They would have to be coaxed. He'd have to prove the chasm wasn't too deep or too wide. And that had everything to do with his determination to fulfill his plans.

"Just what do you think you're doing?"

The sound of Bess's scold, spoken so close that his system recoiled in a shock of tingling awareness, made him slow but not stop.

"Going to work. And I'm running late."

She grabbed his wrist. The heat of her touch brought all his sensibilities to a crashing halt. He looked at her with a wary impatience, careful not to betray how the sight of her all flushed and determined, galvanized his blood into liquid fire. God, she was beautiful in her haughty disapproval—her sweet mouth pursed, her delicate brows furrowed over the bridge of her nose in what she thought an intimidating look. He wanted to applaud her spunk in confronting him, to kiss the stiffness from her lips, but because of the dangerous factors now in play, he merely regarded her as if she was a nuisance.

"What are you trying to do, Zach? Why are you digging up the past? What good is it going to do now?"

"Probably none."

"Then why? Why all the questions? Why stir everyone up all over again? It's not going to change anything."

"It won't change what's already happened, no. It won't give my mother back those seventeen years."

"Seventeen years, Zach. That's a long, long time. What do you think you're going to accomplish?"

His expression closed down tight. "It's so easy to believe the worst about me and my family, but when it comes to one of your own, you just don't want to consider that one of those fine, upstanding citizens is a cold-blooded murderer who would let an innocent woman go to prison to save their own sorry ass. You and the rest of them want to turn your backs and pretend justice was done. Well, it wasn't, Bess, and it won't be until I find out who killed my father." He started to pull away, his features taut, his eyes angry.

"Zach." She let her hand slide down from his wrist until she could lock his fingers in the curl of her own. For an instant he held on just as tightly. "Zach, no one in Sweetheart wants to know."

"Especially not the one who bashed his head in." His grip squeezed convulsively about hers. "Do you think I care that he's dead? I'm just as happy about it as anyone else in this town. Probably more so. If it had been a car crash or a lightning bolt from Heaven, I'd have spit on his grave and said good riddance. But someone killed him, Bess. And that someone is still here, walking around a free man—or woman. And my mother, my family, paid the price. That does bother me. A helluva lot."

She clutched his hand when he tried to wrest it free. "Zach, if you really want to be a part of this town…let it go."

"I can't, Bess." For a brief instant all his pain and fury etched harsh angles into his handsome face.

"You won't," she corrected, releasing him. Realizing she could no longer hang on to something she'd never truly had.

He hesitated, not immediately acting upon his freedom. "I won't win this town over by begging on my knees for forgiveness when I didn't do anything wrong. I'll work damn hard to earn it but I never kowtowed to unfairness, and I won't go crawling now."

"Then you won't win."

"Then I guess I don't care."

He started to stride away, then paused, thinking, finally turning. His expression was quieter but no less revealing.

"I wanted to thank you for letting Faith stay with my mom today. Melody needed to work, and I couldn't get the time off." At Bess's perplexed frown, he reassessed the situation. "You didn't know?"

"I—ah, no, I didn't."

"If there's a problem, I can—"

"No. No, Zach, I have no problem with Faith staying with your mother. In fact, I'm proud of her for offering."

"It's just that she's still weak, and we worry that she'll try to do too much and—"

"I understand. And I agree. Faith is old enough to handle the responsibility. She's a good girl."

"Like her Aunt Bess." He let his devastating smile out a notch, just enough to gel Bess's knees and send her into a flustered retreat.

"Just send her home when you get there."

"Bess?" His soft question stayed her turn. "Don't think the worst."

Bess didn't know what to think.

She tried to concentrate on the books whose hardcover corners had been crushed in shipping, but Zach's comment wouldn't leave her alone.

Think the worst about what? Him? Their situation? His face-off against the town? Her mind went crazy with possibilities. Why had he chosen to be purposefully vague for the first time since she'd known him? Was he hinting that there might be a future for them? It would take more than maddening clues dropped at unexpected intervals to get her hopes up again.

She set aside the packing order and sighed to herself. Who was she fooling? Her hopes where Zach Crandall was concerned would never dim. All it took from him was a glance, a smile, and her anticipation roared ahead like a bullet train. The feel of him was imprinted upon her every receptive curve, the memory of his touch branded upon each nerve ending. She would never as long as she lived stop wanting him. And as long as she wanted him, there would never be room in her life for another.

Disgusted to find she'd accomplished nothing all morning, Bess figured a break from the store was in order. Checking on Faith was just the prod needed for her to visit Mary Crandall without the need for awkward reasoning. She'd swing by the diner and pick up lunch for the three of them. There could be no harm in that; nothing Zach could construe the wrong way. The last thing she wanted was for him to think she was trying to encroach upon his family out of feelings of guilt. He'd be right, but not for the reasons he thought.

"Hi, Bess," Melody called brightly when she stopped at the diner's counter.

Bess marveled at her relaxed cheeriness. Whether it was due to her brother or her mother being home, or both, the improvement was obvious to all who knew the timid Melody.

"Hi, yourself. Could I get three specials to go? One of them's for your mom. I don't know if she has any kind of restrictions, so whatever you think's best."

"You're going over to visit? Mom will like that. She doesn't get much company."

Melody turned away, missing the flash of sorrow crossing Bess's features. "How's your mom doing?"

"Good. We sure appreciate Faith sitting with her. She's so mature for her age."

Bess relaxed and smiled. "You don't need to tell me. Sometimes, I feel like she's the grown-up and I'm the naive little girl."

"Julie's done a good job with her."

"Yes," Bess answered softly. "Yes, she has." She began to fumble through her purse, looking for the right denominations. Melody waved it away.

"Consider it on me. Faith wouldn't let me pay her, so it's my way of saying thank you."

As Bess watched her efficiently wrap and bag the food, she remembered something Zach had said to her. The town of Sweetheart had bent over backward in her time of sorrow, but what, if anything had ever been done for Melody? True, Mel had had that rotten excuse for a husband to keep her from being technically alone, but had she had any friends to rely on, any confidantes to talk to?

She looked at the other woman long and hard and saw a surprising similarity between them. The only difference was she was surrounded by the goodwill of the town, and Melody drifted on the tide of its indifference. She told Zach they'd become friends but was that really true? Or were her overtures as shallow as everyone else's who said good morning and left it at that?

"Melody, did you get a chance to read that book I lent you?"

"Oh, yeah. I meant to tell you how much I enjoyed it. For a man, he sure has an insight into his female characters."

Bess began to smile. "There's a small group of us who

meet at the library once a month to talk books and drink coffee and kick our shoes off. I'd like you to come with me next Thursday night. Faith can stay with your mom, and I know that's your night off. What do you say?"

"I—I don't know." She looked flustered, pleased, anxious.

"Say yes. It's real informal and I could use someone with my same taste in literature to back me up when Mona Fitch gets on her classical high horse."

Melody smiled, just a small glimmer at first as if she wasn't quite certain, then a full wide show of teeth, reminding Bess painfully of her brother. "I think I'd like that. If you're sure no one would mind."

Bess waved off her worry. "We never turn away a new opinion. We'll talk particulars later."

"Okay." Melody passed the meals across the counter. "I'll have Zach bring Faith home right after he picks me up."

"He doesn't have to walk her. It's only a few blocks." Bess hoped her alarm didn't show too prominently at the thought of Zach coming to her door.

"I insist." And the tone of the meek woman's voice sharpened in unusual emphasis.

"Is something wrong, Melody?"

Scared eyes darted about the room before she leaned close to confide, "Our house was vandalized. Zach thinks it's the same jerks he put in jail, but I'm not sure. It makes me nervous just thinking about it. I'd feel better if she didn't go by herself."

"Oh, Melody, I had no idea. What happened?"

"Just some of my hanging flowers knocked down and smashed." She gave an anxious little laugh. "Maybe it was kids." But her haunted gaze said otherwise, and so did Bess's sense of logic.

It was a warning for Zach. And knowing that made her wonder if the incident on the road was an accident at all. If Zach knew, why hadn't he told her?

Bess snatched up the sack, murmuring a quick goodbye before hurrying toward to door.

"Bess?" Mel called after her. When she turned, she was met with a shy smile. "Thanks."

Bess smiled back and gave a wave. Then she was out the door at a jog.

If there was danger at the Crandall house, Faith was right in the middle of it.

The summons to the mayor's office came as no surprise to Zach. What surprised him was that it had taken so long. He stopped just inside the door to study those waiting to shake and bake him. As his steely stare fixed upon each one in turn, some glared back, some glanced nervously away. A split decision in whatever was coming.

"You wanted to see me, Howard?"

The familiar use of the mayor's name brought a twinge of response from those who still thought of him as a young tough instead of as a peer.

"Yes, ah, er, come in, Mr. Crandall."

He smiled, a thin slash of amusement. "It's Zach, Mr. Mayor. No need for formality. I'm on duty, so I'd appreciate you cutting right to it."

Lloyd Baines did just that. "What the hell are you doing, boy?"

Zach met his cold glare with one of piercing frost. "Excuse me?"

"Didn't they teach you nothing in the state academy? Case closed means case closed."

"I know that."

Baines clenched his teeth. "Then why are you poking your nose around in something that's been over and done for almost twenty years?"

Zach let a tense silence build within the room before he replied. "I don't think there's anyone in this room who believes the right person went to jail for killing my father. I agree. And I intend to find out who murdered him. There's no statute of limitations on that."

"We all know Mary didn't kill her husband," Ted Doolin

snarled. "And we all know the someone who did is in this room."

Zach pinned him with a cold, unblinking stare. "I'd say you're probably right. But that someone isn't me."

"Oh, come on, Crandall—"

"Gentlemen, please," the mayor interrupted anxiously. "We're not here to point fingers."

Though he never moved a muscle, an enormous sense of threat suddenly radiated from Zach Crandall. He retained Baines's glare for a long minute before deliberately turning his attention to the mayor, as if the other lawman held no power to intimidate him. "What exactly is the problem, Howard?"

"Folks in Sweetheart are uncomfortable with your questions."

"If they've got nothing to hide, why should they be nervous? I wasn't here for the trial. I'm just trying to tie up a few loose ends for my own peace of mind. Like why there was no murder weapon found."

"We had a confession," Howard reminded him. "It wasn't necessary."

"Unless my mother wasn't guilty. She couldn't produce something she didn't have."

"What did you use, Crandall?" Baines snarled. "And where did you put it?"

Zach didn't favor him with a glance. He was focused on the mayor. "Is there some official reprimand coming? If not, I've got to get back to the station."

"Nothing official," Howard muttered.

"Not yet," Baines added.

"Then we've got nothing else to talk about." Zach restored his dark glasses to mask the intensity of his stare, but somehow the black void was even more ominous.

Elmer Grant came up with one last question. "If you know the case is closed, where did you get the evidence to reopen it?"

Zach paused then slowly drew down his shades. "This isn't an official matter. I'm looking into it after-hours." His features congealed like cement setting up. "It's strictly personal."

Chapter 12

It was Bess's first time inside the Crandall home. When Faith answered her knock and issued her inside, her immediate response was to look at the floor. *Is this where Sam Crandall lay dead?*

After all the stories, all the grim admissions from Zach, all the supposition, she expected to see the Bates house out of *Psycho,* filled with tormented shadows and film noir grittiness. Yet even with the cheery slashes of color and frilly curtains, a certain chill of menace lingered like the stain of a bad memory never completely scrubbed away. Ghosts as frightening as the ones haunting the Crandall family weren't easily exorcized.

"How are things going?" Bess asked, trying to rid herself of the image of a brutish Sam Crandall nearly drowning his wife in the dishwater because she'd stopped to speak to her former beau, Pat McEnroy, while doing the grocery shopping.

"Great. Mrs. Crandall is a doll. She's had a lot of nice things to say about you," the teen called over her shoulder as she led the way upstairs.

"Really?" That surprised her, since she'd never had a conversation with the woman. What she knew must have been learned through Zach. If she had good things to say, they were based on his opinions.

Bess paused before following Faith around the bend in the landing. She studied the closed door at the top of the stairs. Zach's room, the one he'd shared with Fletch, the oldest of his three brothers. She touched the smooth beige paint, noticing variations in the texture where the door had been patched; up high from the assault of a fist, down low by vicious kicks. She wondered how old he'd been, trapped inside, waiting for the protective barrier to give way. She'd seen the marks on him, old scars, bruises, but never had the horror of his childhood been brought so painfully into focus as now, with the evidence preserved within this house.

Trying not to be pulled into the sorrow-steeped shadows, Bess continued after Faith to Mary Crandall's bedside.

Greeting Mary held all the dread of confronting the sins of her past. The tiny, frail woman was propped up in bed, a colorful crocheted afghan tucked about her thin figure. Lines grooved every harsh experience into her wan face but the gaze rising to meet Bess's was warm with welcome.

"What a nice surprise. Come in, Bess."

Feeling like an awkward teen again, lacking every social grace, Bess approached the bed, forcing herself to smile with a confidence missing inside her. "Mrs. Crandall, welcome home."

"Call me Mary. I feel like we're old friends. Zach talked of nothing else while you were tutoring him."

The idea of tight-lipped Zach Crandall gushing about her virtues created an odd constriction within her chest.

While Faith spread out their deli feast, Bess searched for something to say to the woman who'd gone willingly to prison to protect her son from something he didn't do. She was awed by the sense of sacrifice, shamed by her own cowardice in the face of it. She'd been afraid to place her security on the line for Zach's sake. And she was sure Mary Crandall would know just by looking at her that she'd done more to harm than help her son.

"Faith, dear, I could use some of that cold lemonade down in the refrigerator, if it's no trouble."

When Faith sprang to do Mary's gentle bidding, both Bess and Mary looked after the girl fondly.

"A lovely child," Mary murmured.

"Yes, she is."

"Her mother must be very proud."

Bess nodded, picking the crusts off her rye bread.

"I remember your sister but must say Faith doesn't resemble her very much. She must look like her father's side of the family."

The innocent comment froze Bess up inside, but she forced a calm reply. "I don't know. I've never met them. She looks like the pictures I've seen of my father's relatives. I barely remember them. All I have to hold on to is the history."

"History is important," Mary agreed. "Almost as important as knowing your family."

Bess looked up then, her wide eyes studying Mary Crandall's weathered face for signs of any deeper meaning to those casually spoken words. Then Faith reentered the room, and the woman's attention shifted to the teen, her look going tender with the affection one would hold for a child...or a grandchild.

Pieces of bread crust scattered all over Bess's lap and onto the floor and bedspread as she jumped to her feet. Laying her paper plate on the braided rug, she swept up the crumbs with shaking hands.

"How clumsy of me. I don't mean to eat and run, but I just remembered I have to get a delivery ready for pickup." Mess cleaned up, she stood, careful to evade the other two's eyes. "Faith, if you have any problems, call me at the store. You have the number."

"Sure, Aunt B." The teen was frowning slightly, alerted by the frazzled sound of Bess's voice. "I never asked if you needed help with anything at the store. Is everything all—"

"Everything's fine. I just have to get back. I'm not a high-volume retailer so no sale is too small not to be missed."

"It was good to see you, Bess," Mary extended graciously. "I heard about your mother, and I'm sorry for your loss. I never got to know her, but I'd like the two of us to be friends. I hope you can find the time to come visit again, soon."

She held out her veined hand. Bess couldn't not take it. Once the fragile fingers closed about her cold ones, the press of reassurance was unmistakable. Bess risked a glance at the other woman's expression. Kindness, forgiveness, understanding reflected in those sad eyes. Everything Bess had hoped for, had the timing been right, had she been prepared. She withdrew her hand rather quickly to say, "I will. Don't let Faith wear you out."

"I'm enjoying our chance to get acquainted."

And the way she smiled at the girl set panic careening madly inside the staid bookseller.

Once outside the Crandall home, Bess swayed with dizziness, reaching out blindly to catch hold of one of the porch posts before her strengthless legs gave way. She leaned into the freshly painted wood, her eyes squeezed shut, her emotions roiling in sickening cycles of fear.

She knew. Mary Crandall knew.

What would she do with the knowledge? Whom had she told?

"Bess, are you all right?"

She gazed up anxiously to see Fred Meirs coming down the walk. Imagining how she must look to put such concern in the doctor's voice, Bess scrambled for an explanation.

"I was just visiting Mrs—Mary. It's so sad, all the things she and her family have been through."

Doc Meirs came up on the porch to place a caring hand upon her shoulder. "I know. This town and the folk in it haven't been exactly neighborly in the past, and now they're running scared."

"Scared? Scared of what?"

"The truth." He set down his medical satchel and began

to polish his glasses. "The Crandalls were a handy scapegoat for all that was sour in this town. Having the facts come out that none of us are as righteous as we'd like to believe is leaving a bad taste in certain mouths. There's talk—"

"What kind of talk?" Bess prompted, her attention riveted.

"That Mary went to jail for the wrong reason. That someone else killed Sam and that someone else is one of us."

Bess's heart beat faster. "You believe that?"

The doctor sighed. "I got to know Zach, as well as he'd let anyone get to know him. He was a hothead but he wasn't a killer. Whoever struck Sam Crandall down wasn't acting out of self-preservation. The force of that blow was meant to kill, not discourage him."

"I wasn't here for the trial, but I don't remember hearing anything like that come out."

The doctor grimaced. "I was told not to mention it. The trial was supposed to be quick and neat, wrapped up and out of mind."

"Told by whom?"

"Sheriff Baines. The town council. And Mary, herself."

Bess could understand Mary's wish for a speedy verdict. She was protecting Zach and feared evidence might turn up to implicate him. But the sheriff? What motive would he have to sweep the crime under a rug? Especially when he made no bones about believing Zach guilty.

"If we'd been able to recover the murder weapon, I might have been able to make a case."

The doctor's ruminating sparked Bess's curiosity.

"Why is that?"

"It was a very specifically shaped object. Triangular. Like a pyramid. I've been to the Crandalls' hundreds of times over the years and I don't recall ever seeing anything like that in their house. If I could have matched the source to the site of injury, and that source to its owner, I think we'd have had the real killer."

"You think there's a chance it could turn up?"

"After all this time?" He shrugged. "I doubt it. If it did,

I don't know that it would prove any more than circumstantial."

Bess frowned, considering this new slant on the old crime.

"Well," Doc muttered, shaking off the guilt of ages past, "I've got a patient to see. You take care of yourself, Bess."

"You too, Doc. My best to your family."

The conversation wouldn't leave her. All afternoon, as she did the store's operation by rote and tended the handful of customers, Bess's mind was busy processing what Doc Meirs had told her. It helped distract her from the precarious edge her own secrets teetered upon.

The longer Zach dug into the details, thought buried along with his father, the greater the danger that her own involvement would surface. To protect herself and those innocent others who would suffer for what she did, her only recourse was to help Zach uncover the identity of the killer as quickly as possible.

Amateur sleuthing wasn't a skill she'd ever thought to cultivate, but she'd read enough pulp mysteries under the covers as a youth to consider herself familiar if not well versed in the process—at least by Dashiell Hammett's standards of investigation. If Doc Meirs believed the truth hinged upon the murder weapon, that's where she'd concentrate. Perhaps one step ahead of Zach with the information the doctor gave her, she knew where to start.

Melody Crandall was cleaning off the counter in preparation for the dinner crowd. A few regulars loitered over coffee and conversation as Bess slipped into one of the corner booths. After a moment Melody came over, order pad out as she drew a pencil from behind her ear.

"Hi, Bess. I didn't expect you again so soon. What can I get you?"

"Answers to a couple of questions, if you have a minute."

Melody glanced around to see that all the customers were tended, then smiled at Bess. "What can I tell you? The ingredients of the meat loaf surprise?"

Bess's smile strained to conceal her anxiety. She wasn't good at subterfuge so she came right out with it. "Mel, I need to ask some things about the time your father...died."

Color bleached out of the other woman's face. "Oh."

Bess gripped one work-roughened hand for a supportive squeeze. "I know this is hard. I wouldn't ask if it wasn't important."

Melody sucked a shaky breath. "Okay. What do you want to know?"

"Can you remember if you ever had an object in your house shaped like a pyramid? A paperweight, a piece of statuary, something like that?"

Melody's brow furrowed. "I can't think of anything. Why? What does that have to do with what happened?"

"It might be the murder weapon," she confided in a low tone. "If it didn't belong to your family, and we can find out where it came from, maybe we'll be closer to discovering who killed your father."

"It wasn't Zach," came her instantaneous claim, edged in an uncharacteristic toughness.

"I know. I know it wasn't. And it wasn't your mother. Someone else—"

"Someone else in Sweetheart let us take the blame for something they did," Melody concluded. Her serene features hardened in outrage. "No wonder Zach's been so preoccupied. I thought it was because you—" She broke off, flushing darkly as Bess went still in shock. "I'm sorry. That's none of my business. I shouldn't have said anything."

"Melody, can we have some more coffee over here?"

She glanced over her shoulder. "Be right there." Then to Bess she promised, "I'll keep thinking about that pyramid. Maybe something will jolt a memory."

"Thanks, Melody."

As Bess sat recovering from the hurt spearing from her link to Zach and romance, another nearby customer was just as immersed in thought.

A killer thinking of ways to cover a trail thought cold.

* * *

As usual, Bess went from the diner to the bank to deposit the day's receipts. It took her several minutes to escape Lorraine Freemiere's grilling on her personal life, or rather, the lack thereof, and was duly warned that Herb meant to call her soon.

Five o'clock chimed on the courthouse clock by the time she started across the square with the intention of going home for a lonely supper for one. Surprising how little time it took to get used to the company of someone else under the same roof. Quickly, in self-defense, she blocked out the internal clock that warned of summer's eventual demise. The time when Faith would go back to her sister's and the family she knew.

And she'd have to prepare herself for the heartache of loss all over again.

Again she reminded herself she was doing the right thing, the best thing for all concerned. Every year, especially since her mother's death, that reminder became less and less effective in forestalling her silent yearnings. Was it fair for her to have to suffer the rest of her life for a mistake made by a naive teen? Would it be fair for her to reveal the truth now, after holding it in for so long. Too long. More damage would be done in the telling than with the hiding. Her head ached with potential unpleasantness. Far easier to carry her own burden of pain than to wish it upon another.

Unless Mary Crandall spoke her suspicions and took the decision from her.

"Bess? Bess?"

Realizing her name was being called, Bess jerked from her anxious thoughts to glance around. Bernie Sacks, the high school counselor, waited patiently for her response.

"Oh, I'm sorry, Bernie. I must have been on another planet there for a minute."

"Did that book I ordered on deviant behavior come in?"

"I—I'm not sure. We're a couple of hours ahead of them out there in California. Let me call and see if it's been shipped yet."

"If it's no trouble."

She waved it off as was expected. Everyone knew she had no life to get to after-hours. Making a U-turn, she headed back toward Rare Finds, musing uncharitably if the topic was work related or pleasure reading. She sometimes thought Bernie searched for problems in the quiet town to make himself sound important at the school board meetings.

Slipping the key into the antique lock plate, she gave it a turn and pushed the door open. It took her all of three steps into the dim interior to realize she stood in a vortex of utter chaos.

"What the—"

Her astonished gaze scanned the disaster. Shelves were emptied. Books lay heaped upon the floor, delicate spines broken, pages scattered indifferently in every direction as if a tornado had touched down in the center of aisle four. Stackable cases were knocked over like a wall of children's blocks. Her file cabinet stood with drawers yawning wide, their time-consuming data dumped indiscriminately as if someone had searched through them in a violent rush.

Dazed, she came farther into the store, moving numbly at first, then with quick agitation toward her desk, where each drawer had been similarly violated. Who would do such a thing and for what purpose? The pointless vandalism shocked through her like a personal attack. Immediately she thought of Web Baines and his pals, released on their own recognizance just two days prior.

Though it was a job for the town's sheriff, Bess's instinctive reaction was to call Zach.

She reached for the phone, when a rustle of sound distracted her from behind. Clarity came a second too late as brightness exploded through her brain, dropping her down into darkness.

She couldn't breathe.

Choking, coughing, Bess forced her eyes to open against the battering ache in her head, but she couldn't seem to focus. She blinked, her eyes tearing, squinting up. Smoke. The store was filled with smoke. Thick, lung-clogging smoke already heavy at the ceiling and settling fast in a smothering blanket. Over the roar in her temples, she heard crackling, popping. Her books. Her books were on fire!

Groggily she swayed up to hands and knees, but the effort stole her strength, sucking it from her constricted chest. She couldn't see beyond the discarded desk drawers and the black cord snaking behind them. The phone cord.

Crawling forward, she fumbled for it, dragging the receiver end to her with increasing urgency. Coughs spasmed through her as she lifted the receiver to her ear and began to dial. Then she heard the damning silence on the line. No dial tone. Nothing.

Nothing.

She toppled over, her throat raw, her lungs on fire as they worked frantically for just a brief taste of oxygen.

Nothing.

She was about to become a sacrifice on the pyre of her mother's dreams.

Chapter 13

With Melody starting dinner, Zach walked Faith home along the main streets of Sweetheart. The knowledge that Bess stopped by to bring the girl and his mother lunch worked to mellow his mood, making him look upon his escort as a means of touching base with Bess again.

She'd avoided him. He knew why and didn't blame her as much as he blamed himself for giving her cause. He'd hurt her after promising he wouldn't, and all the noble intentions in the world wouldn't change that. The folk of Sweetheart, starting with her own mother, had taken ruthless advantage of her tender nature all her life, just as he'd been guilty of…at first. He'd grown dependent upon her accepting nature, dumping his problems, his woes onto her fragile yet tensile shoulders while selfishly forgetting to recognize the burden she already carried. Forgetting that she had needs and sorrows, too. And still did.

He'd come back to Sweetheart so focused on his own goals he'd ignored her frail feelings. There was no excuse, none.

And if he didn't make it up to her soon, the chance would escape him forever.

His opportunity to close ground was at hand. Or rather, at his elbow.

"So, Faith, how do you like Sweetheart?"

The teen shrugged. "It's okay. Kinda on the slow side, but that's all right. I like the kids. They think I'm a sophisticated big-city girl." She grinned up at him. "I have to admit I like the 'big fish in a small pond' thing."

He smiled, understanding the teenage hierarchy. "Don't you miss your friends?"

A sigh. "I've got a couple of good ones, but the rest, they're kinda shallow. All they talk about is going to the mall, drinking and sex and—" She broke off suddenly, remembering who he was and what he did. He grinned wider to still her dismay.

"That much hasn't changed since I was your age."

She relaxed on an exhalation. "Anyway, the kids here, they're more, I don't know, real? Does that make sense? I thought they'd be dull rednecks, you know, farm kids, talking about the soy market and tractors and 4-H. Not that there's anything wrong with those things," she quickly qualified.

"I know."

Again the grateful smile. "Anyway, we've had some real conversations, about important stuff, like college and the environment and the future. Things I'd never thought much about. I was too busy trying to decide on which designer label to put on my rump."

Zach chuckled at her self-deprecating humor. A tang of wry wit was something they had in common. "There's nothing wrong with that, either."

"I know. But it makes me feel kinda stupid for spending so much time worrying about the "House of Style" on MTV, instead of the House of Representatives."

"You're getting to be a wise old soul, Faith."

"That's what Mom calls Aunt B. I think she was hoping

some of her sensibility would rub off on me this summer. I hope it has.''

''So, what do you think of your aunt?''

''She's the greatest. Not saying that my mom isn't.''

Zach nodded his agreement.

''Mom would get me stuff like new CDs and makeup for my birthdays. Aunt Bess always sent me Shakespeare and play tickets. Brainy stuff, you know. I got so I'd look forward to it. She always made me feel I was smart, like there was more to me than what was on the outside, you know?''

''Yeah, I do.'' And the sense of kinship grew between them during the next few minutes of reflection.

''I'm worried about her.''

The teen's somber confession took Zach by surprise. Alarm bells went off in the area of his chest. ''Why? What's wrong?''

''I never really met Grandma. She and Mom had a falling out before I was born and they never got over it. Mom used to tell me about her, though. She said she was a rigid, puritanical old bi—'' Faith cleared her throat.

Zach filled in the blank mentally. His own reply chafed with friction. ''I know what she was.''

''Mom always worried about Aunt B, you know, being stuck here taking care of her all those years. Grandma broke her hip in a fall when I was just a baby. Guess it never set quite right and she ended up in a wheelchair. Aunt Bess had to take care of her and run the store.'' She kicked at a pebble on the walk, sending it careening into the gutter, growing moody. Reminding him of Bess.

''Mom tried to help out but Grandma wouldn't let her in the house. We kept inviting Aunt B up to visit but she always turned us down. Couldn't get away, she'd say. Guess that was pretty much true the way Grandma had her snared like a greedy old spider. That's not a very nice way to talk about your grandmother, is it?''

''Considering the source, I'd say you're being very polite.''

''You didn't like her, either, I take it.''

"She and I shared a mutual dislike."

"And something in common?" the girl prompted with an innocent lack of subtlety.

"That, too," Zach admitted.

"So, how come you and Aunt B aren't dating now? Don't you still like her?"

Zach nearly choked on those blunt questions. "It's not a matter of liking her. There are other things to consider."

She pooh-poohed his awkward explanation. "Like what? Your reputation?"

He squirmed a bit at her directness but answered truthfully. "Some people never get over things like that."

"And there are other things people never get over, either."

While he considered that profound "out of the mouth of babes" statement, they rounded the corner near the bookstore and Zach drew up short. Their conversation blanked from his mind.

Smoke was curling up from beneath the door of Rare Finds.

"Faith."

The girl looked up, alarmed and alerted by the professional cut of his tone. "What?"

"Go to the diner and call the fire department."

Faith cried out, noticing the black wisps rising on the warm air. Her breathing quickened into gulps.

"Faith, run."

"Aunt Bess—"

"If she's inside, I'll bring her out. Go on. Hurry."

The teen broke into a wild run across the square.

Zach grabbed the doorknob then jerked his hand back from the searing metal. Worse than he thought. Peering through the front window, all he could see was a thick curtain of gray, highlighted against glaring flames.

It was after-hours. All the neighboring businesses were closed. Bess was at home, he told himself, safe and sound. Even as he tried to convince himself, he pulled out his hand-kerchief and wound it about his hand.

The knob still scalded through the cloth, but Zach was able

to open the door. Clouds of smoke poured out, forcing him
to stumble backward. By then other citizens began to race
over, drawn by the billowing blackness. Zach ignored them,
for just inside the hazy opening, he could make out a single
object on the floor.

Bess's purse.

Undoing the top two buttons of his uniform, he shucked
his shirt up over his head to form a protective barrier to the
smoke, keeping a pocket of fresh air close as he barreled into
the burning building.

"Bess!"

His frantic cry was shoved back down his throat by an acrid
fist of smoke. Coughing hard, he pushed farther into the room,
feeling the heat blistering against the bare skin of his back
and hands as he crouched low and began to search. He stumbled over an obstacle course of unseen perils scattered all over
the floor, feeling his way over each one to find unyielding
wood or lifeless volumes. The longer he fought his way
through the dense smoke, the more frequently his starved
lungs sent harsh spasms racking through him. His vision
blurred as disorientation swirled through his lightening head.

God, don't let me pass out before I find her!

His foot snagged, nearly tripping him, as if he'd caught a
low vine. Reaching down, his fingers encountered fabric and
flesh: a woman's stockinged leg.

Bess.

His mind formed her name when his parched throat could
not. Stooping low, he fumbled in the hazy limbo, finding the
rest of her limp form.

So still!

Refusing to let his thoughts linger upon that terrible revelation, Zach gathered her close against his chest, hunching
over her as he made his way toward what he hoped was the
door. He couldn't tell. The smoke gave away no clues as it
continued to mercilessly gag him.

*Hang on, Bess. Hang on, I'll get you out of here! I'll get
us both out.*

Several precious seconds were lost as he searched for a way around a bookcase blockade. Finally freed, he stumbled, falling hard atop Bess's unresponsive form. He couldn't breathe. A strange disembodiment separated his mind's commands from the ability of his body to obey. He sagged over Bess, shielding her from the intense heat, though he couldn't save her from the effects of the smoke. Her hair pillowed his face, filtering his raspily drawn struggles for air.

Not now. Not yet!

Those pleas formed in his groggy consciousness.

Not until I can explain....

He started crawling forward, an agonizing inch at a time, dragging Bess beneath him, with purpose but no direction. A glow formed before his watery gaze. The fire or freedom...he couldn't tell. He continued toward it, slowed by the burden of Bess's slack form. He never once considered leaving her to save himself. They'd be together, either way, and that was enough to motivate him.

He sucked in pure flame. It tore down his raw throat to flare in his lungs. He heard a faint ringing. It grew louder, becoming a shrieking wail. Light flashed and strobed against the harsh dampness blinding him. He pushed ahead, using the dig and shove of his toes when his arms gave out. Movement grew faint then failed him.

Bess. Thoughts of her followed him into a deeper well of darkness. Just as hands followed to grasp at his elbows, at the back of his shirt, pulling him up. But he no longer had the strength to fight the swallowing sense of peace.

Grass. Dry, sharp spears of it tickling beneath his palms, at the back of his neck. He tried to move his head, but something held him fast like a suffocating hand clamped over his mouth. He rebelled against it, arms flailing ineffectually until a calming voice cut through his confusion.

"Don't fight it. Keep breathing in and out, slowly, slowly."

Zach gasped and strangled on a clog of panic. Then air rushed in, sweet, intoxicating, so pure it hurt. Everything hurt.

He blinked sore eyes open. Lumpy shades of gray against glare came gradually into focus, becoming Fred Meirs and several others bending over him where he lay stretched out on the square. His hand fumbled over the plastic bowl covering his mouth and nose.

"Easy, Zach," Meirs said. "It's oxygen. Breathe it in. Your head should clear in a minute."

Closing his eyes, he obeyed, and finally the restorative gas began to work, alleviating the pressure in his chest and chasing the fog from his mind.

Bess!

He tore the mask away, struggling to sit up. Too weak to defy the restraining hands, he allowed them to guide him back down upon the carpet of green.

"Be—" A harsh paroxysm of coughing choked off the rest of her name.

Fred caught his shoulder, squeezing lightly. "The paramedics are with her."

Zach's awareness waned as consciousness threatened to leave him again. Then he fixed upon one horrible uncertainty.

He'd brought Bess out of the burning building.

But had he brought her out alive?

He had to know.

The townspeople pushing in around the opened back of the county's one ambulance parted to give him room. He never saw any of them. His focus channeled down to the sheet-draped figure on the gurney, on the grimy face mostly covered by the bubble of the oxygen mask, on the hand resting in a delicate curl between the rounding of her breasts. That focus didn't waver until he saw that slender hand slowly rise and gradually fall again.

His own breath released in a hoarse shiver of sound.

Thank God.

Faith huddled behind the two paramedics who were measuring blood pressure and pulse rate. Her huge, frightened eyes lifted to find his. Without hesitation, she flung her arms about him, hugging to the dirt and smoke and sweat in grateful disregard as she wept, "You saved her. You kept your promise and saved her."

He hugged her back, surrounding her trembling figure with comforting warmth.

"How is she?" His question grated out in a whisper, each syllable hell to force through scorched vocal chords.

Faith leaned back, wiping her damp and now-sooty cheek with her hand. It shook but her voice was steady. "She breathed in a lot of smoke but she must have fallen and hit her head, 'cause that's what knocked her out. They told me she couldn't have lasted much longer." Her eyes teared up again as she turned back to her aunt.

Zach cupped the back of her head with his hand, murmuring, "You did good, kid. Got them here just in time."

Her gaze flew back up to his. "It wouldn't have mattered, if you hadn't gone in there after her."

Zach followed her stare across the street where firemen worked frantically to keep the fire confined. The front window was smashed out and smoke roiled onto the sidewalk, enveloping all who stood too near. Lloyd Baines and his deputy pushed back the curious to keep them from getting in the way of the tangle of fat hoses snaking across the puddled pavement. Even contained, there was no mistaking the killing fury of the blaze roaring within the store, consuming everything in its path.

As it would have consumed Bess.

A cold chill of consequence shuddered through him as Zach wrapped his arm about the teen, sharing her horrifying glimpse at another possible ending.

The paramedics began packing up their equipment as Fred Meirs took over the examination. Worry ebbed from his lined features as he reevaluated their findings and pronounced them sound. Bess Carrey would be fine.

Sheriff Baines pushed his way in, when Bess's lashes fluttered and she moaned her way back to consciousness. Her bleary stare jumped past him to search the crowd, seeking one face among the blur of those gathered around her.

"Zach?"

He heard her faltery call and bumped Baines out of the way to crouch down beside the gurney. He took her hand up carefully.

"Right here, Bess."

Her lips moved soundlessly for several seconds, making Zach lean in closer to hear the frail words. Then he straightened, his face drawn in taut, immobile lines as they loaded Bess into the ambulance.

Zach watched it edge through the crowd, light strobing but siren silent as it carried her to the clinic for more conclusive tests.

"What did she tell you, Crandall?"

Zach glanced at Baines's impatient features. "Nothing. Just to see Faith got taken care of."

Baines believed him. He shoved his way back over to the smoky scene to assume an authoritative pose, ushering the bystanders away. "Nothing to see. Go on home, folks."

Zach saw nothing but Bess's grimy face. Heard nothing but the words breathed hoarsely against his ear.

"Someone was in the store," Bess had whispered.

Zach recalled the rest with heart banging.

"Someone hit me and left me to die."

Chapter 14

Sunlight streamed across the bedcovers, making Bess blink against the brightness as she slowly awoke the next day. She recognized her own room, preferring it to the sterile hospital surroundings of the night before. A vivid splash of fresh-cut flowers stood behind her digital clock, distracting her from numbers that read 5:43. Puzzled, she squinted, focusing more clearly to see the p.m. dot illuminated—5:43. She'd slept almost all day. No wonder her senses were so groggy and her throat so dry. The moment she dragged her tongue over chapped lips, a deep masculine voice intruded.

"Here. This ought to help."

Too tired to be startled by the fact that Zach Crandall sat at her bedside, she reached for the thermal cup he held and directed the bendy straw to her mouth. Cool water seeped down her throat, cutting through the soreness in a delicious slide. The reason for her lethargy and the charred taste in her mouth floated at the edge of her awareness. She chose not to bring it close enough for recognition. She'd deal with it later. Right now, Zach was here. She was safe in her foggy world.

With a sigh, she settled back against the pillows and gathered the strength for speech.

"Where's Faith?" Her words came out, sounding like the pull of a rusty saw through dry wood.

"Downstairs fixing some supper. She had a friend's birthday sleepover scheduled for tonight, but she wouldn't leave until she knew you were all right. I told her I'd stay with you. If that's okay with you."

The effort of thought was almost as great as the effort for speech, so she just nodded, her eyes closing wearily of their own volition. Content with the idea of Zach watching over her, she drifted again, letting sleep overcome her.

Zach waited a few minutes to see if she'd come around, soothed by the gentle movement of her breathing. The hoarse rattle in her chest that had frightened him in the hospital had eased to a quiet rhythm so he wasn't worried about leaving her alone for a moment.

Faith looked up from the pot of stew she was stirring at the stove. The concern furrowing her brow relaxed upon seeing his expression. "Is she awake?"

"Just for a second. The stuff they gave her will probably keep her out of it most of the night. Smells good."

"It needs to simmer another half hour." She clanked the spoon on the metal edge of the Dutch oven, then restored the lid. "There's more than enough if you want to stay for some."

"Don't mind if I do."

Faith checked her watch. "I'd better call Kathy and tell her I can't come over."

"She's fine, Faith. Your being here, fussing and worrying won't change anything. I doubt that she'll be up for company before morning."

"I don't know——"

"I thought you had a Brad Pitt droolfest planned for tonight."

Faith wavered. "Nothing I haven't seen a million times."

"One more won't do any permanent damage." Zach

smiled, solving her dilemma for her. "Go. Have fun. Leave me a number, and I promise I'll call if she needs you. You know I keep my promises." His conscience winced. Except the ones he made to Bess.

"Oh, all right. You promise?" At his nod, her animation returned. "Kathy has a triple bill planned. I'm bringing the popcorn and bibs to catch the drool. Her number is right there next to Doc Meirs's and the hospital." She paused, frowning, as responsibility chafed at her. "I don't know. Maybe I'd better not. I feel kinda funny running off when Aunt B's—"

"She's fine. She'll be fine. All she needs is rest. Not a teenager pacing next to the bed."

Just a handsome guy sitting next to it. Faith knew whom she'd rather wake up to. "Sure you don't mind?"

"No," he told her softly. "I don't mind at all."

After weighing her worry for her aunt against the possibilities of Bess and Zach alone in the house together, she gave him a look that was intuitively adult then smiled back. "What about your reputation?"

"I'll say I had to stay to get a statement."

"Think they'll buy that?"

"Do you?"

She shrugged. "Does it matter?"

"Maybe it will to Bess."

"Naw. I think Sleeping Beauty would rather wake up to your face than mine. Don't forget to take the stew off the burner."

When he made that promise, she darted for the stairs and the bag she hadn't unpacked, then hurried back, pausing only long enough to stretch up onto her toes to press a kiss to his rough cheek.

"Thanks, Zach." And she was gone.

He touched the damp spot, fingertips lingering there for a long minute. Kids. Not a bad invention when they turned out as good as this one. Something he hadn't thought about before. Kids. Family. His experiences weren't anything that would convince him to plunge right in. But obviously things could work out the right way, if Faith was any indication.

He wondered what kind of father she'd had.

And that led to the uncomfortable curiosity over what kind he'd be. What kind of parents he and Bess might have been together if fate and their families hadn't stood in the way.

Thirty-five wasn't too old to be thinking along those lines. Unwittingly he started the sweep hand on his biological clock ticking.

For the first hour, Zach purposefully kept away from the upstairs room where Bess lay sleeping. He called Melody to check on things there, watched the news, ate two bowls of surprisingly savory stew, then stored the rest and cleaned up the kitchen. He paced. The house made him uncomfortable with its heavy furniture and drab antique decor. He felt Joan Carrey's fierce disapproving eyes upon him as he prowled from room to room, examining everything, touching nothing. This was where Bess grew up, where she continued to live. It was every bit as oppressive as the bookstore; both prisons created by her domineering mother to suck all hope for joy out of her life.

Her mother's fall and subsequent helplessness explained why Bess hadn't left Sweetheart. He thought of her at the old lady's smothering beck and call and wished—

What good did it do to wish things had been different? The only changes he could make were here and now. If it wasn't already too late.

Too restless in the gloomy downstairs rooms, Zach climbed the stairs and walked toward the back bedroom. Double windows were open to invite the warm night air in. Light from a small desk lamp cast a tiny pool of illumination beneath it and left the rest of the room in deepening degrees of shadow. Where Bess lay, her hair shone like pale fine-spun gold. Her lashes feathered along her cheeks, appearing thicker, longer in the slant of light. An angel in repose. Her slender hand tucked beneath her jaw, its ring finger meaningfully bare of anyone's claim. He doubted that any man had ever been

privy to such a glorious sight, and to be the first, and hopefully only, to draw it in, to revel in it, filled him with a possessive panic.

He might have lost her. To the fire. To his lies. That notion
savaged him.

He tried sitting at her bedside in the thinly stuffed chair,
but the rigid position brought an ache to his back where the
skin was scorched and still sensitive. Though fatigue pulled
at his eyelids, he was reluctant to retire to the couch downstairs. What if she woke? What if she needed something?

Finally he did the only sensible thing. He stretched out on
his side beside her, his long form atop the covers, her tempting one safely beneath them. Resting his head on his out-
flung arm, he studied her profile while his thoughts slowed
and gradually sank into slumber.

Bess jerked awake with a gasp, her hand going to her
throat. Her frantic gaze flashed about, grasping at familiar
surfaces to contain her hysteria. Beneath the sheet, her cotton
gown clung damply, absorbing a sheen of cold sweat and icy
chills. A dream. A terrible dream, one of fire and fear, one
where a smoky hand seemed to clutch about her neck, stran-
gling the air out of her. One of unseen threat and seeping
death.

Just a dream.

To drive the horrible reality of it away, she drew a deep
breath. Air scraped rawly down the abused passage to her
lungs, a match head igniting flame in its wake.

Oh, God.

It wasn't a dream.

The smoke…the store…the bludgeoning explosion in her
head…all of it happened!

She tried to sit up. Her outcry clawed up painfully into a
raspy moan as she struggled against the tangle of covers and
an immobilizing weight lying across her middle. A desperate
fear of being trapped, of being burned, of being helpless

flooded her sensibilities until a low reassurance sounded beside her.

"Shhh, Bess. It's all right. It's over. You're safe now."

"Zach?"

Wild eyes darted to the left, to where he lay close. His arm draped over her waist, creating the weight that at first panicked, then comforted her as she rolled toward him. It made a firm bolster along her back, holding her tight against him. Her arms banded his shoulders, her face burrowing into the open collar of his shirt.

"You're fine, Bess. Everything's going to be fine."

His crooning claim couldn't blot out the image of the billowing clouds, darkening all around her as they slowly devoured her air just as the flames devoured—

"The store…?"

"I'm sorry. The fire's out, but I don't know what the damage is." His words, spoken gruffly into her hair did little to quiet her anxiousness. She hung on to him like a life ring, her slender body beginning to quake along his hard lines.

"Someone was inside," she told him, her voice all scratchy and weakened by hoarse gasps of shock. "The place was all torn up. I tried to call—to call you but the ph-phone wouldn't work. And I heard someone behind me."

The calming rock of his breathing became a heaving storm, mirroring the surging terror.

"And?" came his lethally soft prompt.

"And somebody hit me. Knocked me down. And then the smoke, the fire. I couldn't move." Tremors raced along their entwined limbs, hers pressing against his, his becoming shock absorbers. "Oh, Zach, I thought I was going to die."

His eyes squeezed shut, shoving away the swelling panic that came with the remembered sight of her pale, pale face and that small, still hand. "I wouldn't let that happen. You know I wouldn't. Nothing's going to happen to you, Bess. I swear it."

She continued to weep in fractured snatches, her hands

kneading the hair at his nape and the collar of his shirt. Her fear was a fist to his gut.

"Who? Why?"

He shook his head, taking the opportunity to caress the tousle of baby-fine gold with his lips. "I don't know, baby, but I'll find out. I'll find out and there'll be hell to pay. Hell to pay."

The harsh strength in his tone was like a swallow of straight scotch. Searing, then warming, quieting her chills, calming her frazzled concentration.

Giving her a chance to concentrate on other things.

Like him in her bed beside her.

Her fingers went from a frenzied clutching to a restless combing. She pressed closer to feel the hardness of his buttons, his buckle, of his awareness lengthening behind his zipper as he realized the changing direction of her thoughts.

"I'd better—"

"Stay," she finished for him. "Stay with me."

Aw, hell. She couldn't have asked for anything easy…like donating both his kidneys.

"I will, baby. I'll stay. But you have to promise you'll rest. You need—"

"I need you."

"You need your sleep."

She allowed him to push her over onto her back, but the sight of her features, all tear washed and beseeching purged his nobility. Still, he hung on by his fingernails, resisting for the both of them.

"Bess—"

"Zach."

Her fingertips trailed along the rough terrain of one unshaven cheek, creating a sandpapery sound and a flurry of urgent agitation.

"Bess—"

Her fingers hooked behind his ear as her thumb rode the broad ridge of his cheekbone. Intuition shouted for him to get

the hell out while he could, but his treacherous body had
already begun to surrender.

What if he'd lost her?

His lips parted. His eyes drifted shut.

They kissed, a butterfly-light whisper, touching, lifting
away, settling again for slightly longer, then flitting away
again. There was nothing delicate about the way his heart
slammed against his ribs. He stroked her face with his fingers,
filling his palm with her obstinate jaw. And he stared down
at her, his gaze an overcast sky, slated, mysterious, seething
with unchecked danger.

"Bess, this isn't the time."

"Where's Faith?" Her touch skimmed down his neck to
dip into the hollow of his collarbone. Testing the savage thun-
der there.

"She's spending the night with Kathy."

"We're alone."

It wasn't a question, but she answered it anyway.

"Good."

Her succinct reply stripped her intentions bare of subtlety.
She wanted him. Here, now. In her mother's house. In her
spinster's bed. There was no hesitation in that single word.
None at all in her direct-to-the-soul stare. His restraint de-
veloped a hairline crack against the building pressure. When
her lips grazed his, he sandbagged with logic to stand firm.
Then she undercut his barricade, dipping down, swirling her
tongue over hot skin above his top shirt button. He fractured
like the San Andreas.

Hauling her up to him in a twist of sheets, Zach crushed
her mouth with rough possession. She tasted of smoke and
sweetness. He took her down to the mattress, pushing her into
it as he leveled himself atop her gentle curves. His hands
fisted in her hair on either side of her head as his kiss grew
fierce, devouring and openmouthed. He kissed her to the edge
of reason, letting her dangle there in teetering peril when he
lifted away. His glare was hot, naked except for hunger, challenging her to stop him before it was too late.

Too late.

Her fingertips touched his parted lips, feeling the almost-angry thrust of his breath pulsing against them. She sensed the danger involved in provoking such a man, the consequences that once frightened her into second thoughts. The point of no return, once reached, once breached that could mean only commitment. She didn't back away.

"Make it a dream that never ends, Zach."

He caved in upon that quiet request.

"I'll do my best."

His lips hovered over hers, sharing her breath, her shivery expectation, pausing not with caution, but with care, until sinking down to let her taste paradise in the soft, slanting union. She opened for him, welcoming the next level of intimacy as their tongues touched and stroked and teased to the very last ounce of breath.

He lifted up slightly, his husky words blowing seducingly warm against the moisture on her mouth.

"I want to see you, Bess. All of you. And I want you to see me. I want you to know what you're getting, the whole package. If you're ready."

Ready and so willing she hurt.

But as he turned down the sheet and gathered the hem of her gown in one hand to lift it upward, exposing her to the night breeze and his caressing study, eagerness was no match for inexperience. They'd never been naked together. No one had ever seen her without clothing and somehow, right now, that was more intimidating than the explicit secrets they'd already shared.

As the material bunched beneath her breasts, she tucked her knees up tight, and the clench of her hand over his halted her unveiling. Anxious and embarrassed, she didn't expect him to anticipate her modest reaction. But he did.

He returned to the mind-drugging kisses, smoothing her nightgown down to her waist, soothing her fears as he simply held her until her tension eased. She gave herself over to the manipulations of his mouth, sighing into his lapping kisses, moaning as he sucked on an earlobe, licked across the tender flutter of her eyelids and nipped down her neck, distracted from what his hands were doing. They rubbed and kneaded her shoulders, her arms, her rib cage until her legs relaxed and unbent to shift restlessly against his.

His palm rested upon one bare hip, circling in easy revolutions that widened when she didn't resist. He cupped her bottom briefly, moving on when she stiffened, stroking down her thigh and up again, letting her get used to the rough burr of his palm the way he'd gentle a wild horse to the feel of a saddle blanket.

And all the while, he whispered husky encouragements against her mouth, into her hurried breaths, telling her how good she tasted, how good she felt, how beautiful she was, until she quivered with feverish longing, having hungered for those words since their very first kiss. So consumed she didn't think to shut out the glide of his hand up her inner thigh.

That first contact sent a shock of sensation sizzling through her. Her breath caught and held in an agony of suspense as he rubbed her with his palm then began a probing exploration with his fingers. A moralistic alarm tightened the muscles in her thighs but she didn't pull away.

"Trust me, Bess," he murmured alongside her ear as he slipped his fingers inside her. She tensed and sucked a startled breath making him aware that though she wasn't a virgin, in some ways she was still so innocent. He lifted his head, commanding her gaze with the quiet intensity of his own. Her eyes were huge, dark-centered, scared, yet bright with wanting. Rich with trust.

"You wanted to know what it's like being free." He kissed her once softly before adding, "Let me show you how to fly."

Bess closed her eyes and let herself go. She let him coax her with the seductive rhythm of his touch, a rhythm her body already understood, for soon it was moving to the tempo, rocking to an insistent beat not unlike that of her heart. The cadence deepened, drawing untried and unexpected responses, a vibrant thrumming pulled up from a primal source that was woman. Encouraging seismic tremors gathered with cataclysmic force along her legs, through her belly, until they were taut and trembling. Until her breathing began to shudder. Confused, alarmed and gasping, she tried to squirm away and contrarily arched up against his hand as the movement quickened, demanding some answer from her.

"Let go, Bess," he urged, breathing hard and fast.

And she did, peaking in shattering waves of glory, as Zach praised, "Oh, yeah, baby, that's it," until the last fiery spasm rode through her. She stared up at him, her eyes dazed and unfocused, her slender form shivery in the aftermath. He scooped back her hair to kiss her brow, her temple, her cheek before settling for a long, lush sampling of her lips. Her palms pressed to the sides of his face, holding him there until they were forced to part for air. He watched her expression for clues, anxious despite all the evidence.

"Wow," she whispered in awe.

Zach's arrogant grin split wide and white in the semidarkness. "You're damn right, wow!"

She drew a quick breath and smiled shyly. "I had no idea."

"That's because you don't read the right kind of books." His grin muted, becoming a look of unguarded emotion, too complex, too fiercely intense for easy deciphering. His voice rumbled. "And now that you know?"

"I want to know everything."

She sat up slightly, her gaze never leaving his as she pulled her gown off over her head and tossed it aside. She sank back into the covers, her arms opening then curling about him as they kissed again. Her tongue touched his in silky persuasion. A low sound growled through him as he cinched her up tight, his mouth grinding down on hers, pushing the limits of his control. His hands fit over her breasts, the heated contact making her pulse leap then pound faster.

His lips tore from hers, lowering to capture a turgid nipple. He was less than gentle. Her fingers sieved through his hair, tightening, twisting, as pleasure intensified to the brink of torment. He turned his head, his tongue rasping a wet trail up to the other peak as her spine bowed, lifting it for his tender savagery. Her hands pushed over his shoulders and down his back, over muscles so taut they trembled with the effort of control. She tugged his shirttail loose and skimmed her palms beneath it, reveling in the hot, hard feel of him.

"Zach," she said breathlessly, "I want to see you."

He sat up, shucking off his shirt in a single move, his pale eyes glittering like blue flame. As he reached for his belt, Bess's hands were already there, tugging, unbuckling, unsnapping, unzipping, slipping in next to skin, diving deep as if for treasure. Not coming up empty-handed. His breath purged in a harsh rattle, control close to threadbare. Maybe she'd read some of the right kind of books after all.

"Bess, let me do that."

He wiggled off the edge of the bed, away from the gliding touch that had him close to a nuclear disaster. He skimmed out of his jeans, briefs and socks with remarkable speed, drawing Bess's attention from his heavily furred chest to the rocketing eagerness of his sex. The longer she stared, saying nothing, the more uncomfortable he became, not sure of her reaction to her first confrontation with male nudity.

She exhaled slowly through her teeth then rose up to her knees. He didn't move, letting her come to him. Her hands rested on the jut of his hipbones as she leaned ever so slowly into him. Her face nestled into the dark hair covering his breastbone as she melted along him, her pebbled nipples poking his ribs, his hardness pressing into her soft belly, their bodies conforming to a sinfully perfect fit.

His senses were knife sharp, honed to an atom-splitting edge from waiting half his life for this moment, for these exact sensations that were suddenly so much more than he'd ever dared expect.

Show me everything. He meant to, in exquisite detail. At least, that was the plan until her hot little mouth scorched his skin, trickling kisses across his chest. He could have stood even that with a degree of self-control.

But then her tongue curled about the nub of his nipple where it was half-hidden in whorls of black hair and his willpower snapped under the pressure.

The mattress gave under their combined weight. Bess's legs lassoed about him before they finished the first hard bounce. By the second, he was embedded deep inside her, trying not to burst at the feel of her, hot and snug about him. He took her mouth in a series of hard, ragged kisses, his big hands anchoring her hips to greet his explosive thrusts. He wouldn't have believed anything could slow his race toward fulfillment until her fingers dug into one of the raw patches on his back, and the shock of pain jolted through him.

Bess felt his recoil, so sharp and sudden it broke the frantic pace of their passion. He took a moment to blink rapidly, wrestling the hurt back under his control, and would have continued if she hadn't twisted half out from under him. The sight of the blistering burns on his lower back could mean only one thing.

He was blowing hard into the squashed pillow, trying to get his momentum slowed down when he heard her fragile cry. Lifting up onto his elbows so he could see her face was a mistake. Her eyes were round and luminous. Her cheeks shimmered with quicksilver tears.

"Bess?"

She touched his face, her fingertips trembling. "You went in after me."

He didn't want to make a big thing out of it, not as big a thing as she obviously was. He shrugged. "Faith went to call the fire department so I—"

"Risked your life to save me."

He couldn't argue with her conclusion, nor would she let him make light of it as she drew him down for a kiss sweet enough to make angels weep. He could taste her tears and traces of smoke. And suddenly the urgency was gone, replaced by a need to show this woman just how precious she was—worth waiting for, worth dying for.

She moved beneath him, her arms wreathed about his neck,

her damp face buried there as her hips lifted to meet each deep downward stroke. He took his time, quickening the tempo only after he heard her breathing alter into shallow gasps, thinking of himself only after he felt the wild spasms shake up through her legs and grip about him like a tight fist. He went off like a lunar launch.

When he was able, he whispered a shaky, "Wow," and felt her smile.

She kissed his cheek and answered, "You're damn right, wow."

Chapter 15

Bess woke to an exquisite dream, one she'd had since she'd realized that humankind was made to move in pairs.

She wasn't alone in bed.

She'd expected that the uniqueness of having a big male animal intruding upon her space would keep her up all night, alert to every movement, reveling in every resonating breath from the man beside her. To her disappointment, she'd slept hard and deep, oblivious to her special companion.

She half expected him to be gone when she opened her eyes. An illusion, a trick of a lonely mind. Or just gone to avoid complications. But he was still there, making her feel guilty for even considering him cowardly enough to sneak out before they could say their first good morning.

She didn't look at the clock. There was no reason to. She had nothing pending, no work, no job half as important as lingering here, watching her lover sleep.

Lover. A term both exciting and shameful, implying forbidden pleasures best shared in the dark. What would they call what they shared, now that morning brought it to light?

She smiled to herself. Boyfriend sounded so old-fashioned, the scope too regimented to contain the intimate elements they'd enjoyed. A fling, a passing fancy, an affair? Her features took a downward turn. That's not how she wanted to file last night away among her other dusty memories.

Outside her window she could hear the sounds of Sweetheart coming to life. The click of Timmy Bartlett's bicycle as he delivered the morning edition, the barking frenzy of the Pattersons' dog as neighbor, Jerry Posten walked out to his car to go to work. Regular, daily sounds simple in their routine sameness. Outside life went on as usual while in her upstairs room, within her prudish bed, Elizabeth Carrey was lying naked with a man after a long night of impassioned lovemaking. Not just any man, but the town's unreceived outcast.

What would they say if they knew? Would the smoothly timed gears of Sweetheart grind to a halt because she'd had the audacity to slip from her cog?

Blocks away in the town square, the courthouse clock chimed seven.

Zach stirred with a husky mutter.

And Bess went stone still in panic.

She had a naked man in her bed. Not just any man: Zach Crandall, the object of her dreams, her fantasies, her demons. She'd given him her heart and her body when they were teens. Last night she'd added her trust and soul to that package.

What in heaven's name was she supposed to say to him?

Starkly aware of her nudity, she tucked the covers in around her, cocooning her from even the most accidental touch of his big, bare frame.

How was she supposed to act with the man who knew her body better than she did herself? Who'd spent patient hours teaching it to respond with total abandon to his most subtle caress? Would she greet him with weepy-eyed gratitude or sultry confidence? With a kiss or hot coffee?

She wondered wildly where she could find one of those books he'd talked about. Why hadn't she hidden her forbidden copy of *Lady Chatterly's Lover* better, giving her a chance to get to the "good parts" before her mother had discovered it while changing the sheets, and burned it in the fireplace?

Before she could decide on an expression of sweetness or sophistication, Zach turned his head toward her, his laser-bright eyes catching her look of flustered despair. He said nothing for a long minute, giving her a chance to swallow hard and offer up a tentative smile.

"Hi. I was just wondering what you might like for breakfast."

A flicker of desire, dark and volatile, flashed through his eyes, followed quickly by a cooler caution, making her curse the casual way she'd left her statement open for interpretation. The last thing she wanted was for him to feel obligated…for anything. But before she could clarify that, and in doing so make things much worse, he answered.

"I don't have the time. I've got to get home and change before work."

"Oh."

Of course he would. What had she expected? Him to take the day off as a personal holiday?

His expression softened slightly in response to whatever misery artlessly displayed itself in hers. "How 'bout I make coffee while you grab a shower?"

"Okay." *Geez, think you could sound a little more wimpy there, Bess?* she chided herself. She was about to speak up for herself with a more respectable degree of control, when Zach chose that moment to swing out of bed and reach for his jeans. He didn't seem fazed by his nudity, but it hit Bess like a Mack truck.

She forgot to breathe.

Gorgeous. He was gorgeous. Tall, broad through the back and shoulders tapering down to hard flanks and sturdy thighs, every firm, muscled inch molded with raw power. Sunlight detailed each unyielding contour in molten bronze. He tugged up his pants and fastened them in front, the movement creating an image of rippling poetry upon her stunned senses.

Then she saw the splotchy burns upon bare skin, and reality knocked the legs out from under her daydream.

He turned, pausing at the oddness of her expression to ask, "Are you all right, Bess?"

"Fine. I'm fine. The coffee's in the cupboard on the left of the sink."

And those were the first words she exchanged with her lover, discussing coffee and being late for work.

Not the dream she'd imagined.

But when she came downstairs, fresh from a vigorous shower, the sight of him moving easily about her kitchen started all sorts of crazy ideas.

Like how great it would be to see him there every morning for the rest of her life.

Zach leaned back against the counter, coffee warming his hands but not his expression. He'd put on his shirt and shoes. A second cup sat a world away from him on the table. She paused to test the relationship waters. Then he spoke.

"Feel up to some questions?"

She understood without meeting his impassive gaze. This morning it was business, not pleasure, between them.

"Sure. I'll tell you what I can."

She sat down, noticing he put her at an angle to him, not facing him. She stirred a packet of sweetener into her coffee and waited for him to begin. And when he asked, she told him everything she could remember, keeping her voice low and level even as her internal terrors ran rampant.

"So, you've no idea who it was or what they were looking for?"

She shook her head. "None." Then she looked up at him. "Except I think it has something to do with your father's murder."

Surprise blinked through his eyes. Then he was all tough demands. "Why? What makes you think that?"

She relayed her talk with Doc Meirs and with his sister while he listened expressionlessly. Until her conclusion.

"That car running us off the road was no accident, was it? And neither was what happened to Melody's flowers."

Again, his guard faltered.

"Zach, whoever killed your father is getting nervous. We must be getting close."

"We?" He had her by the shoulders before she could register his movement. "There is no 'we,' Bess. You understand? I don't want you involved—"

She slapped aside his hands, annoyed, alarmed by his brusque manner. "Too late for that, don't you think? Obviously someone thought I was involved enough to tear up my store and clobber me."

Leaving her to die. His stark expression finished it for her. Realization stunned her. He was scared out of his mind. That's why he'd pushed her away. That's why he would do the same now—if she let him. Because the thought of separation was scarier than the threat of danger, she made her voice all gentle practicality.

"We have to figure this out before Mel or your mom or Faith gets hurt."

He didn't move, but the calm center behind his eyes blew apart as if she'd applied a twelve-gauge. He started pacing, strides dangerously compact.

"What happened at your store was vandalism. That's what you'll say, and that's what will go in my report. You don't remember getting hit on the head. It must have happened when you fell."

"Zach—"

He put up his forefinger to silence her. "I can't do my job if I'm worrying about you. Now I figure—"

"I figure whoever did it will show himself faster if he thinks I know something."

"No."

"What do you mean, no? I may not read the right kind of

books but I do watch TV. I'll be the bait to draw him out and you—''

''—will wring your neck if you even mention something that crazy again. Dammit, Bess, you sell old books, you're not Miss Marple. If we've got someone's attention, I want him coming after me. I know what I'm doing, and I'm good at it. It's about the only thing I've ever been good at.'' He paused, sucking a harsh breath to smooth the edge of emotion from his words. ''Let me do my job.''

''All right.''

He squinted at her, suspicious of her sudden capitulation. ''Bess, I mean it. This is my—''

''Your what, Zach?'' She surged out of her chair, driven by ungoverned fear. Fear of being isolated from him, of losing him. Faced with her unexpected fury, Zach took a guarded step back. ''Do you see this as your big chance to prove to all the narrow minds in this town that you're not the bad guy? By taking stupid risks, by painting a bull's-eye on your back, by running into burning buildings?''

There was no change in his set expression.

''What does it matter what they think if you're dead!''

''You don't understand, Bess. How could you? No one in this town hid purses when they saw *you* coming. No one pinned everything from firecrackers to B and E on you whether you had an alibi or not. No one refused to talk to your sister at a dance because of who she was related to. No one wrote you off without giving you a chance to prove—''

''What? What do you have to prove to them? You're not that same angry kid anymore, Zach.''

''Yes, I am! To them, I am. They're never going to see me as anything else until I make them open their eyes. I didn't come back here to rub their noses in my success. I came back—aw, hell, never mind.''

She caught his hand as he tried to wave his reasons away. ''Why, Zach? Why did you come back?''

The truth glittered naked and vulnerable in his eyes. ''Because this is my home. It's where I was born. It's where I want to grow old. And I can't, Bess, unless they let me. If they can't accept that I've changed, I can't stay."

Fresh fear catapulted through her. "But—"

"I can't keep fighting, Bess. I'm tired. This is my last stand. Next time I leave, I won't look back. Not ever."

She nodded, accepting his words as fact, because he gave her no choice. She'd never confused his need to belong with his outward indifference. He wanted it as deeply and desperately as she always had. In that, they were alike.

"I don't want you to go, Zach," she told him quietly. "You do whatever you have to. I won't get in your way."

His embrace was sudden and fierce, bonding her to him by sheer force of strength and will. "Liar," he whispered gruffly against her ear. "Last night was incredible. How am I going to think about anything else but you all day?" He kissed her temple in a hard, nearly bruising demonstration before stepping back. "I gotta go."

"Zach...be careful."

His hand was on the doorknob. He glanced down at it then out the back door. "I won't let anyone see me leave." His reassurance held a deceptive calm.

"No, I meant be careful poking around. I don't want you to get hurt."

He crooked a smile at her. "I'm always careful. I don't trust anyone in this town." The intense blue of his eyes muted for the briefest instant as he said, "Except you."

Bess sat in the kitchen for a long time after he'd gone, thinking about that. Those two words that ground her heart down to dust and scattered it on the wind.

Except you.

Oh, what a sentimental fool he was for believing that.

And how was she going to keep him believing it?

He was running a half hour late. There was the quick dash home, through the shower, into his uniform. Endless questions from both mother and sister about Bess...and lots of not-so-subtle inferences that had him grinning in spite of himself. He was striding along the main street when the Drabney sisters emerged from the diner. Instead of sinking back to give him a wide berth, they held their ground in some consternation.

"How is Elizabeth doing?" The elder asked.

"She's doing fine, Miss Lorraine." He paused, smiling at the two old biddies. And surprisingly they smiled back, hesitant gestures that rocked him right down to his socks. "I'm sure she'd appreciate a call if you have time."

"Gracious, yes. Of course, we do. Poor little thing."

"Such a trauma," Myrt added with her own clucking.

Zach started to edge around the formidable pair. "Well, if you ladies will excuse me—"

"Mr. Crandall...Zachary?"

Mryt's hesitant overture stopped his rush. "Ma'am?"

"I understand you received some minor burns while rescuing our Miss Carrey."

"Nothing serious."

She shook a finger at him, ever the scolding schoolteacher. "Burns are not something to take lightly, young man. You go see Johnnie Bishop over at the pharmacy and tell him he's to make you up some of my special ointment. It'll heal you up faster than—" She gave him a nervous glance, her words petering out. That's when her sister stepped in for her own strident two cents worth.

"That was a brave thing you did, Mr. Crandall."

Zach shrugged, feeling itchy beneath the unexpected praise. "Not really, ma'am. A stupid risk, is what Bess called it."

Both ladies smiled in genuine humor, nodding, saying, "Sounds like Bess. Such a sensible girl."

Standing out on the middle of the sidewalk sharing a personable conversation with the two old harpies knocked Zach's focus askew. He walked the rest of the way to the state post in a humbled daze that had him stepping off a curb right in front of the bumper of Bernie Sacks's station wagon. Brakes screeched, but instead of a blast from the horn, the school counselor hollered out his window, "How's Bess doing?"

At Zach's generic response, the man smiled and said, "Good work going in after her that way. Things like that do a uniform proud."

Then he drove off leaving Zach feeling all strange and even more off balance. On the rest of his walk, several more of Sweetheart's citizens stopped to ask after Bess and to compliment him on his courage. By the time he was safely inside the post, he was light-headed from the outpouring of good-will.

It took the sight of Lloyd Baines in his office to supply a cold dash of reality.

"Got your report ready, boy?"

The paunchy sheriff was seated behind his desk, drinking coffee out of his favorite cup. His heavy-soled boots rested in the middle of yesterday's now-crumpled paperwork.

"I will as soon as you get your—self out of my chair."

Baines took his time hauling himself up and waving Zach into the chair with mocking deference. Zach bumped past him to plop down, smoothing out the pages on his work space, each suspiciously left out of sequence by prying eyes.

"So, what did you get out of Joannie's girl?"

The sneer of innuendo was crude and unmistakable. Zach chose to let it slide. For the moment. He looked up at the sheriff, drilling him with a cold glare.

"Not much. Said she intruded on some vandals trashing the store. Figures she must have tripped over some of the books and hit her head, 'cause the next thing she remembers is the hospital."

"She didn't see anyone?"

"No."

"Any ideas on who it might be?"

"She doesn't have any." Before the ruddy features relaxed, Zach drawled, "But I might have some."

Baines stiffened, smirk frozen on his face. "And what might they be?"

"They might be my business for now, until I have proof

of something less friendly than kids playing with fire that got out of hand.''

"Bess?"

"Thinks it's a careless prank that went bad. And I'd prefer she keep thinking that. No sense getting her worried over what's probably nothing."

"Damn right, nothing," Baines growled. "Don't go making no federal case here, boy. It was an accident, plain and simple. There ain't a soul in this county who'd want to see Bess Carrey hurt."

Zach stared at him, saying nothing. He knew better.

Bess knew she wasn't supposed to exert herself, but after Doc Meirs listened to her lungs and pronounced them clear, there was no way she was going back to the house to sit listening to the clock tick while Zach was out provoking trouble.

With Faith along to watchdog her, Bess pushed open the warped front door to Rare Finds. She turned away as the stench of smoke filtered out, then stepped inside determinedly.

It was a disaster.

The fire marshal had pronounced the building structurally sound, but the interior was a charred mass of ashes and soggy pulp from what used to be her stock. Even her records were gone, speaking of long days ahead painstakingly re-creating her inventory by memory for insurance purposes.

"There's nothing left," Faith murmured in hollow shock. Seeing the scope of damage impressed its magnitude of consequence upon her. The knowledge that her aunt could have been as crisped as the rest of the interior shivered through her in upsetting shudders. She turned her thoughts to something else. "What are you going to do, Aunt B?"

Bess nudged one of the volumes with her toe. The structure disintegrated leaving several inches of scorched spine. She scanned the smoke-stained walls, the gutted shelves leaning like skeletal remains against each other. And the books, decades, centuries of collecting literally up in smoke. Her family legacy. Her mother's dream.

Her nightmare.

She was free.

And as quickly as that unbidden thought shot through her, her mind crushed it in proper horror. This was her work, her life. Ruined. How was she going to pay her bills? What was she going to do? How could she let tradition crumple and get swept away like discarded ash?

"Rebuild," she said mechanically. "I'll start cleaning up, then as soon as the insurance settles, I'll start—"

"But Aunt B, why don't you do something for yourself, first?"

She blinked at the teenager as if Faith suggested she campaign for presidency. "But I have work—"

"You always have work." The girl's fright betrayed itself in her frayed tone. Mortality wasn't something a sixteen-year-old dwelt upon. Once faced, it had a rattling effect on everything. Loss was something still fresh in Faith's memory, making time with her aunt all the more precious. "That's always your excuse, for not traveling, for not visiting us, for not joining us on vacation, for hiding in this crappy little store and turning into Grandma Joan."

Stunned by the unexpected attack, Bess lost all color. She couldn't think of how to respond.

Faith covered her mouth with her hands, aghast at having let her feelings escape, then, suddenly, not willing to hide them anymore. She took a deep breath and took a determined stand.

"All the time I was growing up, I listened to my mom talking about how creative you were, how good with people, how generous and warm you were. I never saw any of that. All I got were gifts in the mail, pieces of you that didn't cost anything to send." Tears liquefied her agitated stare. "Okay, so you were busy taking care of Grandma while she was alive, but what about after?"

"The store—"

"Was hers. It's not a part of you, Aunt Bess. Don't you think I could see how much you hated it? Mr. Doolin offered to buy it before. Sell it. Sell it now and do something you want to do. Something exciting, something daring."

"That's your mother, Faith, not me."

"Why not you? Because *she* told you that you couldn't be, that you had to stay and be her sensible daughter, to make all the sacrifices? For what? What kind of hold does that woman have over you that you still think you owe her? You've got a chance at a whole new life. I'm just a kid, but I've seen the way you and Z—Mr. Crandall are when you're together. But how long do you think he's gonna hang around while you board yourself up in this place, acting like the Virgin Mary moral center for the town of Sweetheart?"

Outrage shattered Bess's shock. "Faith Marie, how dare you speak that way to me! You have no idea what sacrifices I've made and why. You horrid, ungrateful child! After all I've done for you—"

With a sob, Faith fled from the store.

But it wasn't the girl's abrupt departure that stunned Bess into silence. It was what had poured out of her: those awful, nasty condemnations.

Shaking uncontrollably, Bess dropped to her knees amid the ash and devastation. Whitened knuckles pressed to her lips as she rocked herself in short, anguished thrusts. It wasn't true. Faith wasn't right. She shook her head, denying it to the only one she couldn't convince. Denying it to herself.

"Bess?" A broad hand eased along the jerk and tremble of her shoulders. "Bess, what's wrong? I just saw Faith run out of—"

She turned and the impact of the blind desolation in her eyes knocked the wind from him. He dropped down beside her, opening his arms just as she threw herself against him.

"Oh, Zach…"

Such wounded agony in her voice, so much desperation in the way she hugged to him. He stroked her hair, his mind spinning wildly. Good God, what had happened to rip her soul apart?

"Talk to me, baby. Bess, talk to me." Her ragged breathing shook him more than anything he could remember. Helplessness twisted inside him, the same way it had when he'd listened to his mother crying when he was a boy. Such crushing helplessness in knowing there was nothing he could do to make her stop.

"Tell me what's wrong," he coaxed, squeezing her so tight he feared he'd break her in half. "I can't help you unless you tell me—"

"I'm not my mother."

The raw wail startled him. Her mother? What—?

"I'm not my mother, Zach. I'm not."

He kissed her temple, murmuring, "Of course you're not, baby. You're nothing like her. Where would you get that idea? From Faith? Did Faith say something to get you all upset?"

Bess's sobs continued, silent, disconsolate, racking her slender body with a pain so deep, he couldn't reach the source to provide comfort. He rocked her, his expression firming into angular planes chiseled from stone.

Damn Joan Carrey.

He'd have a talk with Faith. He'd find a way to explain a creature like her grandmother, a woman so selfish, so proud, she would destroy her own flesh and blood rather than let them go.

"Let's get you out of here, Bess. I was just going for some lunch. Come with me. And don't come back in here for a while. Let the dust settle."

She didn't move for a long moment, pressing into his strength, his heat, as if it could provide an escape from the pain. Vaguely aware she wouldn't find it...because he was part of it.

She'd knelt on this same floor, some seventeen years earlier, weeping with heartbreak while her mother cast a fierce

shadow over her as merciless words filleted her will and whit-
tled away her choice.

*With him? With a boy like that? Are you insane? What
were you thinking, girl? A boy like that isn't going to stay
around for the hard times. He'll up and leave you flat with
all the problems, all the grief. Didn't you learn anything from
all I've told you? He's a loser, bad luck, a bad choice. Tell
him and he'll tear out your heart. Quit that blubbering and
take your medicine. Now I've got to take care of the mess
you've made, you silly, ungrateful child. I'll take care of
things and you'll never see him again, do you understand?
Never again!*

"Zach."

"Right here, baby."

She buried her face against his warm throat, feeling him
swallow, riding the firm, rich pulse of life he'd brought into
her own.

"I loved you, Zach. You have to believe that. You have
to."

He was silent for a few beats, then said softly, "I do, Bess.
I do believe you."

"I'm sorry."

Her voice wobbled under the weight of remorse. Zach held
her, kissed her hair, and he wondered what the hell she was
apologizing for. For being young and afraid? For letting him
go? For allowing him back into her life? Or for pushing him
out of it again?

Dazed and drained, Bess sagged upon his broad shoulder.
Listlessly she let her tears fall, realizing it was too late to
change anything with tears or with apologies.

*You're a wicked child, Elizabeth. Just like your sister. How
could you hurt me so, after all I've done for you? How can
I ever hold my head up in this town again? They'll all see
you for the wanton creature you are, and they'll turn you out,
just like they did him. Bad follows worse, I always said, but
you wouldn't listen. And now, it's too late. It's too late to
change what you've done.*

Bess closed her eyes, becoming that guilt-ridden teenager again. Remembering every ripple of shame and regret that battered her disobedient heart. Remembering how she'd lain on this very floor, the world becoming brilliant prisms as sunlight caught the grandfather clock's crystal pendulum weight, sending strobes of hellfire to flash and dazzle before her eyes.

Her eyes opened. Her grief fell away before a startling awareness. Still clinging to Zach, she lifted her head, looking slowly, slowly behind her to the space beside the front door. Where for as long as she could remember while growing up, her great-grandfather's clock had struck out the hour with gloomy precision.

The case still stood, but the mechanism was silent. Silent for these past seventeen years. Because the clock had broken. The beautiful weight that kept the gears whirring was gone. That beautiful bit of leaded glass that so fascinated her as a child.

That piece of heavy crystal shaped like an inverted pyramid.

Chapter 16

"Feeling better?"

Stretched out on her sofa, concealed by the protective darkness of the cold cloth covering her eyes, all Bess had to do was nod.

Zach had taken her straight home and insisted she lie down. Then he'd fussed over her with tender solicitousness until she was ready to wail for him to leave her alone. She didn't want companionship. She wanted solitude. She wanted some way to explain away what she'd discovered in the bookstore. And the last person she wanted near her while she digested all the possible ramifications was Zach. Hysteria quivered beneath her surface calm, seeking an untimely escape.

"You stay down and quiet for the rest of the day, you hear? Do you want me to call Doc Meirs? Maybe he missed something. Maybe you're concussed—"

"I'm tired, Zach. That's all. Just tired."

Her brittle reply shut him up tight for so long she had to sneak a look. He'd angled her mother's favorite chair so his knees butted up against the couch cushions. His expression was drawn, not with annoyance but with worry. She touched the back of his hand, and his fingers snapped hers up for a possessive clutch.

"Are you sure that's all it is, baby? You should have seen yourself. You scared the hell out of me." He chafed her hand between both of his, the gesture anxious and distracting. His stare was too direct, too attentive. Bess let the cloth cover her eyes again, afraid he'd see the frenzied thoughts swirling behind them.

"I'm sorry, Zach. I didn't mean to. I guess it all caught up with me at once. I folded."

He continued to knead and manipulate her hand within his. "Kids say things without meaning them, Bess. You know that. Faith would never do anything to hurt you."

Bess didn't answer.

Zach's uneasiness grew tenfold.

"Are you sure I can't call somebody to come over and sit with you?"

"Really, I just need some rest, some time to think about what I'm going to do next."

Zach frowned. What was he missing here? Something major he couldn't afford to let slip by. Something big was behind Bess's panic, but he couldn't figure out what it might be. And she wasn't talking. That made him nervous as hell.

"I gotta get back to work, baby. I don't like leaving you—"

She pushed aside the cloth to smile with what could have been a gentle sincerity. But he didn't think it was.

"Don't be silly, Zach. I'm fine. Go to work."

He gave up with a sigh. "All right. Call if you need me. Leave a message. I'll be in and out all afternoon. And I'll stop over after work. If that's all right with you?"

"It's fine with me."

He bent to kiss her lightly, unprepared for the anxious way her arms encircled his neck to hold him in place for a long minute. Again, panic skittered across his intuitive senses, bringing a chill of foreboding.

What wasn't she telling him?

When he straightened, a suspicious shimmer glassed over her gaze before she averted her head, but he let it go, just as he had to let her go for the moment. He had other answers to pursue, then he'd be back to find out what Bess Carrey was keeping from him.

The first part of the morning had dragged for Zach, offering more pieces to the puzzle but no solid edges to frame them into a recognizable picture. Before the computer age, records were haphazardly filed, poorly typed or handwritten in illegible scrawls. He balanced the slow steady pace of his own work with careful study of his mother's trial transcript. It took all his discipline to keep himself removed from the emotional testimonies that sucked him back toward childhood.

Sam Crandall had been a monster and deserved to be dead. But Zach refused to let the man's memory bring harm to anyone else. He hadn't been able to stop the spread of his father's dark influence when he'd been alive, but by God he'd stop it now. He'd see all the ugliness got stuffed back into the grave with his twisted soul.

And now this new worry over Bess.

Tension pounded at the base of his skull since leaving her. The hard smack of his heels on the cement walk wasn't helping. He'd wanted answers. He needed a solution. He had to shake off the clutching stigma of the past. Dammit, why couldn't the bastard just die? Why couldn't he lie in his grave and rot and let everyone else get on to patching up the lives he'd shattered? Zach wouldn't—couldn't—believe the damage was irreparable. That would be too unfair. And he'd had all the injustice he could stand for one lifetime.

He turned up the walk to his house, hoping to have a few minutes alone with his mother before going back to the post, and pulled back in surprise at the sight of a small figure huddled on the steps. He approached with care, unsure of how to handle a fragile teenage heart. His average was pretty lousy to date.

"Hey."

Faith lifted her head from the pillow of her knees. Red-rimmed eyes blinked up at him as she pushed hair, spiky from the heat and tears, out of her face. Her smile wobbled pitifully.

"Hi, Mist—Zach."

He swung down to sit on the step beside her at a companionable distance. Resting his elbows on his knees, he looked down the sunny residential street, purposefully allowing the girl time to pull her thoughts together.

"I screwed up big-time," she said miserably.

He gave a wry chuckle. "Join the club." He tented his hands, studying the triangle they made, thinking tangentially of the object that had killed his father. "Want to talk about it?" Obviously she did, or she wouldn't be weeping on his front steps, but it took her a little more time to get over her awkward pride and humiliation. He gave it to her.

"I said some real bitchy things to Aunt Bess, and I wish I could take them back."

"Things you didn't mean?"

"No. I meant them, I just didn't want them to come out, you know, the way they did."

"The truth has a habit of doing that."

"I really care a lot about her, you know. My mom and dad, they are great parents and all, but they're always on the go, always hurrying to see some new sight or have some new adventure. Sometimes, they wouldn't have a lot of time for me and I'd call Aunt B. She didn't care what time it was or how long I talked, she'd listen. I didn't always take her advice, but it was always good. I really counted on her to be there for me. She made me feel like I was special, you know?"

"Yeah." Zach let his hands dangle loosely. "I know."

"Well, I think she was counting on me today, and I let her down. And I feel really crappy about it. She's pretty good at pretending things don't bother her but—"

"—they do," Zach supplied quietly. "I know, kiddo. And

it's rough to see that. But you want to know something else about your aunt that makes her special?''

The girl tilted her head to gaze up at him. ''What's that?''

''She never closes the door on someone she loves. Even if they've hurt her.''

''Yeah?''

He looked at her and nodded soberly. ''Yeah. But you won't know until you go talk to her. She should be hearing this, not me.''

Faith's arm curled about his neck, hugging tight as her soft cheek pressed to his rough one. ''You're an all right guy, Zach Crandall.''

He sat still, unfamiliar with such unconditional affection. His bland tone masked his surprise. ''Think so?''

''Know so.'' She jumped up, her animation recharging like a battery's. ''Gotta go take care of some things. Later.''

''Let me know how *things* turn out,'' he called after her energetic figure. He waved a hand when she bounced around, grinning back at him.

''I will. Thanks.''

Feeling very old in the face of the girl's quicksilver nature, Zach pushed up to his feet, steeling himself for what he had to do.

His mother was sitting in the living room, watching early afternoon soaps. She beamed up at him. ''Zach! What a nice surprise. I thought I heard you, and was that Faith? Why didn't she come in? Such a sweet girl, just like her mother.''

Zach didn't comment. Instead, he came to sit on the braided rug next to her chair the way he always had as a boy. In a house full of kids, there was never enough furniture to go around. Zach took the floor without complaint, and Mary remembered many a night when he'd fall asleep, his head heavy upon her lap. She continued to rock, waiting for him to speak.

''Mom?''

The somber syllable prepared her for what was coming. She tensed, subconsciously bracing for the memories.

''There're some things I've got to know. About Dad.''

Mary took a shaky breath and touched a hand to his rigid shoulder. He started but didn't flinch away. "Let it go, Zach. Can't you let it go?"

He shook his head.

"Why? What good is it going to do, dragging everything out into the open again? It's tearing you apart. Your sister is having nightmares again. And I just don't want to remember anymore."

"I'm sorry, Mom, but I have to—"

"Why? Why do you have to find out anything? I don't care who killed him. I'm just glad he's dead. The crime's already been paid for."

He twisted, staring up at her through tormented eyes. "But not by the right person."

"I don't care anymore, baby. Leave it alone." She rubbed his taut cheek until he turned away with negating sharpness.

"I care. I care, Mom."

"What good will it do?"

"Everyone will know the truth. Isn't the truth important to anyone but me? This town spit on us for years. They let you go to prison for something none of them believe you did. Dammit, I want to know why! I want someone to take responsibility for those years you sat in jail!"

She stroked his crisp-cut hair with soothing repetitions. "It won't give me the years back."

"But it'll give us our pride back. Mom, don't you see? I want to be a part of this town, and I can't be as long as they all think I killed him."

"Zach, Elmer Grant stopped over this morning. He offered me a job doing payroll for the Super Value as soon as I feel up to it."

"So?"

"So, we talked about you and about how what you did for Bess is going a long way toward changing opinions. The tide's turning, baby. Go with it for once, instead of against it. Don't make things so hard for yourself...and for the rest of us."

His head leaned against her thigh as he closed his eyes. "I don't mean to make problems for you and Mel. I don't."

"I know, baby."

"I want to belong, Mom. These people have never once given me the benefit of anything but their mistrust. But today, they've been greeting me like a neighbor. Mom, I'm scared that's gonna get snatched away from me. I've got to prove that they can trust me, that I'm not what *he* was."

She smoothed her hand over the uniform shirt, saying with pride, "You already did that, Zach."

He shook his head. "I have to prove to all of them that I'm a good risk. The only way I can do that is to sweep out all the dirt and start over clean. They think I killed Dad. They'll go on believing it until I find out who did."

"And what if they don't like what you find, Zach? How are you going to get them not to blame you for stirring it up again?"

"Mom there's a killer in this town."

"Someone who hasn't stepped sideways to cross the law in seventeen years. I say leave it alone. Zach, please. Leave it alone. Don't let him ruin this chance for you."

Zach got to his feet. He didn't meet her beseeching eyes as he bent to buss her cheek and whisper, "I'll see you later."

And the sound of her hitching breath as he walked away left him sick inside but no less determined.

"Why Mr. Crandall, hello again."

Zach leaned his forearms on the counter and gave a deep, dimpled smile. "Miss Lorraine, I was wondering if you could do me a big, big favor."

Wariness sparked in her bespectacled eyes but only for a moment. Then she smiled back, blushing slightly. "I suppose I can, unless you're planning to rob the bank."

He laughed, a low, easy rumble. "No, I don't think so. Wouldn't look good on my performance evaluation. Though I might be tempted to steal you away for the afternoon if I didn't know your husband probably still has that double-barrel he used to pepper my brother's butt with rock salt when he was making off with your pumpkins."

The old woman warmed up like butter swirling in a fry pan. "He still has it, and shame on you for your teasing. Doyle wasn't trying to hit your brother. He's a terrible shot."

Zach grinned, and Lorraine Freemiere buckled.

"What can I do for you, young man?"

"I need my family's bank records from late '79 and '80."

The significance of the date didn't escape her. Her humor fled. "Why would you want those?"

Zach hung his head in a picture of humility. "Everything happened so fast back then. My mom didn't have time to square things away before—"

He took a breath, surprised by how suddenly difficult it was not to let true emotion confuse his manipulation. And that pause what all it took to convince Lorraine of his sincerity.

Her gnarled hand pressed his briefly.

"I'm sure we still have some record of your account. Mr. Tyesdale never throws anything away. If you could stop back just before five, I'll see if I can have them for you."

He glanced up, ashamed, feeling funny about his ruse to get the statements in the face of her sympathy. "I'd really appreciate that, if you're sure it's no trouble."

"No trouble. Tell your mother hello for me."

His smile wavered. "I will."

He couldn't get out of there fast enough. It took a minute for the haze of guilt to clear before he could make his next stop.

Charlie Maitland owned Sweetheart's only cab service, and had for the past twenty years. His main business was delivering groceries to shut-ins or transporting them to Doc Meirs for their checkups. Back when his father worked for Charlie, there was no daily bus route between the neighboring towns, and Sam would do the long drives when not busy putting in a new water pump or turning brake drums. Sam was a good driver when sober, and Charlie never sent him out unless he was sure.

"Howdy, Zach. Heard you was back." Charlie wiped off his greasy hand before offering it. "You was mighty good with engines way back when. Ain't lookin' to moonlight, are you? Sure could use somebody with your daddy's talent for tinkering."

Zach's smile thinned. "No sir, 'fraid not." And when he told the old mechanic what he needed, Charlie spent the better part of forty-five minutes digging through broken boxes and dirty crates before producing what he'd asked for.

"There you go, son. Your daddy's mileage log. Can't guess what you'd be wanting it for, but you're welcome to it."

Zach patted the thin ledger against his pantleg with a force that stung. "Keepsake."

Charlie shrugged. "Whatever. Take care now. Stop on by if you want to tip a few some night and talk old times."

"I'll do that."

Like hell. No way he was planning to reminisce about all the nights he'd shown up after three in the morning to drag his father out of the back seat of the cab, drunker than sin, only to endure his slaps and abusive talk as his old man stumbled out to his beat-up truck growling that he damn well didn't need some snot-nosed thirteen-year-old to drive him. Then, taking the bastard home so the drunk could take out the rest of his temper on his mother, who'd worried that the wretch had wrapped himself around a tree somewhere. Feeling guilty for wishing he had.

Old times. He shuddered and spat on the antifreeze-stained drive. Even after more than twenty years, he could still taste the oil in his mouth from the flat of his father's hand.

He pocketed the ledger, hoping it would provide a clue worth causing his mother's heartbreak.

He didn't have time to dive into the information he'd ferreted up. Just before five, Lorraine Freemiere stopped by to deliver a batch of rubber-banded papers. Before he could go through them, a call came in. A wreck on the interstate wasn't a big deal, but an overturned hog hauler freeing sixty pigs weighing in at over three hundred pounds apiece brought out every man. After two and a half hours of the wildest greased pig contest ever held in the county, the porkers were safely corralled without any of the east or westbound traffic making bacon out of them.

Aching in every fiber and thinking he'd rather wrestle a gorilla in the drunk tank than face hogs anytime soon, Zach sank into his chair with a heavy sigh and turned his attention back seventeen years. Deciding to go over the bank statements first, he opened his desk drawer and stared for a long minute at the empty spot where the papers had been. His brow creased as he plunged his hand back into the drawer, fumbling around in case they somehow got shoved to the back.

But they just plain weren't there.

"Cora Beth?"

The switchboard operator wheeled her chair around the partition at the end of the room. "Yeah, Zach?"

"Was anybody back here at my desk?"

"Not that I recall. Why? Somebody leave you something?"

Yeah, they'd left him something, all right. A big fat nothing to go on.

He reached behind him, to the leather jacket hanging on the back of his chair and knew a moment of thanksgiving when he felt the outline of his father's ledger in the interior pocket. Whomever knew about the bank records apparently didn't know about his visit to Charlie. He wasn't dead in the water, yet.

"Oh, Sheriff Baines stopped in while you were out," Cora Beth yelled back. "But that was to talk to Les. I think he said he was leaving a note on his desk. Maybe he put it on yours by mistake."

Zach leaned back in his chair, eyeballing the desk across the aisle from his. "Must have been what happened. Thanks, Cora Beth." He studied the clean top of Les's work space.

No note. No reason for Lloyd Baines to stop back. Except to retrieve potentially damning evidence.

Against whom?

Cranking off the water at the kitchen sink, Bess grumbled all sorts of dire threats against the person at her back door and their lack of timing. One of Murphy's Laws: no one ever knocks at the door unless you're in the middle of something. Thinking it was probably the Bartlett boy collecting for the newspaper, she swiped a hand through her hair to make it somewhat presentable and pulled open the door. The annoyed gaze she leveled at Timmy's approximate height rose another foot to meet Zach Crandall's grin.

"Somebody forget they were having company?"

His teasing startled her from her surprise, but the way his sassy, smoldering gaze took her in by increments made her aware of how she must look to him.

Wallpapering wasn't the neatest job around, and she'd been at it for hours. She wore her oldest clothes, a pair of ancient jeans with rips across the knees and a snug neon green T-shirt Julie had sent her emblazoned with the saying, "Outside a dog, a book is man's best friend. Inside a dog, it's too dark to read." Wanting comfort as well as casual practicality, she'd opted to go braless, thinking who'd see so why should she care?

Perspiration formed damp crescents beneath her breasts. Water splashed from the sink in her hurried cleanup soaked the snug front into revealing more than it was meant to as her nipples puckered beneath the clingy knit. When she crossed her arms for modesty's sake, his stare flashed up to her face and his irreverent grin returned.

"You've got paste in your hair."

He said it as if he thought her disarray adorable instead of mortifying. Immediately she raked her fingers through the gooey tresses, making matters worse.

Frustrated because he was standing in her doorway looking as cool and fresh as she was hot and icky, she grew testy in her own defense. "I'm in the middle of papering the kitchen. It's not something I do in evening wear."

Instead of looking duly chastised, Zach continued to grin, lines of indecent humor fanning out from the corners of his eyes. "Where's Faith?"

"Deserted the ship, the rat. And after talking me into this project. She went to the show in Chariton. You just missed her."

Nervously, she surveyed the room again, imagining homey craft accessories in place of her mother's dusty teacups. She'd felt guilty at first when packing them away but a sudden urgency filled her to put as much of her mother's memory away as possible. A frantic urgency.

"Want me to help you finish up?"

She shook her head, thinking about the two of them in the sweltering kitchen working in close tandem. "I was about to take a break. There's some sun tea in the fridge."

"Go on out to the front. I'll bring the tea."

The small screened-in porch was a shady relief after the heat of the sunbaked kitchen. Bess settled onto the metal glider and went limp with a weary sigh. The spurt of frenetic activity worked wonders for keeping her worries at bay but the minute she relaxed to let her guard down, they were right there, waiting to exert their pressure. She refused to acknowledge them. Not now. Not yet. She rubbed at the tight muscles in her neck and shoulders, trying to work them out, even as her mind was trying to work out a way to handle Zach. A way that wouldn't hurt everyone.

He paused in the doorway to the house, his big frame boldly filling the space in an affront to Joan Carrey's wishes. Sweaty glasses of tea filled both hands.

"Sugar, lemon?"

"Plain."

"Nothing fancy."

"You know me, Zach."

He handed her one of the glasses along with a cryptic observation. "I thought I did."

She sipped the brew slowly. She expected him to join her on the swing. When he continued to linger in the doorway, she fidgeted. He was building up to something, and she knew she wasn't going to like it.

Then, in typical Zach form, he cut right to it.

"All right, Bess. Suppose you tell me what's going on."

Chapter 17

Ice rattled in her tea glass. "I'm not sure what you mean." She couldn't meet his probing stare, feeling every bit as guilty as a criminal under interrogation. Was she a criminal for concealing her discovery? What did he know? What had he found out?

"The wallpapering. The changes. That have anything to do with this morning?"

She risked an upward glance and found no ulterior suspicions in his handsome features. He didn't know anything, she thought with a rush of weakening relief. It took a second to quiet down her jitters so she wouldn't sound like a crazy woman when she answered.

"Partly. And partly to whatever you said to Faith."

His brows lifted in mock innocence. *"Moi?"*

"She told me you two talked."

"Oh?"

Bess smiled through the strain. "Don't get all squinty-eyed. She didn't mention any particulars."

He blinked his eyes and opened them wide. "So you two mended fences, I take it."

"We're wallpapering them. We've decided to help each other grow up."

A pause, then his quiet summation, "Good."

He crossed the porch to settle on the glider, and for a moment they rocked in silence, both studying their glasses while their awareness of each other built like thunderheads over the sleepy Iowa town. Bess spoke first, her voice thin with agitation.

"Remember when we used to sit out here studying?"

His chuckle was whiskey rich and wickedly warm. "You were trying to study. I was trying to hypothesize on how to kiss you without having you flatten my face with my math book."

She gave a startled little laugh. "You were not. You thought I was a—how did you put it?—stiff-necked do-gooder."

Zach leaned back, his arms draping along the top of the swing, framing but not touching her. "Well, you were, but that didn't mean you didn't have my shorts in a knot for four long months."

"Oh, come on." The subject had her all achy inside, remembering the fear and fascination she'd held for the dangerous Zach Crandall who could have had any girl he'd wanted with a flash of his dimpled smile. Being bad made him all the more desirable to the school's good girls. She'd spent four months of sheer torture, sitting with him, wishing she had the nerve to do something more instructional than dissect $x=y2$ multiplication formulas.

Zach drew a line along her taut shoulder with his thumb, the gesture part chiding, part coaxing. "You were harder to figure out than any of those equations. You still are."

"I'm not complex, Zach."

He made an objecting noise. "It would have taken Einstein to analyze what you saw in me back then. But you saw something worth saving, and damned if you didn't rescue me whether I wanted to be rescued or not. I never really thanked you for that.''

Bess shifted on the hard cushions as a flush of color rose in her cheeks. "Yes, you did."

"I tried to stay away because I was bad for you. Everyone knew it. Hell, I knew it, but it didn't keep me from wanting you. God, I wanted you, Bess. You were every good thing I never had. When you wouldn't leave with me…I never got over it." He gave a soft, wry laugh as if he found amusement in his own desperate straits. Then he suddenly sobered. "That's why I came back, Bess. To get a second shot at the best thing I ever had. And I'm blowing it again."

Surprised, pleased, alarmed, all in one, Bess angled toward him, needing to see his face, to read it in his eyes, but his hand fisted in her paste-filled hair, guiding her head to his chest to deny her a glimpse of his vulnerability. Not sure how to react, she leaned into him, feeling the runaway gallop of his pulse beneath her cheek as she sorted through her own turmoiled emotions.

"Blowing it in what way?" she asked cautiously.

"I can't let it go, Bess, this business with my father."

Her eyes squeezed tightly shut.

"I have to know what happened that night I left. Even if it destroys everything else. I know you can't understand—"

Her palm pressed over his heart, stilling his words. Her own were unbending. "Yes, I do, Zach. I understand. I always have. It's the one thing that's driven you all your life. You can't give it up now."

She felt his harsh inhalation and its gradual release. "I must be crazy to risk so much. To risk losing you again."

"You never lost me."

He went completely still, as if he didn't dare believe her. She continued in a small but sure voice.

"My life stopped when you left. I've been waiting all these years for you to come back and start it up again. I won't give up so easily this time."

"Bess, you don't know what you're letting yourself in for."

"Yes, I do."

"No one in this town wants me to find out the truth."

Herself included. Bess gathered wads of his T-shirt within her hands, horribly torn between the rights and wrongs and middle grays.

"You do what's right for you, Zach."

"I have to do more than that, Bess. I'm not a kid without responsibilities anymore. I can't just run away if I don't like how things are going. I can't leave the people I love behind to get hurt. You could have died in that fire. Someone in this town isn't afraid to play for keeps. I don't want you to take those risks for me."

"Then what are you asking, Zach?"

"I'm not asking you to do anything."

"Yes, you are." The roughness in his voice said he was, and that it was a big thing, one he didn't have complete faith in. Bess sat up within the wrap of his arms. For once he evaded her gaze. "Ask me, Zach." *Trust me, this time.*

"Not now. Not yet. Not until I'm damn sure it's a risk I can let you take."

"I'm a big girl, Crandall. For heaven's sake, I'm wallpapering."

Only he would understand the significance, the cost of that defiant gesture. But it didn't leave him looking any more confident. If anything, he seemed more disturbed.

"I need to do these things first, to put them to rest. I need to know—I want to know if you'll be there when it's over. I want you to know that you can count on me, Bess. Things might get crazy for a while, and maybe you'll change your mind about all this—about me—by the time it's done, but I swear to you, Bess, I wouldn't ask you to hang on if I wasn't planning on something more than dinner out and sex."

She didn't even blush at his bluntness. "I was planning on more, too. And after investing seventeen years, I'm too stubborn to give up on you now."

He was too good at hiding all the pain in his life to allow her to see everything. Just flickers of what he was feeling. Wariness. Fragile hope. And fear, gut-twisting, soul-deep fear.

She touched his cheek. The muscle beneath its sandpapery burr was locked down tight. He stared at her, into her, through her, his eyes fever and fire bright. But he didn't flinch until she spoke.

"Zach, trust me."

He swallowed once, as if pushing down a bowling ball, then again with a convulsive jerk. His stare delved into hers, searching fiercely through the tender mists for some reason to doubt, for some cause for concern. Nervous when he didn't find one.

Knowing that wild things like Zach Crandall grew dangerous when forced into a corner, Bess refused to back down to let him slip safely away. She kept him pinned with his back to the wall, holding him there with the most tenuous of bonds—belief. A belief she'd had in him once, only to have pulled it cruelly away. Was she asking too much to expect trust from him again?

He was maddening in his unwillingness to answer. Perhaps he genuinely didn't know how to. He responded, finally, but not in the expected manner.

His hand clamped on the back of her neck, hauling her up to him with breath-stopping force, to kiss her with mind-stunning fervor. He kissed her hard, trying to prove to her, or to himself, that he wasn't a nice guy deserving of her faith. Gentling the aggressive slant into an endlessly thorough seeking to suggest that perhaps he could be. That he wanted to be. And that was enough for Bess.

She slid off his mouth, standing, taking his hand in hers to lift and lead him to the stairs. He followed her wordlessly to the oppressive heat of the upper story where only a clattery old fan pushed at the heavy air. They paused at the side of her bed to undress, efficiently, without hurry, without concern. And after laying her down, Zach took a moment to provide belated protection. Then he took her slowly, satisfyingly to the edge of sanity and beyond, where she reveled in his hoarse cry of her name and in the explosive pleasure that followed.

She sighed with the gusty relief of a woman totally contented as he nuzzled her heat-glazed breasts and throat, working his way up to her smiling lips. He lingered there for a long, leisurely while before propping himself on his elbows to stare solemnly into her dreamy face.

An arrogant glint of masculine accomplishment gleamed in his eyes, a knowing that he'd rung her bells in a bold rendition of the Hallelujah Chorus. Passion, pride, possession blazed unashamed in that scalding gaze. But it couldn't quite eliminate the veil of caution filtering all the rest from her view. He still held himself back from one hundred percent commitment.

It wounded but she couldn't blame him. Especially since she knew he was right to reserve his unconditional trust.

She averted her head to stare out the window, the world losing its focus behind a sheen of tears.

"Zach, there's something I haven't told you."

She felt his body tense in slow degrees like wet rawhide tightening in the sun. "Oh?"

She released him, letting her arms trail limp and empty to the sides of her mattress. It wouldn't be fair to cling to him now, not as she watched his defenses gather behind a shuttered stare. It took a remarkably short time for the protective barriers to close her out completely.

He eased back off her, movements slow with reluctant caution. Then he turned away from her to collect his clothes, presenting her with a view of taut shoulders as he asked with detached calm, "What haven't you told me?"

She should have come clean with it immediately. Revealing things now smacked of secrets and mistrust. Wedges they didn't need between them.

"I told you what Doc Meirs said about the distinct shape of the murder weapon," she began.

He stopped in the middle of sliding on his T-shirt, then pulled it the rest of the way down. He was plainly puzzled and confused. "The pyramid. Yeah?"

"I think I know what it is." She let that spill out in a rush then took advantage of his silence to sit up and snatch at the sheets to cover herself.

But he didn't look at her. Instead, he asked with a professional remoteness, "So, when did you figure it out?"

"Just this morning, at the bookstore." She paused, waiting to see if he believed her, that she hadn't been withholding the information all along.

"And?" he prompted tonelessly.

She took a stabilizing breath. "And I think my mother killed him."

Zach wrenched about, his brow crowded with furrows, his stare piercing in its intensity. "What did you say?"

"I think my mother killed your father. I think she hit him with the pendulum weight from our clock in the store."

Zach blinked and shook his head incredulously. "Wait a minute, your *mom* killed him?"

Bess hurried on with her tortured confession. "I think she went to your house that night and I think she struck him down. And I think she did it because she thought he was you."

He just stared at her so she blundered on with her conclusions.

"She knew, Zach. She knew you and I had been together. Sh-she told me she'd see you dead before she'd let me be with you again. I—I didn't think she'd actually—" She couldn't finish, her words muffled behind the shield of her hands, as the guilt, the culpability washed through her. She expected Zach's anger, his accusations, but not his cool logic.

"I can imagine her going after me with a gun or maybe turning me into Sheriff Baines, but why would she pick such a—strange weapon to carry halfway across town to take me out in my own house?"

Bess jerked her hands down in dismay. "How can you be

so analytical? I just told you my mother is a murderer! My mother. *My* mother.'' The shock of it just kept getting bigger until her teeth were rattling together with it in the clammy August heat. Then a deeper fear racked her. ''I—I didn't know. Zach, I swear to you I didn't know anything about it. I just found out this morning. I didn't—''

The rest was drowned out as he pulled her into a loose hug.

''Oh, baby, I never thought for a second that you did. You're the one person in this world whose honesty I trust.''

And that assurance burned more deeply than any condemnation.

Because she wasn't being honest with him. And the longer her secret went unspoken, the greater the consequences should it be discovered. The greater the risk of him never forgiving her.

''What now?''

Her tiny voice sparked a huge protectiveness in Zach. He stroked her hair and continued to mash her against him. ''Now I start putting the pieces together.'' When she trembled fitfully, he kissed the top of her head and murmured, ''Baby, we don't know anything for sure. We don't have the weight. We can't place your mom at my house. I've still got a whole slew of questions that are a long way from finding answers. But I promise you one thing, Bess. I won't do anything with what I find out until we talk about it together. Okay? Okay?''

She nodded slightly, and he cursed under his breath, wishing he could offer more assurances. Feeling he had to.

''No matter what turns up, it's not going to change how I feel about you. You hear me, Bess? It won't change anything.''

She remained stiff within his embrace.

He glanced at her bedside clock, then dragged his gaze away from the rumpled sheets, swallowing down a killing wish for the right to snuggle back into them with Bess, to coddle her all night until her fears were put to rest. But he couldn't. He had work to do. Faith would be back soon. His own family was waiting for him. The combination of things conspired to wrest him from where he wanted to be.

"Bess, I've got to go. I wish I didn't have to."

Her head nodded, accepting the practicality of their situation more readily than he ever could. "I know. It's all right."

His palms met the velvety bare skin of her back where the sheet parted behind her. They made small circles, lost in the feel of her. Finally, when he didn't make the first move, she sniffed and leaned away.

"I'll be fine, Zach. Don't worry about me."

Don't worry. His gut did a triple-gainer somersault. How could he not worry leaving her shivery and pale, looking as dangerously frail as blown glass caught in a tornado. The last thing he wanted her to think was that his plan had been to bed her and run. It wasn't. Running from Bess Carrey wasn't an option. But since she valued the town's opinion of her, so should he; a town more 1890s than 1990s in its liberal thinking. That meant no compromising visits, even if it meant compromising his desire to be near her.

"I got my father's cab ledger," he told her, just to talk and ease the ache of separating from her. "Maybe it'll tell us something." He didn't mention the stolen bank records. He didn't know why, for certain, but it had to do with a deep-down need to keep her in the dark where trouble might be lurking. Lloyd Baines was trouble.

"And I've got the kitchen to finish." She managed a wobbly smile that fractured his honorable intentions. His words rumbled.

"I'd give anything to tumble you back into those covers for the next week or two, but since I can't, I'd better get the hell outta here." He kissed her hard and fast, pleased to see some of the resilience return to her gaze. That made it possible, but still not easy, to walk out of her room.

When she heard the door shut behind him in the kitchen below, Bess balled herself up in the still-warm sheets, mind numb with dread.

Her mother, a murderess. Cold-blooded in her manipulations as she preached virtue and practiced the most heinous of mortal sins. How could she? How could she live with what she'd done, go on as if nothing had happened, as if a man weren't lying dead by her hand and an innocent woman imprisoned for her crime? How could Bess not have seen the madness behind her mother's puritanical pride? How could she be so naive as to blindly follow the same rigid rules as a woman who killed to save her name from disgrace? What did that make her? What would that make her when the good people of Sweetheart discovered the truth?

Where would that leave her if Zach uncovered the rest?

Slowly, the guilt ebbed away, leaving a flat, glaring fury. *Mother, how could you do this to me, your own daughter? How could you try to kill the man I love just to keep me under your control? How could you pretend you acted for my good when it was your vanity behind it all?*

You hypocrite!

Wiping her eyes, she rolled off the bed, showered and dressed once more in her shabbiest attire. Then she went down to the kitchen to beat up a batch of fresh paste. And began to apply the patterned paper to her mother's bare walls with a vengeance.

"Zach?"

Tucking his father's ledger behind him, Zach stepped into the living room where his mother occupied her favorite rocker. A book was open across her knees, something he never would have seen years ago. His dad wouldn't have allowed her the luxury of idle time.

"Hi, Mom. How you feeling?"

She wasted no time. "Have you thought about what I said to you?"

"Yes," he told her, his candor gruff and to the point. "But nothing's changed."

That wasn't quite true. Everything had changed since he left the Carreys'. A whole new set of consequences just dropped onto his shoulders. He didn't know how much more he could support before collapsing under the burden.

"Then I guess I'll answer your questions."

He stared at her in surprise, then approached with strange reluctance. Opening up the past was like taking a trip to hell and back, it wasn't pleasant or without tremendous cost. His mother looked so suddenly frail and old. He hesitated.

"Are you sure you're up to it?"

"Let's get it over with, Zach, so we can finally bury it between us."

He nodded, feelings of regret and remorse plaguing him already. He couldn't sit down but instead went to stand at the fireplace. It hadn't worked for as long as he remembered, its bricks loose and chimney soot filled. Like the foundations of his family, it needed a good sweeping and some basic repairs to become functional again.

"What can I tell you that you don't already know?"

"I got copies of our old bank records. Someone went through a lot of trouble to steal them before I got the chance to look at them. Why? What was someone afraid I'd see in a bunch of old deposits?"

She didn't hesitate. "Inconsistencies."

He turned, frowning at her in his bewilderment. "What do you mean?"

"Your father worked for Charlie, driving his cab, working on cars for seven years. He made a decent wage, not an extravagant one. So how did a man with a modest job deposit two thousand dollars in our bank account every six months?"

"Not from tips," Zach murmured as his mind spun with possibilities. "Did you ask him about it?"

"He was furious that I found out. I thought he was afraid I'd ask for an accounting or for a fair share. I didn't get either. And I never asked about it a second time."

Zach's jaw tightened. He needed no explanation. "What did he do with the money?"

"Gambled, drank, spent it on cocktail waitresses mostly." No resentment sparked in her voice, just an age-old weariness.

"How did he get the money? Cash? Check?" A paper trail had to start someplace.

"It just turned up in the account. Sam didn't put it in. He would never have let that kind of money sit in a bank. If he had it in his hands, he'd have spent it right then."

"While you worked two jobs to put food on the table. The son of a bitch."

Mary made no comment. She'd long since given up justifying or apologizing for the brute she married.

So close. He was so close to solving everything. Frustration left a bitter taste. If only he had those bank records... Asking again would create all kinds of questions he preferred not to provoke.

"Mom, did you save our old passbooks?"

"Sam took care of all the finances. They'd be with his things. Melody put them in the attic. If he kept them, they'd be there."

For the rest of the evening hours, he sat in the dusty crawl space opening boxes of memories as raw as unhealed wounds. Touching his father's belongings made his skin crawl with the associations they carried with them. He pushed impatiently through stacks of gambling hunches scribbled out on bar napkins, phone numbers for women named Fanny, Jewel and Starr. His head ached from breathing the stale air in harsh snatches, from the pressure of grinding his teeth in helpless hatred. He stared hard at a collection of photographs: his parents when they were first married standing in front of their new home, his dad all smirky grins, looking so much the way he did now it made his gut hurt; his mom happy, pretty and so alive. He'd never seen her look like that since. He tossed them aside. Family bills. He shone the flashlight down as he flipped through them. Medical receipts and past due notices. For his shoulder, his ribs, his fingers, symbols of what had broken inside him long ago that couldn't be set or mended by time.

He drew in a shaky inhalation and forced himself to concentrate.

Utility payments. Closer.

Mortgage statements. Closer still.

Insurance policies and claim forms for cars wrecked in drunken tangles with posts, poles and abutments.

Bank statements.

He jerked the stack out onto his lap with a fierce elation.

If Sam Crandall came into unexplained wealth, he was either doing something illegal or had caught someone else in the act and was cashing in on it.

"Let's see what you were hiding...."

Chapter 18

The bank records read like a blueprint for blackmail. Only who and why were missing; the important details making the rest absolutely useless.

He'd meant to go through the cab log but, mentally and emotionally exhausted, he put it aside for morning. He slept in his clothes, the papers and book tucked beneath his mattress. Shifting nightmares chased away the benefits of rest; the maniacal figure of Joan Carrey stalking him with murderous intent, Bess's accusations ringing a death knell on all his dreams: *How could you? She was my mother! How could you ruin my family's name just to save your own?* Then the stalking figure metamorphosed from mother to daughter.

He woke in a drenching sweat. Head pounding, thoughts gritty, he stood in a mercilessly cold shower, trying to exorcize the demons that danced behind his closed eyes. His nightmare was just a harbinger of things to come.

He had to consider what it would do to Bess to have her mother exposed as a murderer. Bess, to whom propriety, opinion and past history meant everything. Do what you feel is

right, she'd told him. Right for whom? Not for her, not once
the gossipmongers got their teeth in the scandal. Not for his
mother, who stood to suffer more from the baring of old scars
than she would gain from any revelation of a new truth. Not
for the town who preferred its skeletons remain buried and
its injustices amended with a friendly inclusion but no apology.

He shut off the water and leaned into palms braced against
wet tiles.

Who would benefit from the rectification of a two-
decade-old crime?

His father was dead. A tragedy to none, himself included.
His mother had already done the time, a sacrifice she accepted
to cleanse her soul of blame. The community favor was gradually turning toward him. And there was Bess, sweet, blame-
less Bess who would bear the brunt of it all as a victim to
her mother's last cruel bid for control. No one wanted the
truth to be told. No one cared who killed Sam Crandall. Not
even the man's own family.

So why not leave it alone? Why not let it go?

Dampness fell from his wet hair, from his hunched shoulders, from his tightly closed eyes. Cold chills claimed his
nervous system, rattling through him on a rapidly spreading
rash of gooseflesh.

Who was he trying to punish with his quest for the truth?

A town for turning its back on the misfortunes of his family? His mother for not rescuing them from a life of abuse?
Bess for not believing in him enough to take a risk on his
love?

Or himself, for running away all those years ago, leaving
others to deal with what he was afraid to face? His father.
His failure. His fear of Bess's rejection.

What would change if Joan Carrey was named a killer?

He climbed out of the shower, shaken beyond the capacity
for clear thought. Even a vigorous toweling couldn't restore
warmth.

Carrying his father's logbook and the bank statements, he

walked to Sophie's for some of her paint-stripping coffee.
There was no confident strut in his step, no sassy grin for
those who bid him good morning. He slipped into a back
booth, wishing for solitude, wishing for an answer.

Wishing for Bess to make her regular appearance so he
could purge his heart of its relentless pain.

She hadn't shown by the time he finished his first or his
second cup. To make the restless time pass faster, he opened
his dad's ledger and began to read.

Times, dates, places, names all blurred together in his father's heavy scrawl. Occasional notes were penciled in the
margins, reminders to place a bet on the first race, to pick up
the truck from police impound, court dates, his anniversary.
That made Zach pause, that hint of his father's sentimental
side. Until he realized it wasn't his parents' anniversary date.
Scowling he flipped through more pages of rambling nota-
tions.

Until one date, one fare, one destination brought his whole
future crashing down upon him.

Bess didn't stop at the kitchen. By mid-morning, she had
drop cloths on the dining room floor and was wrestling the
bigger pieces of furniture away from the walls. Geraniums. It
came to her during her fitful attempts at sleep. Salmon-
colored paint and a border strip of colorful geraniums. Out
with the dark, heavy antiques. In with rattan and brass. Off
with the funeral parlor drapes. Up with miniblinds and cheery
swags. A room filled with light. A house filled with life. A
new life for Bess Carrey.

Freedom.

The means to deal in a circumspect way with her mother's
betrayal.

She was up at five taking down curtains and washing
woodwork. By the time Faith stumbled down at seven, she'd
taken all the ugly china out of her mother's monstrous cabinet. Gordon Lake at the interstate antique store had once offered her mother six hundred dollars for the set. That would

nest egg her renovations. The china, the heavy silver she was never allowed to use except on holidays, the dreary cabinet and sideboard crowding into a room already filled beyond comfortable capacity by a huge somber table and tapestried chairs; all of it up for bid. They weren't her. Never had been. They were reminders of silent meals consumed with perfect manners. Treasures to be hoarded but never enjoyed. The same way her mother had meant for her to spend her years.

No more.

Faith stared at her, not quite knowing what to make of this bustling woman who used to be her demure aunt. Bess gave her a chiding smile.

"Well, you're the one who suggested I change."

"I didn't expect it to be from PeeWee Herman to Arnold Schwarzenegger!"

"You don't approve?"

The teenager grinned. "Heck, yeah! Wait till I tell Mom. She'll accuse me of corrupting you."

"Grab a corner and help me drag this hideous beast away from the wall."

Between the two of them, they pushed the massive oak cabinet to allow walking space behind it, then leaned back rubbing sore muscles.

"Geez, this thing weighs a ton. I bet you didn't dust behind here very often," Faith complained, wincing as she rotated her shoulder.

"Okay, lightweight. If you're not going to help move furniture, pedal down to Peterson's and pick up that border strip we measured for yesterday. And have them mix paint to match. Al knows how much I need."

Grumbling about the waning days of her vacation, Faith shuffled out to the garage which had never held an automobile, to wheel out the mountain bike Bess had bought her that spring. She paused to wave before coasting down the driveway. Bess took the last sip of her tepid coffee and paid closer scrutiny to the cabinet.

It was in fine shape, a mammoth piece of workmanship

made to last for several lifetimes. Using a cloth to wipe the cobwebbing from the back, she wondered how much Gordon would give for it, providing they could get the monster out of the house.

"Oh, great," she muttered as the cloth snagged on a loose tack causing part of the thin wood backing to crack. There went a percentage of the profit.

As she tried to salvage the situation by tacking the section back into place, her palm bumped a solid spot in the otherwise hollow space. Something was behind the thin veneer.

What would her mother have hidden behind her bulky china cupboard?

Curiosity became sudden clarity.

Something she didn't want easily found.

Without hesitation, Bess ripped the wood away, moving quickly to catch the shirt box that tumbled free. A box from a department store that had gone out of business ten years ago. Something shifted inside. Something heavy.

Bess hurried into the kitchen, holding the box away from her as if it held a ticking time bomb.

Perhaps it did.

She grabbed up a paring knife and began slicing through the heavily applied packing tape that sealed the top and bottom of the box together. As she slit the final side to free the lid, she hesitated. She knew what she thought the box contained but she couldn't be sure until she looked. And once she saw inside, nothing would ever be the same again. All her past perceptions would prove a lie.

Taking a breath, she jerked off the lid, letting it out in a sob as the morning sunlight dazzled though the triangular prisms. The pendulum weight nested in a bed of loose pages filled with the broken type from her mother's old manual machine.

Her mother killed Sam Crandall. The evidence shot rainbows of revelation across the newly papered walls and ceiling. And over the shadow of a man that suddenly appeared, large and unexpected, at her back door.

With an anxious start, she slammed the lid back over the box and stuffed it out of sight under the sink. Her hands shook. Her breathing rattled like a badly timed window fan.

A knock, crisp and precise.

Zach.

She yanked open the door, her anxiousness spilling her words out almost incoherently.

"Oh, Zach. I found it. You won't believe it where it was. I wasn't even looking, and it was right there the whole time. Come in and see—"

She'd grasped his forearm but didn't realize something was wrong until he pulled free with a sharp jerk.

"I didn't come here to talk about that." His voice rang flat and factual. Not his professional tone. This was something very different.

Only then did she look up and really see him. Her mouth closed with a snap. Nothing moved in Zach's expression. Nothing. His eyes were pale glaciers, cold, lifeless, devoid of any sign of warmth. Fear stabbed through her, fear and a truth she wasn't ready to recognize.

"Zach, what's wrong?"

"You tell me, Bess." Again, the slow, deadly calm, the clipped pronouncement of each syllable through fiercely clenched teeth. "Tell me something you should have told me a long, long time ago."

Panic immobilized her. Her mind refused to work, her body to respond. She could only stare up at him, lost in the savage sea of blue his eyes had become.

"Oh, Zach, I'm—"

He sucked a breath, and the wall of his composure crumbled. "Don't you dare say that you're sorry. Sorry won't even come close to—" He gripped his lips together until they paled from the pressure. His eyes strobed pale fire, then grew frighteningly opaque. "How could you talk about trust and not tell me about our baby?"

Light-headed, she groped behind her for the edge of the table. *He knew.* How, didn't matter. The only thing that mattered was her keeping it from him. And why. She had to make him understand.

"I was seventeen years old. I hadn't even graduated from high school. I didn't know what else to do, Zach."

"You could have told me." Blunt, unarguable words.

"I was afraid."

"Of what? That I might want to keep a baby we made between us? That I might want the chance to prove I could support a family? That I might turn out to be a better father than mine was to me?"

"Zach—"

"But you never gave me the chance, Bess. You never gave me a choice. *Damn* you! Didn't you think I had the right?"

She flinched beneath his harsh condemnation, deserving his anger and the cut of outrage slashing through his words. But his pain was more than she'd prepared for. Anguish ripped through his voice in a hard pulse of betrayal, a sorrow so raw she wept in ceaseless shame. No forgiveness could ever come from so deep a wound.

Even as grief worked upon his taut features, his glare grew colder. When he spoke again, bitterness speared through the racking misery in a direct thrust to her heart.

"Or wasn't I good enough to be the father of your child?"

"No, Zach," she cried, desperate to reach him before he withdrew completely behind the impenetrable wall of blame. "It wasn't that. It was never that. I was scared. I didn't know what to do. My mother—"

"Your mother." He spat that out like the vilest curse. Shaking hands shoved back through his short hair making fists behind his head as he fought for a thread of control. "I would have stood by you, Bess. I would have moved heaven and earth for you. Why didn't you tell me? Why didn't you trust me to do the right thing? You let me go without ever giving me the chance to prove how much I loved you."

His back to her, he expelled his breath in a noisy rattle, head hanging, hands moving in fierce clenches. Sobbing into her hands, Bess watched him gather strength, saw him dredge

up the control it took to force down sentiment as he squared
his shoulders on a deep inhalation. When he turned, the ter-
rifying blankness masked his expression once again.

He dropped his father's ledger at her feet.

"It's all in there. How your mother took you to see a Dr.
Boyd about seventeen years ago. Look in there and tell me
you didn't abort my baby!"

She lost a precious second to shock. Then Zach continued,
his fury freezing to the bone.

"Your damned reputation. Well, you don't need to worry
about me soiling it anymore. Keep your secrets. Wallpaper
over it and pretend it never happened. Hang on to the vanity
of being Saint Joan Carrey's daughter. You earned it, and my
family and I paid the price for it."

He yanked open the door, then turned briefly, impervious
to her tears, to deliver one final blow.

"Your mother would be so proud."

The door slammed behind him, glass rattling as Bess dis-
solved in nerveless shivers. She'd lost him to her weakness,
her fear. She'd failed to trust in the goodness she knew he
possessed, as a teen, as a man. Instead of facing the truth,
she'd buried it, just as her mother had buried her sins in a
box and allowed another to pay the consequences with her
lies. Bess made Zach pay with her silence.

And now, after all she'd done to him, after all her family
had done to his, he was willing to sacrifice the vindication
truth would bring to spare her its shame.

How much more plainly could he say he loved her still?

She heard the crunch of Faith's bicycle in the driveway
and dashed away her tears with a purposeful swipe. Time to
act, not cower. Time for some belated bravery, even though
it was too little, too late.

Bess gave Faith no chance to express her alarm upon seeing
her ravaged expression. She pushed a small sack into the
girl's hands.

"Take that to Zach. Give it to him and tell him…tell him
to do the right thing."

* * *

Zach dropped into his desk chair, grabbing desperately for composure. A satisfying yet hollow thud sounded as his father's bank statements met the bottom of his wastebasket.

That was the end of it.

The past was behind him, with all its secrets, all its shame. He wasn't that same confused kid, teetering on the edge of right and wrong. He'd made his choices. He'd stood firm upon them and wouldn't waver now even though every wounded corner of his heart cried out for him to cut and run. Run far and fast, away from reminders that would never cease to torture with what might have been. Away from scars he couldn't erase, from a stigma he couldn't escape. Run back to what he'd been, to where he'd come from. To what he'd worked so diligently to rise above—a sense of worthlessness, the inheritance his father left him.

An inheritance he'd refused to accept.

He scrubbed unsteady palms over his face, clamping down on the runaway emotions that spiraled him back into helplessness and despair. He wouldn't go there again.

He sat, breathing deeply, drawing upon a discipline of mind and body. Using both to combat an inconsistency of heart, a weakness of soul. And as those perceptions struck a manageable balance, a detached logic began to sort and shift through the panicked disarray of the past few hours so he could look at them again.

Shock and surprise finally ebbed, leaving spirit-bruising sorrow but also a degree of reason. Looking back, he could understand what had happened and why. He could empathize with a young and vulnerable teen faced with an overwhelming decision, one so frightening, so life altering she allowed herself to heed the wrong counsel. But who was he to say that what smacked of wrong to him wasn't right for her? Because he hadn't put himself in her place. And he hadn't asked the most important question.

Had she made her decision before or after he told her of his plan to leave?

Had his abandonment forced her to make a soul-shattering

choice? Had she seen the years ahead, alone, as too threat-ening to consider?

Had he known, had he stayed, would things have worked out for the better? Would he have been capable of reaching out of the wild, unstable place he'd been in to establish a firm foundation for a wife and child? Or would the situation have fed off his immaturity, twisting his intentions, frustrating his desires until he was warped into a man just like his father?

He had no answer, and she'd had no certainty when she was forced to choose.

There was no right or wrong, just what was. And he could accept it and move on, or he could let it eat away at him like an emotional cancer until there was nothing left but bitterness.

He'd been there.

It was time to move on.

Time to step back and heal. Then he could look at things again, then he could think about Bess again. But not now. Not while the hurt was so new, so impossibly huge.

Bess's lack of faith wounded, but it wasn't a killing pain. He could get past it if he tried, if he wanted it badly enough.

If he wanted her badly enough.

Oh, God, what a mess.

He couldn't forget what Bess had done, but knowing her reasons, understanding her fear, he could give the one thing he'd wanted so badly to receive when he'd returned to Sweet-heart.

Forgiveness, and the right to begin again.

"Zach?"

He glanced up blindly, fighting his way out of his consum-ing thoughts to acknowledge the girl beside his desk. He stared at the sack she placed on his blotter.

"Aunt Bess said you were to take this and do the right thing. Whatever that means."

With a wary reluctance, he opened the bag then poured the heavy glass bauble out onto his desktop.

The sins of the past. Trusted into his care by the woman he loved, at this moment, more than pride.

Fractures of light brightened, dazzling him until he blinked away the blur of emotion. After all he'd put her through with his damning recriminations, she'd placed her future in his hands, just as she'd done so subtly since his return every time she encouraged him to find the truth, a truth that would expose her deeds and leave her at his mercy.

The significance had him trembling.

He looked up at the anxious teen, seeing concern etched into her pretty face. Looking again. Seeing for the first time with crystal clarity beyond her vivacious youth to eyes as uniquely blue as his own.

Awareness shot through him, a lightning bolt of realization.

Faith was his daughter. His and Bess's.

The product of a past infatuation. The evidence of an enduring love.

An inarticulate sound escaped him. He clamped his hand over his jaw suppressing any further outbursts while shock had the advantage.

His daughter.

He swiveled his chair away from her, breathing fast, mentally scrambling to overcome the surprise. The *joy!* Because Faith obviously didn't know, just as he hadn't known, the secret Bess had shared with the one person she could count on for unconditional support. Her sister, Julie.

He swallowed hard, commanding his pulse to slow its frenzied spasms, ordering his brain back on line before the girl thought he was having some kind of attack and called 911.

He risked another glance at her, choking on unfamiliar swells of pride and possessiveness. Fighting down the fatherly need to hold his own child.

"Zach, are you all right? What do you want me to tell Aunt B?"

Vision skewed by emotion, he said, "Tell her to trust me."

Chapter 19

Drained by the encounter with Zach, Bess carried the box of old papers out onto the porch. She sat, rocking, staring at the faded type, waiting for the numbness to wear off, for the pain of loss to set in. She waited, but it didn't come. No swelling tide of sorrow. No twisting misery of past recriminations. No heartbroken sighs over what had slipped away.

Instead, as she moved the glider to and fro in the same soothing rhythm two young lovers had enjoyed so long ago, something else began to build, layer upon layer. Something she didn't recognize for what it was until she identified the tandem emotion. Anger.

She would not give up Zach Crandall without one hellacious fight.

Determination steadied her, strengthened her. Instead of falling back upon past failures, wallowing in their familiar comfort, she looked back dispassionately, seeing that time for what it was, her mother for what she was.

Then Zach had happened into her life, dangerous, dark, disreputable, one of the *Crandalls*. And when she should have been properly horrified, she'd let herself be swept away by every evil her mother had warned her to watch out for. Sensation, sin, sex, hot, unbridled experimentation. Love. Desperate love between two fragile souls. A love that created the most perfect result imaginable.

She was through feeling ashamed of that fact. And through feeling guilty for doing the only thing she could under the circumstances.

She and Zach shared a wonderful bond, one fate had denied them for far too long.

And she'd let the need to please others rule her life for the last time. She had a second chance to claim the only man she would ever love.

She wasn't going to lose him.

Not over her mother's machinations to save a reputation that meant less to her than love. Not to preserve a lie, to hide a crime, to uphold a legacy that made her a prisoner within her own heart.

If her mother killed Sam Crandall, she would not perpetuate a crime of pride. She would not allow Mary Crandall and her children to be victimized anymore. In her lap, she held the answers.

She picked up the first sheet of paper and began to read.

What we're doing is wrong, but I can't seem to help myself.

A journal, written in her mother's florid style.

Todd has been gone over a year. His letters seem written by a stranger. I wake up at night and can't remember his face and cry myself back to sleep knowing this stranger will someday be home and my life will no longer be my own. My only reprieve is in the arms of a man who's not mine to love.

He told me again that he planned to divorce her. I have to believe him or I shall go mad.

Bess stopped reading, too stunned to go on.

Her mother, her pious, straitlaced mother, had an affair while her father was fighting overseas. What she held in her hands were private thoughts, reflections of a tortured soul trapped within this box for years.

Who in Sweetheart had been Joan Carrey's lover? What married man had caused her to cast off all her moralistic codes for the sake of lonely passion?

The answer had to be somewhere in the shuffle of unsequenced confessions. She picked up the next sheet.

He lied.

He told me what he knew I wanted to hear so I would damn myself with the sin of adultery. When I went to him after learning of Todd's death, I expected him to share my relief that we could finally be together.

He laughed at me and called me a fool. He was right. I have been a fool to lust, a slave to pleasure, a hypocrite to all I have tried to instill in my daughters.

They must never find out. And they must never make the same mistake I have.

Bess shivered. She could hear the echo of her mother's zealous fervor building in those words. She picked up another page.

I am betrayed.

After all I've done, after all my careful teaching, she gave herself to that Crandall boy and is pregnant with his bastard. The wretched girl. Acting the whore and expecting me to forgive her. Never! How could she do this to me?

Bess's initial shock gave way to pained anger. She crumpled the page in a convulsive fist, no more room in her life for her mother's vengeful spirit. Shaken but still determined, she read on.

The devil came to my door last night and I vanquished him.

To think he believed me weak enough to give in to his extortion. To save my family name, he said, reeking of liquor. He thought I would pay him, just as my old lover paid him for his silence. With enough money, he'd see his demon boy would never come to make a claim on my Elizabeth. Oh, he had no idea how far I would go to do just that. When I told him I would see him in hell, he laughed at me and pushed

*me down. I fell against the clock and that's when it became
so clear.*

I did it for my Bess. For the sake of her salvation.

And then I called him to help me conceal the crime.

He owed me that much.

*Crafty devil that he is, he arrived with the perfect plan—a
way to rid me of the menace of the boy along with the threat
of the father.*

Bess's hands shook too severely to make out more words
typed with such savage glee that the keys perforated the cheap
bond.

She held her mother's confession to murder.

And Joan Carrey's unnamed lover was her accomplice.

"Melody, have you seen Zach?"

Melody paused in her gathering of the dirty plates to give
Bess a quizzical look. Beneath the questions lay a harder
sheen of accusation. Bess had no trouble interpreting it. *What
have you done to my brother?* The waitress's reply was cool.

"Not since this morning."

"I have to talk to him."

"I'll tell him if I see him."

"Mel, this is important, not just to Zach but to your whole
family." That made the other woman's hostility ebb in curiosity. "Do you know where he might be?"

"He's not at work?"

Bess shook her head, growing frantic with the delay.

"Ted, Mayor? Have either of you seen my brother?"

Howard Anderson glanced up to smile. "I saw him go into
Doc Meirs's just a little while ago. Something wrong?"

"No," Bess said, her voice a little too brittle, her smile a
tad too tight as she regarded the two men. "Just have something for him. I'll just leave it at the post."

The men went back to their conversation and Bess
squeezed Melody's hand.

"Tell him I'm looking for him," she said in a low aside.
When she started away, Melody caught her hand.

"Bess?"

She paused at the other's intensity.

"Zach loves you. No matter what happened between you, remember that."

She knew in her heart, but hearing it spoken out loud with such surety brought a sheen to her eyes and a gruffness to her voice.

"I know, Mel. And I won't forget."

Sheriff Lloyd Baines looked up from his paper-strewn desktop to scowl at Zach and Fred Meirs. Something in Crandall's smug smile, in the hard glitter of his glare, warned him that it was payback time.

"I'm busy," he growled, trying to disguise his uneasiness. "Make it quick."

"Lloyd," the doctor began with a quiet professionalism, "we've got new evidence in the Crandall case."

He gave a nervous snort. "After seventeen years? What did you find? A confession signed by Elvis?" His eyes narrowed. "C'mon, we know who killed Sam Crandall, and I don't have to look very damn far to find him."

"We have what we believe to be the murder weapon," Meirs continued. "The dimensions from my initial examination of the body match, but we'll know more conclusively when we get reports back from Des Moines."

Baines's flabby features tightened. "You've already sent it off?"

Zach let out a slow, thin smile. "Knew you'd want it done right away before anyone could tamper with the findings."

The sheriff's jaw worked fiercely before he ground out, "It's my case. All evidence should go through me."

"Professional courtesy," Zach drawled. "I knew you didn't have the right facilities here to check for possible blood, hair and tissue matches so I sent it to the state lab boys. They're very thorough. Nothing gets by them. They'll send you a copy of their findings."

"Well, thanks a helluva lot for including me in my own case."

"Oh, you're going to be included, Sheriff. Don't worry."

Baines glared at Zach, agitation edging in next to anger. "So who did you find to take the blame for you, Crandall?"

"Nothing I want to speculate about yet."

He sneered, "Yeah, I'm sure. If you're done wasting my time on this fairy tale…"

"Actually, I've come to request your official assistance, this being your case and all."

Again, the suspicious glare. "Doing what?"

"I've reason to believe the killer didn't act alone. Since some might consider me too personally involved in the case, I'd like you to handle the questioning of our primary suspect."

"Do you want me to question you now or shall we do lunch?"

Zach's smile played out firm and final. "We're going to pay a little visit to a friend of yours."

Lloyd Baines grew suddenly very serious.

Having just missed Zach at Fred Meirs's office, and with messages scattered all over town, Bess returned home to anxiously wait for one of them to catch him. She couldn't relax. What she planned to do would either tear her world apart or it would put it all together. No guarantees. So many times she'd shied away from risks, choosing what was safe and predictable out of fear of disappointing anyone. Now the only one she worried about failing was herself…and Zach.

She'd made up her mind to roll with the consequences that came, no matter what they might be, to depend on her untested inner strength to support her in lieu of public opinion. She'd survive. And she would prosper, if not in Sweetheart, then somewhere new. She would not take another step back to what was. Now was the time to go forward. The truth would take her there as a key, not the lock.

Then she needed to tell Zach about Faith and trust him to

do the right thing with that knowledge. If he couldn't forgive her, she might not get over it, but she would go on.

"Trust me," was the message he'd given Faith to deliver before the teen left to visit Mary Crandall.

It was time she did.

To fill the interminable minutes, Bess started through her mother's journal entries again. Not pleasant reading. Each page described the workings of a repressed and disturbed woman who sought to use her children to repair her own mistakes. Julie had refused to be manipulated, but she had been the perfect faithful foil of her mother's increasing madness. She'd been too close to see what was so obvious to her now.

Most of the rantings centered on her mother's hatred and mistrust of men; on the father that deserted her when she was a teen, on the husband who went off to war and never returned, on the lover who made promises he never planned to keep. On the wrong-side-of-the-tracks boy who corrupted her daughter and stole away her last chance at redemption.

Bess read the accounts of her mother's plots to destroy her relationship with Zach, turning each page with deeper and deeper distress. She recognized the patterns of emotional abuse heaped upon a naive girl. Just as damaging as the ones Zach wore on the surface, hers scored psychologically on her spirit instead.

The two of them had never had a chance. Not then, but perhaps now.

Then the text grabbed her full attention again. Its next few pages held hints of something darker than her mother's mania.

Someone's been in the house.

Nothing's been taken but I know things have been moved.

He's searching for the evidence that his sin is as great as mine, but he won't find it.

A violent chill shook through her. Someone had prowled through their rooms, perhaps while they were away, perhaps while they slept. She immediately thought of the violation at the bookstore.

I live in constant fear.

Bess's gaze flew along the page. With each paragraph she experienced her mother's panic, drawing on the scent of smoke, the feeling of suffocation as she'd lain helplessly waiting to die. Was it the same man terrorizing both mother and daughter?

How foolish of me to think Crandall my only danger. Last night, I confronted my oh-so-successful lover to tell him to leave me alone or I'd give my souvenirs to his wife and his adoring public. I've never seen him in such a fury. When I would not give him my keepsakes, I thought he was going to kill me, too. He threw me down the basement stairs in his rage. I'm left crippled and would be at his mercy if not for these records I've maintained so carefully, and for Bess who is my guardian angel. He will do nothing while she is with me, so I must see she stays ever near.

Her mother's fall, no accident, just as the attack on her at the bookstore had been no accident, nor the incident on the road. What had her mother kept to place them in such jeopardy? She'd found no mention of the man's name, only admissions of her mother's own guilt.

Or did the box contain more than the weapon used to take Sam Crandall's life and the tortured ramblings of the woman who'd killed him?

Bess shuffled through the loose and yellowed papers until she discovered a small bundle near the bottom. She lifted out a stack of credit card receipts, all rubber-banded together. She flipped through them: numerous dinners at Haven's, records of various hotels from neighboring communities. Her mother never drove a day in her life, so how had she reached these rendezvous?

Awareness struck, like the glancing blow above her heart, providing the final piece to the puzzle before her.

She returned to the kitchen with the papers and snatched up Sam Crandall's cab log, comparing the dates, the places. Joan Carrey had relied upon Charlie's cab to take her to adjacent towns. The destinations were always legitimate: stores, banks, libraries. But where she was dropped off was not where she was going. That's what Sam Crandall discovered, probably by following her and putting two and two together to make extortion.

Realizing she had the final answer in her hand, Bess checked the other side of the charge receipt to find the embossed name from the plate and the affirming signature at the bottom.

Just as everything fit together with a stunning force, a knock at the door distracted her from it.

Zach.

She ran to open it, anxious to tell him of all she'd discovered.

But it wasn't Zach standing on the back porch.

"Hello, Bess, got a minute?" He pushed his way into the kitchen without awaiting her response.

Trying to act naturally, Bess smiled to conceal her fear and said, "If this is another attempt to buy the store, I'm afraid the answer is still no. I've decided to do some renovations."

Ted Doolin smiled back, the gesture slick and sincere. "Really? I admire your tenacity. If you need extra funding, just come to me at the bank."

Bess's features stiffened around her fixed grin. "I think I'll have enough to remodel with the insurance money from the fire. Some of our books were quit rare and valuable. Mother had the foresight to get special riders on them."

"A clever, methodical woman, your mother. Anticipating the worst and always ready."

Bess's heart began to pound so fast and loud she couldn't believe he didn't hear it. She had to get him out of the house. She had to get the evidence to Zach. Then her dismayed gaze jumped to the box sitting open on the kitchen table. And she glanced up in alarm to find Doolin following her movements with grim purpose. He stepped over to the table and gave the papers a quick perusal.

"Actually, I came over to discuss some things, but now I can see that talk isn't necessary. You've done my work for me.'' He gathered the log, pages and the receipts, setting them in the box, replacing the lid. "Now all I have to do is get rid of the loose ends. You'll have to come with me, Bess. Please don't underestimate my willingness to hurt you."

"I won't," she answered, and he chuckled at her sudden temerity.

"Full of surprises, just like your mom. I underestimated her more than once. But this should take care of those miscalculations. Come along, my dear. My car's in the drive."

"Aren't you afraid someone will see us together?"

"Why would I be? I'm an old family friend counseling a distraught young woman who's just discovered her sainted mother to be a killer."

"Zach already has the murder weapon," she said, stalling for time, trying to think her way out of the situation.

"That's good. It should prove a solid case against your mother."

"And what about you and your part in it? She called you to take Zach's father to their house. It was your idea to frame Zach."

"True, but you have no evidence against me. I was very careful. And once I dispose of these," he tapped the box, "I can sit back with the rest of the town council and express my shock over the tragedy."

"And what about me?"

"You're a smart girl. I can see you've already figured that part out. I'll leave the appropriate pages from your mother's diary clutched poignantly in your hand. I think it would be rather poetic for Crandall to find you…after your suicide."

Her breath seized up imagining it. "He won't believe it."

"Yes, he will, and think of his guilt, knowing you took your life because you couldn't bear the pain of what your family had caused his to suffer. A rather classic ending. I think your mother would have approved." He tucked the box under his arm and gestured toward the door. His smile vanished. "Shall we go?"

She shut off all thought except survival. She couldn't afford to be distracted by visions of Zach's shock and sorrow upon finding her dead. He'd blame himself. She knew he would. And so she couldn't allow Doolin to go through with his plan. She headed for the door in front of him, alert, more alive than she ever thought possible, as she looked for her chance to escape her planned fate.

Doolin grabbed her arm as they started down the back steps. She saw his car parked beside the house, a big tank of a black Buick. And on its shiny front bumper was the unmistakable rubber burn from Zach's motorcycle tire.

She walked toward the car slowly, meekly, letting Doolin think she was scared witless. It wasn't hard. She was terrified right down to her cotton socks but her mind was functioning in overdrive.

Did he have a gun? Could she slip away and run for help? How far would she get before he overpowered her? He wasn't young, but a man of vanity, he'd stayed fit. One thing was certain, if she climbed into his car, she wasn't leaving it alive.

The clarity of hindsight amazed her. She could see Ted Doolin seated at Sophie's having coffee at the table next to her when she confided her doubts about Zach being the killer, and again this morning when she'd spoken to Melody all flushed and excited. How hard could it have been for him to put two and two together and guess his charade was about to see light? When she'd refused to sell him the bookstore so he could demolish it along with any proof her mother might have hidden there, he'd done the next best thing in trying to torch it himself. He left no doubt in her mind that he had no compunction about taking another life.

She slowed her steps. When Doolin pushed her forward, she turned, thinking to delay him with questions. Didn't killers love talking about their genius after having to hide it from the world?

"I don't understand why you let yourself get involved with Sam Crandall's murder."

"I had to make sure he was dead. The bastard had been blackmailing me over Joan for years. It was my chance to be rid of him, once and for all. And I couldn't risk your mother doing something stupid, like confessing everything to save her twisted soul."

"So you helped her put Mary Crandall in prison. Didn't that bother either of you, an innocent woman going to jail?"

"I didn't lose any sleep over it, and your mother sure wasn't going to speak up at the trial, not and let Crandall's boy get his hands on you. She was one crazy broad, your mother."

"But smart enough to keep you sweating for seventeen years."

Doolin scowled, unamused. He gave her another shove and Bess pretended to stumble on the loose stones. Caught off guard, Doolin's grip slackened and Bess took advantage to explode into a run like a sprinter coming out of the blocks.

It seemed like a good idea.

At least until the banker snagged her arm and swung her into the side of the car with enough force to rattle brain and bone. Dazed, she felt herself manhandled around so the door of the Buick could open. Propelled inside its dark stifling heat, she fell face first upon the scorching black vinyl but immediately was scrambling for the other door. She kicked against the hand on her ankle, gratified by a fleshy impact and dire curse. She fumbled for the handle. It wouldn't open. Panicked, she reached for the lock, popping it, pushing the heavy door open, spilling out onto the gravel just as Doolin charged across the seat after her.

Right into the big bore of Zach Crandall's revolver. The banker looked up in disbelief to see the lawman's wide satisfied smile.

"Going somewhere?"

Chapter 20

Pinned by the ice blue stab of Zach's gaze, Ted Doolin scuttled backward only to discover the other door blocked by Lloyd Baines's bulk.

"Git outta there, Ted," the sheriff snarled. "You ain't going anywhere but to jail."

While Baines dragged the submissive banker out of his car, Zach risked a quick glance downward. "Are you all right, Bess?" He heard her soft sob of breath, and a killing quiet took control of his voice. "Did he hurt you?"

"No, no, just a little banged up, but okay."

The sound of her shaky words let the knot in his belly out a notch, but he was still wired tight as a fence line. "Sorry I'm late. I just got your message."

Bess tipped back, dropping on her fanny in the hot driveway, leaning back against the open car door to grin up at him with a wobbly relief. "Your timing was just fine."

Sitting there all scraped and trembly, still managing to look as composed as a Sunday schoolteacher, Bess Carrey made his heart kick start back into its regular rhythm. A tensile steel threaded through her fragile figure. Her eyes were huge, tired, scared. And brimming with accomplishment as she said, "We got him."

He didn't know whether to strangle her or grab on and never let her go. If he gave in to the latter idea now, he'd forget the rest of the world existed. So he held on, remembering procedure, clinging to his discipline. Trying to keep himself from blowing a hole through Ted Doolin the size of a hubcap for making Bess Carrey cry.

Only she wasn't crying. Not even close.

"Zach—"

He heard a million meanings in her quiet tone and he would listen to every one of them. Later. When he could give her his undivided attention.

"Go inside, Bess. I'll have Doc Meirs come over and take a look at you while I book this sonofabitch for murder."

"Murder?" Doolin rounded on him, white-faced and furious. "You can't—"

"I can. Two counts of attempted on Bess and one full boat for my father."

"But Joan killed him."

"Hit him, yeah. But she didn't kill him. Doc's got some interesting theories that you wouldn't let him explore seventeen years ago. Says the first blow knocked him out but it wasn't fatal. It was the second one, delivered with more strength than a woman like Mrs. Carrey could have managed, that caved in his skull."

"You're the last one who should be crying over that. You wanted him dead, too."

Zach failed to react to his baiting with emotion. Instead, his statement was coolly candid. "I'm not arguing that. I'm just saying you should have been man enough to admit it instead of letting my mom do your time. You could have worked up something, smart man like you, that would have made it look like self-defense."

"But I was the mayor of this town running for reelection and you—you were nobodies."

Zach's features firmed to cut stone. "Not anymore. See how far your credentials get you in prison. Get him the hell out of here."

Baines grabbed the banker's arm, hauling him down the drive to where his squad car angled across its end. Zach relaxed his grip on his revolver and replaced it in his holster. Picking up the box of damning evidence, an odd sense of disappointment overcame him. He frowned. He thought restoring his family name would bring a light from above or something, some grand sign that all had changed. But he felt no different than an hour before or a day before. And he suddenly realized it was because all the changes affected the past, not the future. Only one thing would do that.

He glanced around, but Bess had already gone inside.

"Crandall, the meter's running."

Scowling down at Baines then glancing back at the house, Zach began to walk toward the street, uncomfortable with the feeling of things unresolved.

He'd be back to settle them. Later.

Holding open the cell door, Zach let Baines do the honor of pushing Doolin inside. The clang of the lock sounded very permanent. Baines gave Zach a sideways glance and grumbled, "Guess you think I owe you some kind of apology, don't you?"

"No. Just some explanations."

"'Bout what?"

"It always bothered me that you thought I was the guilty one and still you never made any attempt to find me. You rushed my mother to trial so fast, I have to question that due process was served."

"Her trial was legal, boy. Regrettable, it turns out, but judge and jury made the calls, not me."

"Is that because you were sitting on some of the evidence? Deputy, would you relieve Sheriff Baines of his side arm, please?"

A beefy hand slapped over the top of the holster. "What are you, nuts, Crandall?"

"My dad was blackmailing Doolin, and I imagine those papers Bess has will tell me why. But I know my father. He wasn't too bright and he was a greedy SOB. He wouldn't have settled for a piddling two grand twice a year. So I figure someone else must have been holding him back."

Inside the cell, Doolin chuckled wryly. "Give it up, Lloyd. I'm not the only one going down for this."

Baines glared at the banker. "I didn't have nothin' to do with killing Crandall."

"Yeah," Doolin sneered, "but you were in on his blackmailing scheme. How'd that happen? He offer up that juicy bit of scandal to get himself out of jail? Is that how you got to be his silent partner? Not too silent when you got me to back your reelection campaign. Not too silent when you shushed up the murder investigation so none of your dirty dealings would surface. The one bright side in this whole mess is knowing that you'll never get another red cent out of me, you parasite."

The deputy moved Baines's hand and slowly took possession of his firearm.

When word circulated that Zach Crandall not only had Ted Doolin in jail but Lloyd Baines stripped of his badge pending investigation, he became an instant celebrity. A status that wore hard on a man with other things on his mind.

His plan was to stop in at Sophie's to assure his sister that everything was under control and to call his mom to arrange for Faith to remain there until he and Bess had a chance to talk. Like most best-laid plans, his was quickly shot to hell.

The customers at Sophie's descended upon him, battering him with questions and compliments he would have enjoyed at any other time. But not now.

The fickleness of the town's loyalty bemused him. He'd thought Baines and Doolin their leading heroes. Come to find out, he wasn't alone in his dislike of their bullying ways. With the cell door shut, more and more citizens were willing to come forth, expressing their regret over what his mother endured. Hard as it was, Zach vowed not to feel bitter. The people of Sweetheart weren't guilty of anything a little honesty couldn't cure. They'd been led astray by the wrong men long enough. All were just waiting for the chance to make amends.

It was his town. His home. And he'd be damned if he'd give any reason for hard feelings to continue.

But even as the farmers and businessmen pumped his hand and clapped his back, he was mentally gauging the amount of damage control needed to clean up the toxic spill of words he'd spewed in Bess's kitchen. While the senior ladies, led by the blushing school librarian, expressed apologies over their rush to condemn—something he'd never in his life expected to hear, let alone from the upper crust of Sweetheart's hierarchy—he nodded and smiled and wondered how long it would take to work his way toward the door to slip their attentions. Even Mayor Anderson put in an appearance, politically shrewd enough to plant the germ that Sweetheart would be needing a new sheriff—someone inside their community. At first Zach didn't realize he was the one targeted until Howard nudged him slyly to the delight of his future voters. But even the long-sought sense of inclusion couldn't hold him when heart and mind were fixed upon a certain gutsy bookstore owner across the square.

"That's something to think on, Howard. But right now, if you'll all excuse me, I've got some busi—"

As he spoke, he heard another jingle of the front door. More well-wishers, he thought with a groan as Lorraine and Myrt cleared the way like bulldozers in orthopedic stockings. Clearing a path so Bess Carrey could approach him.

Thoughts of escape disappeared. Thought, itself, eluded him as he watched her come closer, closer until they were toe-to-toe right in front of everyone in the crowded diner. Close enough to see the small abrasion on her chin. Close enough to lose himself forever in her smoky gaze. Close enough to think about her petal-soft lips as they parted.

Close enough for her to have only one thing on her mind.

He took a startled step back then her hands were on either side of his face holding him still. And she kissed him. Not a chaste peck of gratitude but a full-contact, tongue-thrusting, heart-stopping kiss that left him too dazed and surprised to do anything but stand there, hands limp at his sides, brain limp in his head, while other parts of him were anything but.

She stepped down, a sassy smile inviting him to make something of it, as her wrists locked behind his neck. Her eyes searched his without a trace of playfulness, her stare somber, worried, even frightened.

Then he realized why. She came to him, making a grand statement of devotion, while not sure he'd accept or return it.

Her faith, her courage, dropped his pride to its knees.

He made no attempt to lower his voice when he said, "I love you, Bess. Always have, always will. I came home for you. We've got some talking to do."

As he followed her out the door, Zach heard several very distinct comments. His sister saying, "It's about time." Lorraine Freemiere hushing Herb Addison's grumbles with a curt, "You had your chance, so quit your bellyaching." And town crier, Alice Barbor, sighing, "I always said they'd make a beautiful couple."

Sun slanted across her mussed bed, glowing soft and warm on the two of them as they lay side by side beneath the occasional caress of the oscillating fan. Her fingers twining through the whorls of black hair on Zach's chest, her bare foot rubbing along the coarse length of his calf, Bess was content in body but yet anxious in mind.

"Zach?"

He made a questioning noise but didn't open his eyes.

"There are some things you need to know."

He turned his head to look at her then. "I know Faith is our daughter." And while Bess struggled for some way to explain that wouldn't hurt him any more than she already had, he smiled, a slow, sexy, satisfied smile that had her heart flip-flopping. "She's terrific. We did good, baby, didn't we?"

The tender stroke of his fingertips along her suddenly tear-dampened cheek encouraged her to return his smile. "Yes, we did. She's the best of both of us." She caught his hand and pressed her lips to its broad palm before continuing. "Zach, I never ever even once considered—"

He silenced her with two fingers. "If I'd been thinking straight, I'd have known that. Seeing that entry in my dad's log—I didn't know what else to think at first. If I hadn't decided to leave, would you have told me?"

She wouldn't lie to him, not now, not about anything.

"I don't know, Zach. I'd like to think I would have, but I just don't know. My mom found out. She took me to that doctor to confirm it, and she wanted me to get rid of it—of Faith—right then and there. I couldn't, Zach. I just couldn't. She was part of you, part of us.

"Mom was furious. You'd have thought I was the only woman since Hester Prynne to conceive out of wedlock." She tried to smile but the gesture was unnecessary. It was no use trying to convince Zach that she hadn't been terrified, both morally and emotionally, of the position she'd found herself in. So she quit trying. Her sigh was ragged.

"We came up with a compromise. Or rather she came up with one, and I didn't have much choice. I'd finish school, then I'd go away and have the baby and put it up for adoption. And I'd never see it or you again."

He got very quiet in mood and voice. "So that's why you let me go."

"No. I let you go because I thought I was doing the right thing. If I'd told you, you'd have stayed and been honorable. I never doubted that for a minute. But there was nothing for you in Sweetheart, Zach, and I couldn't make myself ruin your future. I'm not going to try to second-guess what might or might not have happened. I let you go, and I've had to live with that decision, but it made me realize I couldn't let go of all you'd meant to me. I couldn't give up Faith.''

So she'd called her sister who was married and settled, as much as Julie could ever settle in one place, in Des Moines. Julie did the rest. Her husband, Michael, suffered from juvenile diabetes, the disease that eventually claimed him. They'd been afraid to have a child of their own for fear of passing along that dreaded gene. Bess's request seemed an answer to their prayer. Michael arranged for the lawyer, and while the red tape was peeled back layer by layer, Bess graduated and went to live with her sister for the summer.

And in Sweetheart, Mary Crandall confessed and was imprisoned for her husband's murder.

''By the time Faith was born, all the adoption details were confirmed. I came home alone, and Faith stayed with Julie. The hardest thing I've ever done was staying away while she grew up. Julie was great. She sent pictures and letters and encouraged phone calls...'' Her voice tightened as the lump of anguish in her throat increased, until it shut off further sound.

Zach said nothing for a long while, thinking how easy he'd had it, not knowing. Thinking of all she'd suffered alone to give him the opportunity to find the strength and the good inside himself. Characteristics she'd never doubted that he possessed.

''Baby, I've been in combat situations, I've had to take men's lives or lose my own, but I've got nothing on courage compared to you.''

She shook her head, refusing the compliment. ''I'm not brave, Zach. Look at all the damage I caused by not speaking the truth. I let my mother coerce me into not saying I'd been with you the night your father died. I kept silent and let your mother go to prison thinking she was protecting you. I thought she was guilty, Zach, or I would have spoken up. I would have.''

''I know.'' But that reassurance couldn't absolve her.

''I let everyone continue to believe you were guilty to spare my own reputation. I let myself think more of this town's opinions than your feelings, after I swore to you that I wouldn't. That's not brave, Zach. I hid my head in the sand, and I'm not proud of it. And I don't expect you to forgive me for it.''

The last thing she expected was his soft chuckle.

''Baby, I can't forgive you when I don't hold you to blame. I was the one who was ashamed of who I was. I was the one who was so weak I had to run away. You counted on me to be there for you, and I wasn't. That won't happen again, Bess. It won't.''

She didn't dare look at him. She didn't dare speculate on what his words meant as he wrapped her up in his embrace and pulled her against him.

''What about Faith?'' she asked, knowing that was one part of the past they couldn't ignore.

''What does she know?''

''That Julie's her mother and I'm her Aunt Bess and you're the gorgeous bad boy who roared into town to shake the dust off her favorite aunt.''

She felt his grin against her hair. Then he grew serious once more.

''Guess that'll do for now, at least until we get married and talk to Julie. She's done way too much not to be included now. Think she'd mind us taking Faith over the summers while she does her globe-trotting?''

Bess came up on her elbows and was staring into his face, hers pinched with uncertainty.

''What?'' he asked, slightly alarmed. ''You don't want her over the summers?''

''I want to know how you could slip something like 'until we get married' into a sentence and just keep talking.''

Zach gave her an exasperated look. ''Well that's been the plan for seventeen years. Don't tell me you want to change it now.''

Moisture glittered at the ends of her lashes. ''No, I don't want to change a thing.''

"Except this house." He shuddered. "I can't live here with your mom scowling at me all the time."

"I expect you to help me finish the wallpapering and redecorating. When I'm finished, this will be *our* house."

"And the store?"

"It's been in my family for centuries," she told him with a proper pride. "I like being a bookseller. But new books, new ideas, not the old, moldy stuff that refuses to change with the times. Faith and I were talking about making it part new books, part coffee shop, the way they do in the big cities. Think Sweetheart could stand the shock?"

"I think it'd be good for them." His tone dropped an octave. "Just like you're good for me."

They kissed, long and slow, with the leisurely confidence that there was no reason to hurry. When he lifted her off him, she was grinning. She traced the shape of his smile with her forefinger as she spoke the final truth to him at last.

"I love you, Zach Crandall. You might be all respectable now, but I'll always see you as a bad boy who loves to stir things up when they get dull. And I like that about you."

Then came his husky promise.

"I'll do my best to see you're never disappointed."

* * * * *

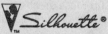

BEVERLY BARTON

Continues the twelve-book series— 36 Hours—in April 1998 with Book Ten

NINE MONTHS

Paige Summers couldn't have been more shocked when she learned that the man with whom she had spent one passionate, stormy night was none other than her arrogant new boss! And just because he was the father of her unborn baby didn't give him the right to claim her as his wife. Especially when he wasn't offering the one thing she wanted: his heart.

For Jared and Paige and *all* the residents of Grand Springs, Colorado, the storm-induced blackout was just the beginning of 36 Hours that changed *everything!* You won't want to miss a single book.

Available at your favorite retail outlet.

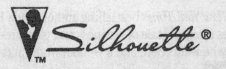

ALL THAT GLITTERS

by *New York Times* bestselling author

LINDA HOWARD

Greek billionaire Nikolas Constantinos was used to getting what he wanted—in business and in his personal life. Until he met Jessica Stanton. Love hadn't been part of his plan. But love was the one thing he couldn't control.

From *New York Times* bestselling author Linda Howard comes a sensual tale of business and pleasure—of a man who wants both and a woman who wants more.